The Trouble with DATING a Movie Star

The Red Carpet Series

The Trouble with Dating a Movie Star is a work of fiction. Names, characters, places, and incidents are either the products of the author's imagination or are used in a fictitious manner. Any resemblance to actual persons, living or dead, or actual events or locales is purely coincidental.

Cover design by Jada D'Lee Designs
Cover Images by: iStockphoto / Alphavisions ©
Shutterstock © / Karuka © / Cutts Creative ©
Book design by Integrity Formatting
Editing by Donna Wolosin

Z. N. Willett
Visit my website at www.znwillett.com

ISBN-13: 978-1499137286
ISBN-10: 1499137281

Thank you to my family
for always cheering me on,
and to my BFF for encouraging me to find my voice.

To René

THE TROUBLE WITH DATING A MOVIE STAR

Book One in the Red Carpet Series

Z.N. WILLETT

love ya, all the best

CHAPTER ONE

Have you ever experienced that moment when your body starts to tingle uncontrollably, and your heart speeds up? When you start fidgeting as you try to gain control over your breathing before your mind becomes totally blank? That moment when you see him for the first time....

Except mine was in a movie theater. Along with hundreds of other women, that all gasped when Andrew Hughes walked onto the screen.

The trouble started when my best friend Erin brought me to a movie that she had been raving about. It was during midterms of my freshman year of college, and we both needed a break.

The moment Andrew walked on screen, my heart ached. My hands actually started to tingle, and the air in my lungs collapsed at the first sight of him.

It was an unexplainable attraction and my body responded in ways it never had before. I couldn't take my eyes off of him and wanted more of him. That day changed my life forever. I couldn't get him out of my mind. Every waking moment, he was there teasing me and then haunting my dreams. I wouldn't say I was obsessed, or even a fangirl. *But,* I was motivated. I had found my muse.

Six years later, that muse has helped me to become a best-selling romance author. No one except Erin knew that Andrew Hughes was the reason to my success, and the primary reason I was able to overcome writer's block. Writing about romance and having non-existing relationships of my own wasn't motivating.

Seeing the fairly new actor on film had opened up my mind to all sorts of possibilities. Possibilities I would love to explore with him if the opportunity ever became available. However, he *was* a movie star with a long-term girlfriend made it an impossible dream. It also didn't help that they were Hollywood's sweetheart couple.

Word on the streets was that Brittney Price and Andrew Hughes started dating during their first film together and have been going strong for about three years. There had been rumors of secret rendezvous throughout the years, but the more recent break-up rumors had received a lot more press.

One could hope.

Yet, Andrew would always be available to me anytime. I just had to close my eyes and imagine his sexy, bronze, messy hair gripped in-between my fingers as we kissed vigorously. His ever changing hazel-green eyes locked to mine. As his hand inched down my arm while his fingertips lightly circled my bare flesh. Goose bumps followed his touch...

I needed to write that down.

It was raining and cold, but it came as no surprise as I was in Washington, D.C. right after the election. I was on my way to Erin's house when she called and asked me to meet her at The Anchor first. The Anchor was in the heart of Georgetown, and was our place in college where we would go to grab a pint and hang out. I missed Erin and couldn't wait to see her. She also wanted me to meet her new boyfriend, Miles.

Since I had started working on book number two, papers and reference books in my tiny office in Dallas had taken over my life. I had no time to talk or catch-up with friends and family, few as they are.

My publisher, Elena, said that I needed someone to help me with my upcoming book tour as well as to organize my life. I wouldn't say I was disorganized. I just needed an extra hand. Especially now that I was getting offers to turn my first book into a movie. I welcomed the help and my new assistant, Keira.

The Anchor was a short drive from my hotel, and my plane had arrived early. I usually flew into Washington Reagan, but for this trip, I flew into Dulles in Virginia. The Washington D.C. metro area encompassed parts of Virginia and Maryland. The District was surrounded by the two states. It was common to cross the borders and mostly a necessity to get anywhere. My hotel was in Arlington, Virginia, which gave me enough time to shower and change before I was to meet with Erin at the pub. I still ended up arriving before her, forgetting that she was always fashionably late.

The place was crowded, and no tables were available, which was typical for a Friday night. I worked my way up to the bar and sat down on a stool gaining the bartender's attention. "What can I get you?"

"A Shandy, thanks," I yelled over the crowd.

People were mingling all around me, and I decided to watch the game until Erin arrived. Two pints down and Erin *still* hadn't arrived. I sent her another text. She was on her way, but that was fifteen minutes ago and now three beers later. It was time to find the ladies room.

As I stood up, I turned into what seemed to be a human tank. As we collided, his drink spilled down my blue blouse. "What the—I'm sorry, miss! Hey Jack! I need a towel," he shouted towards the bartender.

"It's okay," I said as the sticky liquid continued to slide down my chest. "Was that a full glass?"

He laughed and started patting down my shirt. "Here, let me help."

"Ummm...that's okay. I can do it." He actually blushed as I grabbed the towel from his hand. The tall, muscular guy looked sweet, and he had the cutest dimples when he smiled.

"Hey Wade, how long does it take to get my beer?" a voice asked from behind me.

"Drew. Sorry man. I kinda gave it to her."

"Well, how nice of you," he said, amused.

I turned around to face the idiot. "Yes, how nice of him indeed. Maybe, if he hadn't been in such a hurry to get you your damn drink, it wouldn't be *on me*!" And *that's* when I wished I had just shut the heck up.

The first thing I saw was his perfect square jaw and plump rose-colored lips as they curled up to one side. Then, a pinkish hue made its way onto his olive cheeks as I made contact with clear hazel-green eyes. His smile grew wider as his thick brows arched up amused. My mouth dropped.

Andrew Hughes.

Wet and hard were two things I often dreamed about when I dreamt about Andrew Hughes, but that night was a nightmare.

All I could do was gawk at him as his eyes drifted from mine to my very wet chest. I didn't have to guess what he saw. My blouse was drenched. I was cold and had on a new very sheer bra. The coldness mixed in with the fact that Andrew Hughes stood only inches from me....

Yeah.

When he looked back into my eyes with that intense stare of his, my heart raced. Everything I felt the first time I had seen him on screen didn't compare to the sensory overload my body was now experiencing. There was something new this time around, and I couldn't breathe.

"Hey, are you okay?"

Still. Couldn't. Breathe.

"Ummm, Wade, something is wrong." I heard the panic in his voice.

"Miss, are you okay?" Wade came around and started to wave his hand. "Drew, I think something's wrong with her."

"Should we call 911?"

"No!" I gasped as they both looked at me. Shaking my head as I tried to catch a breath, words finally spilled out, "I'm fine. Give me a minute."

"Are you sure? I think you may need help."

I did. I was standing in front of Andrew Hughes, wet and embarrassed. Never in my strangest dreams had I *ever* imagined meeting him like *this*. "No, sorry...I think I'm just...cold." Both of their eyes fell to my chest. I needed to get out of there. "Excuse me," and I ran to the restroom. Heading immediately to the mirror to confirm what I already knew—yup, wet and hard. I then used the hand dryer to dry myself off, but the damage had already been done.

I had made a complete fool of myself in front of Andrew Hughes, and there was no changing it. First impressions were everything. I wrote about them. It's your moment. The one that both of you would always remember. I looked in the mirror at the large beer stain, and decided I couldn't face him again. My moment was over.

I high-tailed it out of the restroom and headed straight for the door, diverting the bar at all costs. Almost outside, I felt a bit of relief rush over me until a large hand wrapped around my arm, halting my movements. "I hope you're not rushing out because of me. I am sorry, miss..."

"Andria. It's Andria, and no, I just needed to be somewhere." I kept my gaze on the door, wishing I could just appear on the other side of it.

The gentle giant looked at my blouse. "At least let me take care of your shirt."

"That won't be necessary." I was already embarrassed enough.

"I insist, and Andrew wanted to speak to you—"

"No! I'm fine, really." Seeing Andrew again was the last thing I wanted.

"Hey, Wade. Did you find her—hey," Andrew said smiling.

I stared, and then finally forced myself to smile. What the hell was going on with me, I thought.

6

"Miss—"

"Andria. Just Andria," I stumbled out again.

"Well, Andria, I'm sorry for...being rude. I'm Andrew." He extended his hand to me.

I couldn't stop the huge embarrassing grin from breaking out across my face. "Nice to meet you, Andrew," I said as I shook his hand.

"This is Wade, my brother-n-law and beer-spiller."

"It wasn't entirely his fault," I let out a humorless chuckle.

We stood there for a moment looking at each other. I could feel myself starting to get dizzy, and then realized I had forgotten to breathe again.

Wade spoke up. "So Andria, please let me take care of your shirt."

"Thanks again, but that's okay. It will come out in the wash."

"You were heading out?" Andrew asked.

"Yeah...I need to meet someone." It became difficult to keep eye contact.

"Oh." He sounded disappointed, but that had to be my imagination.

"Well it was nice meeting you, Andria." Wade sent me a huge grin.

"You too, Wade." I turned and looked one last time at Andrew. "It was nice meeting you too, Andrew."

"Likewise," he said.

I knew I stared a little too long, but I wanted to hold that moment—even if it was a disaster—for a little bit longer. What I couldn't understand was why he was staring back. I smiled, and he returned the gesture. We stood there smiling for what seemed liked forever, even though it was probably just a few seconds. "Well, I better go." I turned around and walked out the door. Actually, I ran straight to my car and sat there. I wasn't sure how long, but eventually I heard a knock on my car window, which startled me as I yelled out, "Erin! Geez, you scared me!"

"Why are you sitting in your car, Andria? I have been trying to call you! When I couldn't find you in The Anchor, I was going to take off. But, I saw what looked like you sitting in a car. Surprise, here you are. Why? What's going on? Have you been here all night?"

"Erin get in, you won't believe what just happened."

I filled Erin in on the grand cluster fudge of meeting Andrew Hughes for the first time. She poured us drinks as we sat on her couch. "Wow, Andria. Just wow. You've thought about this moment since..."

"Forever and I messed it up! I actually raised my voice at him, Erin. I don't know. I was mad, and wet, and mad. Not sure why. Wade was a sweetheart, but when Andrew came up...how could I have made such a fool of myself?"

"You didn't make a fool out of yourself. It wasn't your fault, and you handled yourself well," she said and placed a comforting hand on my arm.

"How, Erin? I couldn't speak!" I was frustrated with myself for being so incredibly stupid.

"That's better than saying something stupid." Erin winked playfully at me.

"Not helping."

"Look on the bright side. You finally got to meet Andrew, and you said he sought you out."

"No, Wade sought me out."

"He came right behind him. Hey, cheer up. You met Andrew Hughes. Cheers." She clinked her glass to mine.

"When do I get to meet your new boyfriend?" I desperately needed a change of subject.

"You are going to love Miles," Erin sighed and smiled brightly, as her hazel eyes twinkled with happiness.

All I knew about him was that he was an accountant by day and a musician by night. Erin had met him when he was assigned by his firm to handle Erin's finances.

Erin and I were childhood friends and grew up together in Arlington, Virginia. We were total opposites. She was interested in beauty pageants and clothes while I spent most of my time reading books or at the Smithsonian. She was taller than me, thinner than me, and had a body that I would kill for. Her golden brown skin was always flawless, and Erin's curly brown hair was maddening. I had inherited my wild curly auburn hair from my mother. Even though her hair was redder and her curls tighter, I inherited the unruly part. As I grow older, it has changed, and now that I straighten it, it's become more manageable.

Both of our fathers were in the Military and Erin's worked at the Pentagon. We even went to college together at Georgetown. While I majored in English lit, she majored in art. She went on to work in fashion, and now manages a high-end clothing boutique. Erin was also my official stylist. I was her guinea pig, but most importantly she was like a sister to me.

I was the only child of Dan Moore and Sophia Thompson. Dad now lived in Baltimore, Maryland and was counting down retirement from his military desk job, while my mother and her husband Bob lived close to me in Dallas, Texas. Mom stays home, and Bob's a contractor.

Erin and I stayed up late into the early morning talking, until I was reminded that I had an early meeting with one of the interested studios regarding the movie deal in six hours. I was stunned when people liked my book enough for it to be a best seller. But I was more than shocked when several studios told me they wanted to adapt the book into a film.

Erin was the one who encouraged me to write. At first, it was just a way to express my thoughts. I was never one who felt comfortable speaking, and she pushed me to write my thoughts down and not to be embarrassed by them. I spent most of my freshman and sophomore year in college writing stories that eventually became chapters for my first book. I shocked her—myself more I think— and she said I had finally let loose my inner freak. Sharing them, however, took another several years. When my publisher, Elena Martinez, took me on, my life changed.

Four hours later, I stumbled out of bed, took a shower and grabbed some coffee in the lobby of my hotel on the way to my meeting. I was thankful that Erin had already preplanned my outfit since it was an important one. Nothing over the top: navy suit, white button down blouse, and a pair of ridiculously high-heeled shoes—I barely could walk.

Elena had flown in the publishing house's attorney and I was to meet him at a building downtown. For some reason, the studio people were in town for an event, and I was thankful it was during my Thanksgiving visit with Dad. I was heading to Baltimore the next day to have dinner with him and his girlfriend, Pilar, along with her family.

On my way I grabbed a hot coffee to go, and noticed a lot of commotion in the lobby. Nothing too unusual, but I sensed something was off.

The hotel was old, grand, and beautiful. The lobby had large chandeliers that stretched from the entrance to the front desk. The furniture was made of dark wood and rich tapestries. It looked as if you had stepped into the nineteen twenty's where men wore dinner jackets, and women sat in the parlor with spectacles in hand.

While I waited for the Valet, I could hear people frantically speaking, as well as a couple of girly squeals. I turned around and spotted a mob surrounding what looked like one person. I watched as they all walked in unison to several waiting black SUV's.

I watched them dispersed as I took another sip of my coffee. At that moment, I also made eye contact with Andrew Hughes. I choked, and the hot liquid burned down my throat.

There I stood and watched as Wade shoved him into the car and then jumped in the front seat. We both stared at each other and I tried to look as if my throat didn't just receive second-degree burns.

I smiled and waved at him, and he smirked—meaning he gave me the most incredible sexy smile—before his expression turned to panic and then frustration as they drove off. I sadly waved goodbye, and the Valet pulled up with my rental car.

The meeting went well. It looked as if my book, *Deception* was one step closer to becoming a film. To be honest, everything was way over my head. Thankfully, the lawyer Elena had sent, Don Reed, was great. He explained everything to me in layman's terms, and once the deal is made, I may find myself earning more money than I ever could have imagined.

On our way out of the office, a tall lankly man and a curvy woman displaying too much cleavage walked in. We said our goodbye's as Don greeted them. "Frank, it's good seeing you again."

"Don. You're here for the premier?"

"No, a new deal. Have you met Andria Moore?"

His bright blue eyes flashed my way as he turned to me and smiled wickedly. "Andria," he elongated, "Such a beautiful name, fitting for such a beautiful woman."

As nice as that should have sounded, the man was creepy. His eyes swept over my body as his tongue darted out. "Ummm, nice to meet you," I responded sheepishly.

"This is a new deal? I want a piece."

"Frank, she's the author."

"Smart and beautiful..."

"I'm Amy," the tanned woman said interrupting, wearing a scowl on her face. She flipped her streaked brunette locks as she reached out to me with her limp hand.

"Nice to meet you. Don, I will talk to you after the holidays. It was nice meeting you both," I said.

"Hey, are you guys coming tonight?" Frank spoke up again, just as I was about to make my escape.

"I'm heading back out today, Frank," Don politely declined.

"Well, Andria you have to come. Everyone will be there, and since he's back in his old stomping ground, it's going to be huge."

Who was he talking about?

"I planned to spend some time with friends and family actually, sorry, maybe—"

"I won't take "no" for an answer. Here are two passes. Invite whomever you want. If you need more, here's my card. Call me. The only thing I ask of you is that you find me when you arrive." He placed them and the business card in my hand.

"Thank you, but..." I noticed the logo on the tickets.

It was the logo from the studio, but this one had a gun in the middle. It has been displayed everywhere. It was the logo for Andrew Hughes's new film. I looked at them closer and confirmed they *were,* in fact, two tickets for Andrew's new movie.

"Do you like Brittney Price? She's in this with her boyfriend. I represent him."

All I could say was, "Ah, ya?"

"So you'll come?" Frank asked, stepping in closer.

"Frank, we really need to start," Amy interrupted harshly.

"Come. You'll enjoy it, and the after party will be great," he said as they walked toward the conference room.

Both Don and I walked out of the office to wait for the elevator. "Andria, you should go. This is a great opportunity to get a little wet, and you can start early with networking."

Funny, I already "got wet" and networking was the last thing on my mind.

The first thing I did was drive over to Erin's shop. The second thing I did was speak a hundred miles an hour regarding the meeting, Frank, and the fact that I had two VIP tickets to Andrew Hughes's premier. "Why didn't I know there was one here?"

"It had slipped my mind. It's been on the news," Erin said as she looked at me innocently.

"Erin! How could that have slipped your mind? That's why he's here?"

"No. He's here because he's *from* here and went to school here." She furrowed her brows at me as if I already should know this information.

"What? I thought he was from New York?"

"Andria, what kind of fan *are* you? Do some more research! His family is from New York, but he grew up here in Middleburg. He went to Georgetown! The same school we went to?"

"I didn't know. OMG! He was so close! He's always been close..." I couldn't help the frown that fell across my face.

"Why do I know more than you?"

"I just watched his movies, Erin." She raised a brow. "Okay, and maybe looked up pictures of him online, but that's about it. I have been busy."

"Busy dreaming about Andrew Hughes." She rolled her eyes.

"What?"

"Nothing. Let's find you something to wear for tonight." Erin's eyes shined bright, thinking about dressing me up.

"I'm not sure if I should go?"

"You're going, and you're going to look incredible."

"Are you coming?" She looked sheepish. "Erin Young! You *are coming with me*!"

"Andria, of course I would go, but Miles's parents are coming into town, and I'm meeting them for the first time. Sorry, Hun, but I will make sure you look fabulous!"

Yeah, as if that's totally going to make up for not going with me

I was going to back out and say I wasn't going, but I had already messed up my first chance with Andrew, and hopefully this could be a make-up.

So, I assumed the position and let Erin play dress up until she was happy with the right dress. "You're going to make all the men go crazy!" She gave me a wink and let out a squeal of delight.

I didn't care about making *all* the men go crazy, just *one* man.

CHAPTER TWO

If I had known last night that I would be walking down a red carpet for the first time, let alone at Andrew's premier, not only would I have worried myself to death, but I would never have shown up.

I thought about turning the car around the entire drive from the hotel to the theater. It was only fifteen minutes away, but I was stuck in traffic for over an hour and a half. I had plenty of time to change my mind. Don had told me if I decided to go, to leave early. I thought he was just being punctual, but he was right and I was late.

I was thankful that Erin still lived close by in Alexandria, and she knew how to quickly select the perfect dress. It was always a challenge to find one that fit me perfectly in all the right places. I was an average size, with average breasts, but my inherited rump would make dresses pull around my hips. Yet, the long black jersey dress we both had settled on was perfect. It was a halter dress—not so great in cold weather—but she insisted that I had to wear it.

Another twenty minutes had passed, and I had finally arrived at the drop off point. I grabbed my overpriced wrap, to cover up my shoulders so that I wouldn't freeze to death. I wanted to wear a turtleneck style dress, but Erin said I didn't know what I was talking about.

Even in the cold, the place was buzzing with activity outside of the theater. People with radios were escorting everyone down the red carpet. Reporters were staggered along the way conducting interviews and photographers were stationed for pictures by sponsor billboards.

Large security men with dark glasses lined the fences as fans screamed and yelled behind them for autographs. It was a chaotic, yet still structured mess that seemed to work.

As I walked down the carpet, I looked for Andrew everywhere but couldn't find him anywhere. I did see Brittney, and thought, *I was cold.* She was wearing a strapless green dress with cut out sheer panels. It was breathtaking, and with her ridiculously fit body, she had to be one of the only people who could have pulled that dress off. Her platinum blonde hair was pulled up into a structured up-do, and her make-up was dark and heavy.

Brittney was one of the most beautiful women in Hollywood, but there was something I didn't like about her.

It wasn't jealousy.

Right.

Something about her seemed pretentious. I couldn't figure out why someone like Andrew would date her. Andrew seemed to be a genuinely nice guy, and he was known to be someone everyone respected and liked. Brittney's reputation was the complete opposite. She was a wild child, and was always saying or doing something that placed her on the front page of the tabloids. I knew not to believe everything I read or heard, but something about her was off. I know opposites attract, but....

I watched as Brittney continued to pose for pictures. I wasn't sure why I suddenly felt dispirited, but I knew staring at her wasn't helping my mood. Something about it all seemed too surreal. Again, I thought about leaving, but I wanted to see Andrew. Unfortunately, it looked as if it would be only on screen.

The movie was nothing less than fantastic. Andrew was an incredible actor and could do just about anything. My favorite roles to see him in were ones such as this one, where he was in control and powerful, with a little bad-ass in him.

When the cast came out to greet everyone, from about thirty rows back, I saw glimpses of Andrew's blue-striped suit that fit him like a glove. Seeing him in jeans and a t-shirt was incredible, but seeing him in one of his signature designer suits was mouth-watering. He had a great sense of style, and always seemed to surprise everyone with his color selections.

Andrew's Mother and Father were in attendance, along with his older sister. He thanked them and said how wonderful it was finally to have a premier in his home town.

Frank was hanging back on the side of the stage, scoping out the audience. When I spotted the back of his long dark hair, and he turned looking in my direction, I ducked. I was supposed to have let him know I had arrived, and should have since he was the one who gave me the tickets. But, the guy was strange. Not to mention that he made me feel uncomfortable.

The entire event inside the theater didn't last more than two hours. Everyone mingled after the movie, and many people were looking for a way into the exclusive cast party afterwards. I spoke to a couple of people who sat next to me, then said my goodbyes before heading back to the hotel. The cast party was being held at the same hotel I was staying in. That gave me time to freshen up before going down to the private affair. I was on a mission, to find Andrew Hughes.

The ballroom was large, but it was set-up with intimate sections scattered throughout. There were sofas and floor pillows in certain sections, and tables and loungers in others. It was semi-dark, lit by different colored lights that reflected off the walls. It created an amazing spectrum giving the room a club like feel. There was a DJ spinning house music while people mingled, eating from the many food stations positioned around the room.

I grabbed the first cocktail I saw pass my way as the server walked by. As I tried to look casual, I searched for Andrew, but couldn't find him anywhere. I walked around the entire premises twice; after all, I was on a mission. Unfortunately, it was one that seemed to be a bust. I didn't see any of the major cast members, and soon realized I may never see Andrew again.

What was I thinking?

I met Andrew—once—and I thought if he saw me again, we could have a do over, but that was only a dream. There was no such thing, and he was here for his movie premier, with his on-and-off again girlfriend.

What did I expect?

That thought made me drink more. I wasn't sure what I was drinking, but it was tall and tasted like cola with a splash of sweetness. After my second one, I realized I should have asked what it was, but it was too late as I felt my body relax. I had been a tense ball of nerves the entire evening, and for the first time, I felt at ease.

I thought about going upstairs, but in the back of my mind, I still hoped that Andrew would make an appearance. Still, I walked the entire place again and didn't catch a single glimpse of him. When the server offered me another drink along with his number, I knew that it was a sign to leave. When the only person talking to you is the staff, the party is over.

I walked out of the ballroom and headed straight for the elevator. The lobby was pretty clear, it was after two in the morning, and everyone else was dancing in the other room. As I stood waiting for the elevator, the hairs on the back of my neck suddenly stood up. I could feel warmth lightly caressing the back of my neck as heat touched my naked back. "Every time I see you, you're running away."

Frozen, yet relieved to hear his golden voice, I answered. "I'm not running away. It was getting late."

"Have a drink with me," he whispered in my ear.

The man made me speechless.

"Andria...one drink," he said as he slowly brushed my hand.

My fingers stroked the outside of his hand as he held onto my fingers and walked us to the small lobby bar. My hand tingled as he released it letting me slide in the booth first before sitting next to me. We didn't say anything, just smiled at each other until the server came and took our order. "A bottle of your best champagne," he said, not looking up at her.

"Right away, Mr. Hughes."

I grinned as I watched her response. She had to take a moment before she left our table. No one could blame her; I was literally dying inside myself.

"I came back for you, Andria."

I turned my head back to him in shock. "Excuse me?"

"This morning, when I saw you from the car, I didn't realize the driver would take off so quickly. Before I could tell him to hold on a minute, we were gone. I told him to take me back, and by the time I returned you were gone."

In shock, I looked down at my wringing hands. "Sorry. Ummm...there was a meeting I needed to be on time to." I swallowed the lump in my throat.

"So did I."

Looking up into his intense stare, I started fidgeting uncontrollably and nervously bit my lip.

What the hell?

I could have sworn he growled a little as his eyes focused on my mouth. I released my lip, and he smiled. He actually smiled at that. "Ah...your movie was wonderful."

"You were there?" He looked surprised.

"Yes. I actually received an invitation after my meeting today. I didn't know you were...the premiere was tonight and here."

He scooted closer to me. "It's the first time that I was able to do it here. This was a special one for me, and now it seems special in more ways than one."

"Well, it was incredible."

"Thank you and you look beautiful, by the way," he said as he moved in closer.

My mouth dropped, and I couldn't control that. What could I do? The drinks before helped, but to have him say

I looked beautiful, how was I supposed to respond? "Thank you?"

He laughed. "Why do you sound surprised?"

"I'm surprised that you're sitting here with me, having a drink, and telling me I look beautiful." I didn't mean to blurt that all out.

He looked humored by it. "That's a given, Andria. You're incredibly beautiful."

I could feel every part of me turning red. My face and chest felt flushed. "Andrew..."

"You blush too, making you even more irresistible." His eyes perused across my body.

My heart stopped.

Thank God the server interrupted with the champagne. "What should we toast to?"

He thought for a moment before saying, "To spilt beer." And with that, I drank.

The entire glass.

One empty champagne bottle later, Andrew and I were still in the intimate booth at the hotel's lobby bar. It was amazing how easy it was to talk to him. I felt nervous at first, but he put me at ease right away.

Andrew did most of the talking, which I appreciated. He talked about growing up in Virginia. How he was into the music scene as a teen—I had no clue he played the piano. He said his Nanna and Mother forced both him and his sister Taylor to learn; they were very involved in the arts. They nurtured them to experience many things, including studying music and art abroad.

His Mom was an Oncologist at the world renowned South District Cancer Center, and his Father was currently the CEO of a small automobile technology company his grandfather Duke had founded. His older sister Taylor was a model, and one with brains. She works alongside her father as an engineer, and is head of operations. Seeing Andrew's family earlier, it was obvious he was blessed with the family genes of beauty. Yet now, I can add brains to the list of attributes.

Listening to Andrew made me realize I should have known *some* of these things about him. The way Erin spoke, it was common knowledge. I would sneak a peek at a magazine here and there, and click on a website now and then, but I really didn't know as much as I should have known about him.

Andrew smiled the entire time while he talked. He questioned me a couple of times if I really didn't know all these things. I would tell him I had no clue, and then he'd smile bigger.

Andrew was discovered by his manager in high school, but decided to wait until after he had graduated to start his acting career. He started college majoring in Political Science, planning to go on to law. But, the opportunity Andrew's manager offered was too great and his studies could always be finished later. Nine years later, and at twenty-eight, he was finally considering continuing after his next film.

Even though Andrew didn't finish college, he experienced the social side of it during the few terms he had spent there. He also told me that he would visit his childhood friend a lot in high school during his time at Georgetown. I was surprised that he was speaking about Wade, who looked a lot younger. Not only was he his brother-in-law, but also his bodyguard. Taylor and Wade were childhood sweethearts and had gone to college together. Andrew would spend some weekends and school breaks visiting them. They would take him to The Anchor, and it became a special thing for him. "The Anchor was the place where my best friend, Erin and I would hang out when I went to Georgetown."

He seemed shocked. "Too bad I didn't see you."

"You wouldn't have. I was in Dallas then."

He thought about that before asking, "Having a dad who was in the military, wasn't that..."

"Hard? For me, not at all, but it was for my Mom. They divorced when I was five. When he decided to take a desk job later, I saw him more often. Then, when the opportunity came to attend a private school in Maryland, my mom encouraged me to take it."

"Where you a military brat?" he asked and smiled.

"Not at all. I was more of a loner and didn't really have friends, except Erin and my friend Brandon."

His eyes squinted. "Who's Brandon?" he asked with a weird tone.

"Brandon and I grew up together. After my parents' divorce, I would visit my dad during the summers. Both he and his friend John, who is also Brandon's father would go hunting and bring us along. This was *horrible* because I hate hunting. We would camp out and Brandon and I would play while Dad and John did their thing. Brandon and I went to different schools in high school, but we remained close friends."

Andrew leaned forward while his hands ran through his hair. "Are you two still close?"

"I still consider him a good friend."

Andrew's face hardened unexplainably. "Were you more than friends?"

"Ummm..." Andrew's intense stare was not only making me uncomfortable, but I found it was weirdly...hot. "We tried it for a minute, but after...we remained friends. I'm also friends with his wife, Jamie."

He sat back in his seat, brushing his thumb over his bottom lip as he continued to stare into my eyes. All I could focus on was the movement of his thumb. "So you two dated?"

I looked down a little uncomfortably by the line of questions. "Not really 'dated', dated. Just tried it out for a moment, but it was awkward and wrong."

"Uh-huh."

Looking back at Andrew, I couldn't quite read him. He had what seemed like a million facial expressions, and each one could tell his mood. But the look on his face was one that was hard to read. We sat in a moment of silence while he pondered over whatever it was he was thinking. It was then that she popped into my head. "And you and Brittney?"

He made a scowled expression when I said her name. "Don't believe everything you read, Andria."

What was that supposed to mean? Lately, the press was saying they're not together. So, were they? They sure looked like it today.

"I don't believe everything I hear or read, but surely you can see why I would think that you two..." It didn't sound right coming out at the time, but if he could ask me about Brandon, she was fair game.

He gaped at me for a moment as he searched my eyes for something I was unclear of. "Andria, in my profession, things are meant to look one way even if they are not."

"Okay?"

He leaned in closer as his voice lowered. "Like my movies. I play a part, but in real life I am far from that image. Do you understand?"

"Yes...no." He laughed. "Are you trying to tell me you two are not dating, but *dating*?'" I confused myself.

He placed a wicked smile on his face as he came in closer saying, "Oh, Andria. I love your—"

"Andria!" a voice stretched out my name— interrupting—as we both looked up at him.

I saw the last person I wanted to. "Hi, Frank."

He spoke at my chest. "I knew you would come. Why didn't you find me?" Then he finally noticed Andrew. "Andrew, what are you doing here?"

Andrew sat straight up. "I was going to ask you the same thing."

"Amy and I were looking for someone, but I have found something better," he said, scoping me out.

The guy was really starting to bother me.

Andrew rested his arm on the back of the booth behind me as he asked, "You know my manager, Frank?"

I moved in closer to him and saw a gleam of approval in Andrew's eyes. "No, not really. We met today. He was the one who gave me the tickets."

Frank looked between the two of us. "We met at Grant's. Her meeting was before mine. How lucky was I? When I saw her...she was with Don."

"Is that so..."

"Don is our attorney," I blurted out. Not sure why I felt the need to explain. The look on Andrew's face was just telling me to do so.

"Beauty and brains, Drew. Her book is up for a film adaptation."

Andrew's arm tightened as his eyes filled with surprise. "You're a writer?"

I looked at Frank who seemed smug that he knew that and Andrew didn't. "We haven't gotten that far."

"Who do you write for?" He asked in a clipped voice.

"Ummm...for me, and EM Publishing."

"What *kind* of writer are you, Andria?"

I wasn't sure why the conversation was turning into an interrogation, but I answered. "I am a romance writer, Andrew. I wrote *Deception*."

"You're A.P. Moore?" Frank asked loudly. Andrew looked pleased that Frank didn't know as much as he had originally implied.

"You know my book?"

"Everyone does." Andrew answered smugly.

"Come on," Frank interrupted. "*You* really wrote that hot book?"

He was really getting on my nerves. "Ummm, yes, I wrote *Deception*." I answered with a glare.

"You're full of surprises, Ms. Moore." Andrew said coated in honey as he placed that smirk on his face.

I couldn't take my eyes off those lips, which made me unaware that Frank was bent directly over me before he asked, "So, Andria, would you like to have a nightcap—"

"Frank, she's having one now," Andrew growled out.

Did I mention the man was hot when he was annoyed?

Frank placed an evil grin on his face as he looked directly at Andrew. "Drew, don't you need to find Brittney?"

In that moment, my heart fell. No matter how incredible he was, and how interested he seemed to be, he was her's. I could not nor would I compete with her. "I better go—"

"Andria, wait," Andrew said as he looked directly at Frank. "Why don't *you* go find Brittney since you're so interested in her. Andria and I aren't done. You can leave, *now,* Frank."

Frank rose back up with both hands up as if he were surrendering. "Drew, hey man, I was just—"

"I know what you were doing Frank," Andrew said glaring at him.

Frank never dropped the grin as he looked over towards me. "Andria, you have my card," and with that, he walked away.

Andrew ordered a drink on the rocks as he sat there looking at me with a penetrating stare. It made me uncomfortable, yet again hot as hell at the same time. He didn't say a word, and when his drink arrived, I watched as he swiveled the cold glass in his hand before taking a sip from those beautiful lips. When his tongue swiped the liquid from them, it made me a little woozy.

I finally had to break the awkward silence. "I was going to tell you I was a writer."

"I know you were. I should have asked what you do, but we got caught up in the past. So, you're here for business?" He asked and leaned in.

"It coincided with my Thanksgiving trip. I stopped here first to see my best friend Erin, before going to Baltimore tomorrow."

He took another sip as I watched. "And you live..."

"In Dallas."

"I see."

Something had changed between us. I wasn't sure what, but Andrew seemed heavy in thought, and the night turned the moment Frank had interrupted.

"Well, Andrew, it's getting late. It was...this was nice," I said standing up.

"Let me walk you back to the elevator." He placed some cash on the table as he followed me from behind.

We said nothing until we stood facing the front of the main elevators. I didn't want the moment to end, but it was time. I peered over to my side for one last look at Andrew, memorizing every detail before finally saying, "Andrew. Thank you again for the champagne and..."

He stepped directly in front of me with his back towards the elevator door. "I want to see you again."

My heart stopped.

I know I was supposed to say something, but I couldn't think rationally. I was sure my ears were playing a trick on me, and my brain became scrambled. "Ummm, I'm not sure," was I crazy? My mouth was having an insane moment. "What about Brittney?"

Maybe not that insane.

"There is no Brittney." He stepped closer.

I couldn't take my blue eyes away from his hazel ones that radiated as he smiled.

"Don't always believe what you read, Andria. You, of all people, should know that." He winked. "I will call you," and with that, the elevator door opened.

He did not take his eyes off of mine as he stepped to the side. I entered the elevator as my eyes never wavered from his until the elevator door closed.

CHAPTER THREE

The next morning I woke up in a daze, reeling from my conversation with Andrew Hughes last night. He said that he wanted to see me again, and I still couldn't believe what I had heard. At first, I thought that I had to have dreamt it, but if that had been the case, creepy Frank wouldn't have appeared.

It had taken what seemed like forever, to finally fall asleep last night. All I could do was to think about Andrew over and over again. He was very different from whom I had imagined, and better looking in person, which was hard to believe. He had a wicked personality, and he was sexy-as-hell. ...Well, a little like I had imagined—but meeting the real Andrew Hughes was eye opening.

When I finally decided to get out of bed, doubt started to creep into my mind about him. As I was in the shower, I started to have thoughts like: He probably hits on a lot of girls. He was probably drunk. No, I know he was drunk. We did have a lot to drink.

It's Andrew Hughes. Andrew, *freaking*, Hughes, I was talking to. And he wanted to see *me* again? There was no wrapping my head around that.

Erin and I were meeting up for breakfast with Miles before I left for Baltimore. We met at a diner in Old Town Alexandria that was close to her brownstone. I was officially meeting Miles. He was a tall—very slender—good looking guy with a nice smile. He had long sandy brown hair, a pale complexion and had a heavy southern accent. He had moved to Virginia a couple of years ago from Baton Rouge, Louisiana to work as an accountant for his current company.

Miles had some other talents as well. When he first came to Virginia, he met a group of guys at a bar, and soon discovered they were looking for a guitar player. He offered up his skills, and they've been a band ever since. Erin mentioned that they were really good. They're an alternative band that uses a bit of southern influences. I thought she was biased until she sent me one of their CD's. I loved it and often wrote to their music.

Miles seemed to really love Erin, and treated her like the spoiled princess she was. I couldn't ask for anything more.

It was hard for Erin and me to talk about what happened last night without being rude to Miles. He said it was all right, and let me tell the gist of it. But, I didn't want him to think that I wasn't interested in getting to know him. It *was* our first meeting.

When Miles went to the restroom, Erin attacked me. "So, are you going to go out with him?"

"What kind of question is that, Erin? *Of course,* I'm going to go out with him. But, I don't think he'll call."

She rolled her eyes. "Are you joking? He will call."

"We were drinking, and he didn't even ask me for my number. Oh, my, God, Erin. He never asked for my number! It was just..." I started to panic.

Erin placed her hand on mine. "Andria, please stop. He can easily find your number, and he wasn't *that* drunk."

"How, Erin?"

"Don't worry about the *how*, just start preparing for the *when*," she said sternly.

"Miles is a great guy, FYI."

She smiled big. "He is! He hinted about taking me to meet his family. This makes me totally nervous," she laughed as Miles sat back down.

"So, Darlin', what did I miss?"

"Oh, nothing Miles, just a little girl talk."

With that simple statement, I was back to getting to know Miles.

I drove back to the hotel to pick up my things before heading to my dad's. I looked around the lobby for any sightings of Andrew, but it was a bust. I grabbed my things and headed to the front desk to get a copy of my bill. "Ms. Moore, there was a message left for you." The agent walked to the back and returned with a large basket. "It was actually this," she said as she placed the basket on the counter.

Peeking into the basket, I saw bottles of The Anchor's house bottled beer, with The Anchor printed t-shirts, snack items, bottle openers, and a bunch of other novelty items. As I opened the card, my eyes grew wide when I saw Andrew's signature. I grabbed the basket as if it were a bomb, and ran to my car. Throwing it in the front seat, I sped out of the hotel like some crazed maniac. Then, like all maniacs, I started to laugh hysterically.

Coming to my senses, I pulled into a parking spot and read the note. Yup, it was only the sight of his signature that made me go mad.

> A.P. Moore
>
> A.k.a. Andria,
>
> I understand how a day with the family can be cooped up for the holidays, hopefully this will bring you some cheer.
>
> Talk to you soon,
>
> Andrew

I reread the note five times before starting on the road again. I glanced at the basket numerous times and started to eat the nuts half way there.

As I pulled into the driveway of my father's home, I realized that nothing had changed. There were a few new shrubs, but everything looked exactly the same. After my parents' divorce, my father stayed in my childhood home until I was around ten. That was when he moved closer to Baltimore. The small single-family dwelling has been home ever since.

Dad walked out rubbing his graying beard. As he walked straight towards me with open arms, I noticed his mustache had vanished. "Andria, you're late."

I hugged him, "Good to see you too Dad. There was some traffic. You shaved your mustache?"

I have asked him to shave thousands of times, but he always said it was a part of him. He shuffled his boot-clad feet kicking up snow on his jeans. "You...ummm, Pilar likes it. Hey, you've asked me to and...whatever. I'm just glad you got here safe, Kiddo. Let me get your bags." I grabbed the basket, and we walked into the house.

He brought my luggage upstairs to my old room while I placed the basket in the kitchen. "Andria," Pilar said as she wiped her hands before giving me a hug. "We're so glad you could make it."

Her wide brown eyes were bright, yet tired as she placed loose strands of long black hair into her bun. "Thanks, Pilar. Umm, you didn't have to start dinner. I was going to—"

"Nonsense! You've done enough of feeding Dan for all of these years. I'm glad I get a chance to do that now."

My father was a horrible cook and the only reason I had done most of the cooking was because I couldn't stomach his cuisine. The man cooked everything in a crock-pot, and chili every night quickly got old. "Ah, yeah. I bet he's happy with that." I smiled as I grabbed a soda from the refrigerator.

Pilar and my father met at one of my school functions. Her daughter Jaimie was one grade ahead of me. They both were single parents and started meeting for lunches and then dinners and so on. Pilar also has a son Carlos, and her son-n-law happened to be Brandon. Jaimie and Brandon dated their senior year in high school, eventually getting married.

Even though Brandon and I were good friends, Jaimie and I had never seemed to mesh well. She treated me as a threat. Brandon said it was her personality, and she was like that with everyone, but I wasn't naïve. I knew she only tolerated me because of him. Now that her Mom was my dad's girlfriend, that didn't make our relationship any better. You would have thought with Brandon marrying her, she would be comfortable around me. But, unfortunately, that wasn't the case. For his sake, I tried to make sure I was civil, even with her occasional snide remarks.

"Hey, you didn't have to bring me a gift." Dad's blue eyes gleamed as he picked up a bottle of beer.

"It was actually given to me by a guy I met."

"I don't know how I feel about some guy giving you a basket of beer. You don't know this fella." Dad's eyebrows furrowed, and he gave me a concerned look.

I grabbed the bottle opener and opened a bottle for him. "It's not like that Dad. Everyone kno—it was just a joke."

"Still not sure what a basket of beer has to do with a joke, Andria."

"It's from that pub I hung out in at college. Hey, how was your hunting trip yesterday?"

I knew the topic of hunting would change Dad's focus. I laughed when Pilar knowingly shook her head and continued to season the turkey. "It was a good day. We did a little ice fishing, as well. I was telling Pilar we should have a boil tonight. I can pick up some fresh seafood at the market." He winked at her. Then pinched her side rolls as she swatted his hands away from her stomach and continued prepping.

It was weird seeing my dad...playful. "That sounds like a great idea. I'll do that, and we can give Pilar a break for the night."

She stopped patting the turkey with butter. "Oh Andria, you don't have to—"

"I want to," I smiled. Seafood boil was now on the menu.

Carlos, Brandon, and Jaimie came over to join us for dinner, along with a couple of Dad's army buddies and their families. It was a house full of people, which felt strange because it had always been just Dad and I. We weren't very social and it seemed to work for us, but things had changed. It wasn't too bad. I always wanted to know how it would be to have a large family around for the holidays.

After dinner, I went upstairs to my room, and called Erin to fill her in on the gift Andrew left for me. It had been busy, and that was the first time I had a moment to breathe. We giggled and laughed like schoolgirls before I hung up. On my way downstairs, I saw Brandon heading to the bathroom. "Were you trying to get away from us?"

I positioned myself against the wall. "I needed to call Erin, and *no*, I was just thinking it felt strange having a house full of people."

"Funny how things change, huh?"

"Yeah..."

That made me a little sad not having my mom here, but my parents were happier people apart from each other.

"You look good," he said as his eyes swept over me.

I crossed my arms. "Thanks. How's married life?"

He shifted from one foot to the other. "Not what I expected."

"What do you mean?"

"I'm not saying I don't love Jaimie, or enjoy being married to her. It's not as simple as I thought it would be."

I walked closer to him. "Are you two having problems?"

He nervously looked over my shoulder down the stairs. "No, nothing like that. It's just...like you said, it feels weird having a house full of folks. It feels weird being married, that's all."

I hadn't spoken to Brandon much since he and Jaimie were married last summer. But, I knew my friend, and something was definitely up. "Do you want to talk about it?"

"It's nothing. Hey, I finally read your book."

I gave him a special copy, but I never thought he'd actually read it. "You really read it?"

"Of course I did. It wasn't too bad." He sent me a teasing smile.

"Well thanks for that compliment. I thought you said it was a chick lit."

"It is, but it wasn't too nauseating." He laughed.

"I still can't believe I have a book out there."

"Yeah. Ummm...Andria..." He looked hesitant and uncomfortable. "How much of it was about me?"

I stepped back confused. "What?"

"The parts and all..."

It had taken me a minute before clarity came. "Brandon, *nothing* was about you."

"Ouch." He stumbled back placing his hand over his heart.

"Did you want it to be?"

"I'm not saying that. I was only curious."

I looked around us, to see if anyone was near. "Brandon, that night was a mistake."

"I know," he whispered. "I was just wondering."

"I see. Now *I'm* curious as to what parts you thought were about you."

"Well, actually. None of it, but I thought maybe you had embellished."

"I would have had to embellish *a lot*."

"Andria!" he half shouted.

"Sorry, I didn't mean it like that. You know it was awkward and—"

"Not good."

We both stood there staring at the other before we started to laugh.

"Can you believe I'm a romance writer, and my first experience was almost with my best friend? It would have been horrible."

He looked hurt. "Hey! Not horrible. It would've be—"

"Wrong," I said as he nodded in agreement. "Although, I will never be able to thank you for being so kind to me."

He looked puzzled. "How was I supposed to be?"

My eyes glanced down to the floor. "I don't know, but it could have gone all kinds of wrong." I looked up at him, and his half grin before he turned to enter the bathroom.

I was on a date with Joe Walter. He was one of the popular boys in high school, and I was stunned when he had asked me out on a date. I was so excited, even though Brandon and Erin both warned me not to go out with him. Erin had a sick feeling that something was going to happen, and Brandon said he had a bad reputation. I blew both of them off, and that was something that I'd always regret.

Everything seemed to go fine at first. We went to see a movie and then had pizza at a restaurant before Joe took me home. Dad was away that evening working the late shift, and I mistakenly invited Joe inside. We sat and talked for a while before he made his move. I was thrilled and excited at first—I was a virgin in every way—and he was my first kiss. I naively thought that was as far as it would go until he started grabbing and groping me. Even though I said to stop, he continued on.

Panicked, I started to scream, but he reminded me that no one was home and that I had been begging for it all night. I realized something horrible was about to happen, and I only had a quick window of opportunity to do something to stop it. I thought back to everything Dad had taught me about defending myself. Then I shoved my knee hard into his groin, pushed him off of me, and ran to my room. I grabbed the phone and called Brandon, knowing he was at the auto shop he worked at down the street. While Joe continued to bang on my door.

Soon, Brandon came crashing in. He was working out then and was built like a tank. His mere size was already intimidating, yet the anger radiating out of his blue eyes was horrifying. He beat the crap out of Joe.

After, Brandon said he would call Dad, but I asked him not to. I let him in the house knowing I wasn't allowed to have boys over, and at the time, I blamed myself.

I knew *none* of it was my fault. But, at that time, I wasn't thinking rationally. Even though Brandon told Joe he was going to tell Dad anyway, I wouldn't let him. However, I did let him and his friends from school beat the crap out of Joe, before telling him never to look or speak to me again.

Erin and Brandon rotated staying with me at night when Dad was working the late shift until I felt safe again. It was during those nights that Brandon and I got closer. Eventually, I felt better and Erin stopped coming over, but Brandon would stop by to check in after his shift at work.

One night, I asked Brandon if he thought I was attractive. Of course, he looked at me as if I were crazy, but he said I was. I confessed to him that I was still a virgin with no prospects, and Joe was the first and only guy I had kissed. He was appalled and said he would rectify that immediately.

The kiss Brandon and I shared was sweet and nice. Nothing heavy or heated—at first—then something happened, and he kissed me more firmly. I wasn't sure then, but I suspected Brandon and I had totally different feelings for each other. Even though I could see why a lot of girls were attracted to his dark and handsome features, I wasn't into Brandon like that. I didn't want to hurt him. I was the one who had asked, and I stupidly decided to see where it went.

I opened my eyes to see if he was getting into it. His eyes were closed, and the sounds he was making made it obviously clear how he felt. I froze; I halted my lips and stayed as still as possible. Brandon took that as an opportunity to unbutton my blouse and jeans at the same time.

After the initial shock that he actually thought I would have sex with him ended, I grabbed his hands as they fumbled with my buttons. He asked me what was wrong, and I told him "everything." The whole thought of what we—no he—was about to do was wrong.

He panicked and said he should have been more sensitive after the whole debacle with Joe. He wasn't thinking. I told him it had nothing to do with Joe. I wasn't sure why he looked so hurt, but he joked about getting carried away, and of course nothing more would have happened.

I loved Brandon, but I wanted my first experience to be...everything.

As I turned to head back down the stairs, my cell rang in my pocket. Usually, I don't answer private unknown numbers, but when I looked at my cell, I had a weird, unexplainable feeling. "Hello?"

"Hello, I'm looking for Andria Moore."

I stopped walking. I knew that voice. "This is Andria."

"I hope I'm not interrupting anything important."

My mouth went dry. "No. Ummm, I was...ah, I was just finishing talking to Brandon."

Why did I sound like a bumbling buffoon?

"Brandon is there, Andria?"

With that, my mouth watered as my entire body hummed with excitement. Andrew's tone was clipped, yet all sorts of visuals flashed in my head.

He dragged out. "Andria?"

"His mother-in-law is dating my dad. How did you get this number? I mean, I didn't give it to you, and I wanted to tell you thank you for the basket."

"I'm a pretty resourceful guy. I'm glad you liked it."

"My dad really likes it," I laughed. "You didn't have to—"

"I wanted to. Are you busy this evening?"

"We just finished dinner..." Not quite sure why I whispered the last part.

"I happen to be in the area and thought I could see you."

I slid down the wall, sitting on the floor. "You just happened to be in Baltimore? It's a two hour drive."

"Yes, I know, but once I drove out of DC, I was heading in the direction of Baltimore."

I smiled big. "I see. Well, since you're in the area, I would love to see you again."

"Good, I will be there within the hour."

"Oh, okay. Do I even need to give you my address?"

"No, need."

"Should I be scared of your ability to track me down so easily?"

"You can trust me Andria. I won't bite."

And with that, I was a little disappointed.

CHAPTER FOUR

It had been over an hour, and I started to worry if I had imagined the whole conversation. Andrew was late, and since it was our first...whatever, I had nothing to compare his sense of time to. I thought of calling him, but I didn't want to seem too eager or desperate.

What was I thinking? The man tracked me down, was driving *two* hours to see me, and *I* was worried about looking anxious? Well, maybe a little. I tried my best not to act like a fangirl, but Andrew Hughes was driving to my home to see me. *Me*, Alexandria Paige Moore. It didn't matter how successful I was. Or the fact that Andrew wasn't the only celebrity I had met. Every insecurity a girl could have came flooding over me. Even ones I never thought I had.

Having rushed everyone out of the house, I asked Pilar to cover for me with Dad. I gave her my credit card, treating them to a movie. I knew Dad was suspicious with my sudden "headache," but I wanted everyone out.

When I heard the doorbell, my heart nervously beat faster. I slowly counted to ten before opening the door, and finding Andrew soaked from head to toe. "Oh my gosh, are you okay?"

I didn't even realize it was raining, and by the looks of it, it was turning to ice and sleet.

"Come in before you freeze to death."

"I think it's too late," he coughed out as he entered.

Even though I felt sorry for the wet man who stood in front of me, my lady bits started tingling at the sight of a wet Andrew. His hair was darker and somehow sexier, and his lips were plump and red from the cold. The gray jacket he wore was open, displaying the black wet t-shirt that defined every inch of his chest. Thoughts of Andrew in the shower came to mind before hearing him cough again. "Let me get some towels, please, come and sit down. I'll make some tea." He followed me into the kitchen.

As Andrew took a seat at the table, I ran upstairs to collect a bunch of towels. I put a few in the dryer to warm-up and gave him the others. I poured a cup of tea that I had made and placed it in front of him. "Drink, you could catch pneumonia. What happened?" I asked, sitting next to him.

"I had a flat tire and a low battery cell. This made it impossible to keep a signal when I tried the auto club. I had to change the tire myself in this weather," frustratingly saying as he ran his hand through his hair.

"Oh, Andrew."

He took a sip of the hot liquid. "Thanks for the tea," he sneezed.

I stood and grabbed his coat as I headed upstairs to get the warm towels. I threw his coat in the dryer, and grabbed my hairdryer before returning downstairs to wrap the towels around him. "This should warm you up, and I placed your jacket in the dryer. Do you want to dry your hair?" He nodded and started to dry it off with a towel. "I had a better idea."

Turning on the hairdryer, I started combing through his wet hair with my fingers. He let out a contented moan that spoke directly to my girly bits. It didn't help that I was thinking of grabbing and pulling said hair.

"Andria," he purred. "That feels so good."

There was only so much of that I could hear without mounting him right then and there in the chair. "I think you're dry now," I said turning off the dryer.

"Thank you," he cooed as he placed his hand on my wrist.

I stood looking at his hand for a moment. "It's the least I could do. You did come all this way. Why exactly?"

"For you," he said directly into my eyes.

"Okay?"

"Am I scaring you?"

I wasn't sure what Andrew saw on my face, but I wasn't alarmed that he had found me; I *was* scared as to where it would lead. "Andrew, I've been hurt—"

"Never by me," he said confidently and with finality.

I gaped at him, lost for what to say next before asking, "Are you hungry? Why don't I fix you something?"

"You don't have to do that." He squeezed my wrist.

"I want to. It will only take a minute. We had a seafood boil, and there is plenty left. It'll only take a few minutes to heat up. I'll grab some French bread for dipping and make a salad to start," I said and began to cook Andrew Hughes dinner.

Watching Andrew eat was worse than watching him drink. I was envious of Dad's utensil as he placed the fork in his mouth. "This is incredible, Andria. You're a terrific cook."

"Thanks. My dad isn't the best cook. As a kid, I got tired of his cooking quickly, so I started to do all the cooking for both of us. When I come home, I try to cook for him as much as possible. Things have changed now that he is dating Pilar, but I wanted to do this for him today. Pilar can cook on Thanksgiving," I said smiling.

"Do you like Pilar?"

I started to collect the empty dishes. "I do. I've known her for...what seems like my entire life."

"She's this Brandon's mother?" His brows furrowed.

"Mother-in-law." I smiled to myself.

He finished his food and insisted on helping with the dishes. It felt weird and normal at the same time. We fell into a fairly comfortable domestic flow. I washed, he dried, and after wiping down everything, we sat in the living room and talked.

"I can't believe you came all this way to see me," I confessed.

He slid closer to me on the sofa stretching one arm behind me. "You were the first person I thought of when I woke up this morning."

I was literally left speechless.

He moved in closer as his free hand started tracing imaginary circles up my arm. "There seems to be some sort of connection between us, Andria. Don't you feel it?"

Heck yea! But, all I could do was nod my head.

"I have never just dropped in to see a girl that I just met, but you are not just any girl, are you, Ms. Moore?"

His voice sounded like pure sin, and I wanted to give him my soul right then and there. I sat staring as his fingers continued to move up and down my arm while goose bumps followed in their path.

"May I kiss you, Andria?"

Looking into his burning eyes, my entire being was nervous and excited by what I saw in them. He continued to make me speechless, yet I nodded, and then he leaned in.

My chest heaved as Andrew stopped within an inch of my face and looked intently into my eyes. My mouth watered as he glanced at my lips before tilting his head forward.

Seeing his beautiful face up close was too much, and I closed my eyes. His lips were warm and soft, and I found it difficult to breathe. As he pressed his lips into mine, I slightly opened them, and he followed leaning into me.

Andrew kissed slow and gentle, and as I felt his arms wrap around my back, I stiffened up. I willed my body to relax, but I *was* kissing Andrew Hughes. I was a total wreck inside. I kept telling myself to breathe, but my body wasn't listening. When his hands soothingly started to caress my back, my mind and body finally relaxed in his arms.

After several more warm kisses, I threw caution to the wind and opened my mouth a bit more. I then felt his smile on my lips as he followed and pressed harder.

That should have been my first kiss, I thought.

As the kiss deepened, my body began to have a mind of its own when my hands found refuge in his hair. My fingers wrapped themselves around the silken strands as I pulled Andrew in closer. The moment that I heard myself hum in satisfaction, he shifted closer and the kiss heated up.

When I say heated, I mean, it heated the *hell* up.

I couldn't get enough of him, and the sounds vibrating off Andrew caused my thighs to rub together. When he pulled me in tighter, it was really getting harder to breathe. Our mouths seemed to fight for dominance, and I surrendered gracefully to the master that was Andrew Hughes. When his hand glided around to my breast squeezing, a wanton, "Andrew, yes!" escaped me.

I was on sensory overload. My mind couldn't focus on one specific act as my core pulsated. Andrew broke the kiss, seeking air along my neck as he nipped and kissed up and down creating a heated trail. When he reached my collarbone, he inhaled with a low rumble. "Need you now, Andria."

I wasn't sure what happened first, but all I remember was a group gasp at the same time I felt a breeze on my chest as Andrew ripped open my blouse. I could hear the buttons hit the hardwood floor at the same time I heard my Dad yell, "Andria!"

"Dad!"

We both looked over, and I saw fire in both Dad and Brandon's eyes as Pilar and Jaimie grinned widely while Carlos looked on in disgust. "Geez, Andria. I'm going to be scarred for life," he said.

"Alexandria Paige Moore, what the hell is going on, and who the hell is he?" Dad asked as he stormed toward us.

"Is that Andrew Hughes?" Jaimie pointed her long fake nails towards us.

"Answer him Andria," Brandon added coming behind Dad.

"Guys, could you give us a minute," I pleaded.

I watched as they all headed to the kitchen, leaving Andrew and me alone.

He took my hand before saying, "That wasn't exactly how I wanted to meet your father."

I think I was more in shock that he thought of meeting my dad versus my dad walking in on us. "I am so sorry. I didn't realize what time it was—they're early."

"Why are you apologizing?" He smirked. "I was the one who got carried away. Andria, I hope you don't think this is why I came here," he said, looking a bit concerned while he collected my buttons.

"No. Ummm...no, of course not. I hope you don't think I would...and we just met."

We both sat there awkwardly before hearing my dad say, "Anytime!"

My eyes had widened in horror before Andrew shook his head laughing. "I am totally embarrassed, but please believe me when I say that I don't normally do this."

He took my hand and placed a soft kiss on the inside of my wrist before saying, "Andria, if I were being honest, the only thing I regret is that they came home early."

My mouth opened.

Feeling the cold breeze hit my bra clad chest; I excused myself as I ran upstairs to grab another shirt. When I entered the kitchen, everyone was seated, including Andrew having a cup of coffee. "Do I need to introduce Andrew?"

A gruff came out of my father as he folded his arms. "No, he took care of that. Why didn't you tell me he was coming?"

I looked around the crowded kitchen as everyone waited for an answer. "It was a last-minute thing, Dad."

"Is that so? A last-minute drive from Virginia, Andria."

I glanced at a guilty Andrew. I wasn't gone *that* long. "Dad..."

Pilar placed her hand on my father's arm. "Dan, leave Andria alone. She's an adult. Andrew, please excuse Dan. It's hard sometimes for fathers to see their little girls grow into women." Dad grunted. "It's true. Even for Mothers with their sons. Last month Carlos told me he had a girlfriend. Even though I said he was too young. "She glanced over at him.

"Mom!" Carlos said wide-eyed and embarrassed.

"But...I had to face the fact that my little man is growing up."

"That's all nice and dandy," my father added.

"Anyway. So Andrew, do you know you look a lot like that movie star?"

"I get that a lot," he grinned at me.

"Pilar, he *is* that Andrew."

It had taken her a moment before the light bulb turned on. "Oh, my. Well, how did you two meet? Are you going to be in her movie?"

I stood next to Andrew. "It's not *my* movie, and things aren't finalized. We met at Andrew's premier last night."

It was easier to say that, than when his bodyguard/brother-in-law spilled a drink on me. The questions would start flying.

"I now see where the basket came from," Dad mumbled under his breath.

Brandon stepped in front of me. "You two only met last night, and we find you—"

"Brandon!" I eyeballed him.

"So you're Brandon?" Andrew glared at him.

"What's it to you?" He pushed toward him as Andrew stood up.

I stood watching the two men puff themselves up like roosters, and I noticed that Jaimie didn't see anything humorous about it either. "What's it to *you*, Brandon?" she asked eyeballing her husband.

"Babe, he was all over her—"

"None of your business, Brandon," I interrupted.

"You're my—"

He stopped himself, as Jaimie and I both scowled at him. Andrew looked pissed, and Dad looked content. Carlos smirked, and Pilar looked horrified as she walked up to Andrew saying, "I apologize for my children. They don't seem to have any manners. Are you staying for Thanksgiving?"

They all looked at him, including me. "Thank you for the thoughtful offer, but I need to return back to Virginia. My parents are expecting me for dinner tomorrow."

"You drove out of your way to see Andria?" Dad asked.

"How romantic," Pilar added wrapping her arms around Dad's forearm.

"She's not that easy," Brandon stated under his breath.

"After meeting your daughter Mr. Moore, I couldn't help myself. I have the utmost respect for Andria. Even if she's a romance writer," he grinned.

I lightly punched his shoulder, sneering before smiling. "I'm so glad Mr. Hollywood overlooked that little flaw."

Andrew squinted his eyes at me and smirked. I so wanted to be back on that couch.

"I had better head out. It was nice meeting all of you," Andrew said as he collected his things.

"I'll walk you out."

Pilar stopped us as she hugged a surprised looking Andrew. "Hopefully, we can see you again," and with that, we walked to his car.

We stopped in front of the passenger door. "I'm sorry about...that." I nodded toward the house.

He moved a stray hair off of my face. "Don't be. They seemed nice, and I can't blame your father, but what's with Brandon?"

I was wondering the same thing. "He's like my older brother, Andrew. He's protective."

"Uh-huh."

"Ummm, about earlier, I hope you don't think I do that... that quick." I couldn't look at him.

"Tonight didn't change anything except that I want to see you again. I need a redo of this date."

I looked up. "Was that what it was?"

"I was hoping it could be. It wasn't exactly what I had planned. I thought I would take you out for dessert before the tire fiasco, but I did have dinner—which was wonderful, by the way. It's just not what I had planned, although I did enjoy the evening very much." He smiled.

"So did I."

"You'll be back in D.C in a couple of days, right?"

"I promised my best friend Erin that we would go shopping for black Friday before I return to Dallas."

"I was planning on returning to LA Friday morning, but how about we try this again?"

It was hard to contain the burst of joy I felt. "Sounds...ummm...great."

"This time, it will be a proper date. I'll call you. Till then, Andria."

He stepped in closer; entwining his hands with mine as he bent down to kiss me. It was soft and sweet. I wanted to hold on to that moment forever, but he pulled back. "I thought I heard a shot-gun."

We both looked over to the front door, and there stood my father holding a hunting rifle. "Dad!"

"Dan, get in here!" Pilar yelled.

I was appalled, but Andrew laughed it off, and said, "Your father kind of scares me."

"Dad's harmless." I kissed him that time before walking to the driver's side. "Goodnight Andrew."

"Goodnight Andria."

I watched as he pulled out of the driveway and headed back to Virginia, and then turned toward the house. Dad had no right pulling that crap with the gun. I was twenty-four years old! "What the hell was that?" I asked, storming into the house after Andrew drove off.

"Watch your language young lady. I was only joking. I always wanted to do that."

"You thought *now* was a good time?"

"You're lucky I didn't load it. I enter *my* home, with a strange man pawing at *my* daughter, on *my* sofa."

"Yeah, and this guy seems like a prick!" Brandon jumped in.

"How would you know that?" I hissed.

"Come on, it's obvious. You just met, and he's trying to get into your pants."

"I think you need to focus on your own relationship and stay out of mine."

In hindsight, saying that in front of Jaimie wasn't the best idea, which didn't make our holiday any more festive. Brandon should have known not to cross me. I wasn't proud of it, but when provoked, I've been known to have a temper.

Usually, I respected Brandon's opinions when it came to guys. I have made my fair share of bad choices, but Andrew was different. For some reason, Brandon didn't want to hear that. I wasn't sure what was going on between him and Jaimie, but he needed to butt out.

CHAPTER FIVE

The drive back to Virginia usually was soothing, but after the Thanksgiving fiasco, I was ready for a relaxing day with Erin. Nothing about black Friday was relaxing, unless you enjoy crowded stores full of pulling and shoving people. It was the Superbowl for Erin, for me, not so much. When she suggested going to the spa in the afternoon, I gladly accepted her offer. But, when we arrived at the spa, Erin had another agenda. I told her how far Andrew and I had gotten on the sofa, and she was determined that I needed a full work-over.

I wasn't lying to Andrew when I said that I usually don't fall into bed with every man that I meet. Yet, I did have a secret. One I wasn't ashamed of. It was private, and no one's business other than my own. Erin knew—of course. But, because of the nature of my work, I couldn't reveal it to anyone else. I was a virgin. You could see why I had kept *that* a secret. I wasn't sure how many books I would have sold if the public knew that A.P. Moore was a v-i-r-g-i-n.

I could hear them now, "What does she know about sex and romance?" Well...a few things since the book became a best seller. But sadly, I was afraid that wouldn't stop the ridicule. There were a couple of times I thought I was ready to get up on the horse and ride the saddle—no pun intended—but every time it felt...wrong.

When I had first arrived at Georgetown, I went to a party and met this guy who had seemed nice. We went out a couple of times and then I thought what the heck. I didn't want to leave college and not experience everything it had to offer.

One night, he wanted me to go down *there* on him. I couldn't. It was too intimate of an act for me, and I really didn't know the guy very well. When I told him that I felt uncomfortable, he laughed, and said I was the first girl who had refused. Then I thought about how many there were before me.

I left.

The last guy was a year ago. I dubbed him my first "adult relationship". He wined and dined me, and it was nice, but when it came to sex, it was a total flop.

He had planned the perfect evening at his place—flowers, music, low lighting. It was going to be our first time. I wasn't in love with him, but I figured that would come later—I was ready to get my v-card punched.

Everything was going along like a romance movie—nothing was unexpected. He kissed me and then led me to his bedroom. I went into the bathroom to make myself comfortable. When I came out in the prerequisite teddy, he told me how beautiful I was and placed a glass of champagne in my hand. He laid me down gently, and started to kiss my neck and proceeded down my stomach to *my* happy place. I held my breath in anticipation as he told me he was going to make me feel so good.

I waited.

And waited.

The big "O" never came.

I was starting to believe that the big "O" was a myth. I must say that he did put in a lot of effort, but I felt nothing. I thought about faking it so that we could get it over with, and that's when I suppressed a giggle.

So, I thought.

When I saw the irritation on his face as he was really putting in an effort, I slipped out another giggle. As much as I wanted to lose my virginity, I didn't want to "get it over with."

Before I could say stop, he asked me to leave, frustrated from my lack of enthusiasm. I didn't understand why it wasn't working, and I tried to explain to him that it wasn't him it was me. But he didn't want to hear that, and I couldn't blame him.

Yet, I *was* starting to think it was me.

I confided in Erin, who assured me that it wasn't me. But, I soon realized, I couldn't just sleep with a guy for the sole purpose of being deflowered. Don't get me wrong, I was all for the empowered women—I wrote about them. I respected those who wanted to wait until marriage, and I couldn't judge those who hadn't.

I lived through Erin's escapades. She happened to lose her v-card a long time ago, but I wanted...more. I wanted the intimacy, and I definitely needed to be in love with the guy. So, I made a pact to myself—no sex until I was in love.

Did that include Andrew Hughes?

The jury was still out on that one. I had to admit the thought that Andrew would be my first both thrilled and frightened me at the same time. This had now brought me to the spa with Erin. In her words, "You always need to be prepared, and you need to clean the cobwebs out down there, Andria." I would be insulted if anyone else had said that to me. Sadly, she was right, and I did need an overhaul. I got waxed, plucked, scrubbed and kneaded. I was in so much pain; I wished that I had thought about it sooner and not the same day as my date with Andrew.

"Do you know where he's taking you?" Erin asked while rubbing ice over her neck.

"No, but he told me to dress comfortably."

She took a sip of water. "Huh, so that crosses out dinner at D.C's finest."

"I don't care where he takes me." It was getting too hot in here.

"So naïve," she said as she lay back down.

I stared at her as I stood under the cold-water shower. "Why would you say that?"

"I swear Andria, A.P. Moore had to be another person. *She* would have wanted something romantic and grand," she said, sitting up.

"Whatever." I grabbed a towel and headed out of the steam room.

"You're late."

Andrew smiled coyly. "My apologies. It's a bad habit that I picked up in LA. You must be Erin."

Erin didn't seem fazed by Andrew's fame. "Nice to meet you, Andrew."

"Is Andria ready?"

I watched from the hallway as they both acted like this was an ordinary thing. Taking one last look in the mirror, I walked out. "Hi, Andrew." He stood smiling in a pair of dark denim jeans that fit him perfectly, and a long sleeve green polo shirt with a leather jacket. "You look nice."

Chills coursed through me as I watched his eyes glide over my body. "I was about to say the same thing, except, you look incredible."

I had on a pair of dark gray jeans, with a gray printed tank top that had a sheer silver blouse overlay. Erin said it was casual enough, but insisted that I wear a pair of studded designer heels for accent.

We said goodbye to Erin and walked out of her brownstone to an expensive looking sports car. It was dark the other night, but I was sure that this car was different from the one Andrew had driven to Baltimore. I wasn't good with cars—never was really interested—but I had to ask. As Andrew opened my door, he said it was a prototype that his sister, Taylor helped to design.

I sat in and crossed my legs—he paused for a moment, and looked down at my shoes. Andrew stood in thought as he eyed my shoes before closing the door. I wasn't sure why it took so long for him to come around to the driver's side, but when he finally got in, he started the car and sped off. "So, where are you taking me?"

He looked at my shoes again as he shifted in his seat. "A little place that I thought you might like."

We drove for about twenty minutes before pulling up to our destination. I didn't realize at first that we had stopped. Andrew was explaining that he was able to test drive every car that Taylor and his Father worked on. They had several European contracts, and when a new feature was designed, he offered his services to try them out.

Before exiting, Andrew put on a baseball hat and glasses with darkened green lenses, and walked around to open my door. When I stepped out, I stopped in my tracks. "You're taking me to The Anchor?" my voice cracked with surprise.

"I thought we needed a do over."

At that moment, I was rethinking that vow of celibacy.

Andrew reserved a quiet spot in the back, partitioned off away from the main dining area and prying eyes. We were in a high booth and no one else was seated in the section. He took off his hat and glasses, and it looked as if I would have Andrew all to myself.

We drank beer and talked. Actually, I drank Shandy's. He found it humorous that I wasn't a fan of beer. I explained that I picked it up on a London trip. It's the only way I drank the stuff, and I wasn't going to a pub and order white wine.

Andrew ordered every appetizer on the menu and surprisingly ate most of it. I couldn't help laughing as buffalo sauce dripped down his full lips. "What?"

I stared as the sauce dripped further and my mouth suddenly watered. "Nothing. You seem to be enjoying the food."

I leaned over and scooped up the sauce with my thumb. One edge of his lip curled up. "The only time that I get to eat like this is usually when I'm with Wade—or at a game. My cook doesn't believe in junk food, and my mother would be disappointed that I was here."

"I see." I wasn't sure why all of a sudden I felt like he didn't care enough that it was okay for me.

"Did I say something wrong?" he asked and stopped eating.

"No. I'm...umm, glad that you feel comfortable to bring me here."

He tilted his head in thought. "The only reason I brought you here was because this was...it's where I first saw you. It wasn't under the best circumstances," he chuckled. "You told me this was your place in college, and I didn't want it to be tarnished because of me. When I said that I wanted a redo, I was serious. I wanted at least one happy memory with you here."

"You didn't have to—"

"I did, and yes, my mother would be very upset that my attempt of a second date with you is here. But under the circumstances I think that she would understand."

I smiled at him and asked, "Are you close with your mother?"

He sat up straight. "I love my mother and respect her. She was the one who taught me how important it is to respect all women." He laughed to himself as he continued saying, "She would take me on 'mommy and me date nights' telling me it was good practice on how to treat a lady."

"That is really cute."

He picked up his glass. "It wasn't as a child, but I grew to like them. I'll let you in on a little secret. We still have them," he smiled before downing his beer.

I went into a trance watching his adam's apple bounce as the liquid flowed down his throat. "Could you be any more perfect?" I thought, but apparently said that out loud when his eyes squinted. "Umm, sorry, I didn't mean—"

Then that incredible laugh of his erupted from his chest, the one that always forced a smile on my face every time that I heard it. "I am going to hold you to that. When I mess up in the future, I will remind you of this day."

"You say that with such confidence."

His fingers started to sweep back and forth over the top of my hand and electricity sparked to every nerve ending in my body. Andrew sat quietly in thought watching his movements as I studied his face.

His eyes made contact with mine, holding them hostage as he asked, "Would you like to take this somewhere private, where I can show you how confident I am?"

What could I say to that?

When Andrew told me that we were going to his place, I assumed it was a hotel since he lived in LA. "This is a hotel?" I asked as we pulled up to a very expensive high-rise.

"No. This was mine and Taylor's place to use during college. It was a gift from our parents. Taylor and Wade used it while they went to school, and I was supposed to after I graduated from high school. Now, I use it when I'm in town, or they use it when they're in the city for a medical conference or an event."

He stepped out and opened my door. "I thought you were staying at the hotel during the premier?" I asked as we walked to the elevator.

"I did stay at the hotel. I let Mom and Dad use the condo, and since Wade was working, Taylor stayed at the hotel with him."

Andrew punched in a code, and the elevator opened to a private floor with only two doors. Andrew opened the first door, and we walked into an incredibly furnished apartment for two college kids. It looked as if Andrew's parents were doing quite well. "Did it always look like this?"

"It's changed a little, but yes."

Even though the place was spacious, it was very homey. The bottom level was one large space and the kitchen was adjacent to the living room. The furniture was plush with fluffy cream pillows, and the kitchen was very modern. I loved the dark hardwood floors, blending throughout the unit with the clean crisp colors of blue, cream and dark brown. The upstairs held a loft that could be seen from the living room. "There's a playroom upstairs." I coughed staring at him with wide eyes. "Not *that* kind of playroom. It's our recreational room," he said amusedly.

I turned from Andrew and walked around the large open space. "This is a beautiful place, Andrew."

"Wine?" he asked softly behind me.

The hairs on the back of my neck stood on end. "Yes, please."

He stepped to my side, walking to the kitchen asking, "White?"

"Please."

Per his instructions, I made myself comfortable on the large puffy sofa that I immediately sunk into. Andrew sat the glasses down and then sat next to me. I took a sip of the incredible tasting, obviously expensive wine. "This is really good."

"It's something that I found in Africa. Do you want to try my Roobernet?"

I watched as he swiveled the glass. "Maybe later. Do you travel often?"

"It comes with the job. It used to be enjoyable, but now it's a chore."

"I don't think that I will ever see it that way."

"Wait. One day you'll wish you were back in your own bed."

Taking another sip of wine, I imagined Andrew's bed for a moment. "I can see that happening, but not for a while. I'm excited to travel."

He placed his glass down and turned towards me. "Are you planning on doing that soon?"

"My book tour starts in two weeks. First, the US, then I'm off to Europe. I've been excited about it for months."

His face dropped. "How long will you be gone?"

"It's scheduled for six weeks."

He reached for his glass and took another sip. We didn't say anything for a while, and I wasn't sure what to think. I sat quietly until he asked out of the blue, "How did Andria Moore become A.P. Moore?"

"Well, it was Erin actually. She helped me to find my inner voice and encouraged me to write things down in a journal."

His brows furrowed. "You're saying you did *all* of those things?"

"No! Ummm, no. It was in my head. You read my book?" I thought, please no. It's embarrassing. Then I thought, you wrote the book, Andria.

"Sadly, I haven't read it—yet. But I bought it after we met. I plan to start it soon, actually."

Andrew was going to read my book, and I wanted to climb under the coffee table.

"I hear it's very good. I did flip through it. It seems different from what I thought you would write," he said with a sly grin.

As I turned closer to him intrigued, I asked, "How so?"

"We haven't known each other long, but you seem so...then the other night at your father's..." he trailed off. "When I skimmed your book, I saw another side of you..." and his grin became something more.

"It's fiction."

He licked his bottom lip. "It's pretty detailed."

The room started to feel warm. "Most romances are."

"Ah-huh." He scooted over.

"Pure fantasy, Andrew."

"Your fantasies?" He smirked.

Yes!

I didn't answer as I picked up my glass and took another sip of wine while Andrew watched. Something about him watching me sip my wine stirred feelings deep inside. As I sat the glass down, a vision of us on Dad's couch came to mind, and a low moan escaped from me. "You're killing me, Andria. Shall we finish where we left off?" With that, Andrew hovered over me.

As I breathed out "Andrew," it sounded more like a 'come hither'. You know that growl deep inside that says, I want you, *now*.

He achingly placed soft wet kisses along my neck, taking his time and making me very frustrated. I could feel myself getting heated down there, and I wanted more; but he was going too slowly. I moved my hands up his back until I reached what I wanted. I had a thing for his hair—I couldn't understand why, but pulling it gave me great joy and made me very, very...well...wanting.

As I pulled his silky locks, he kissed me harder, lower, and positioned himself on top of me. The weight felt incredible. I yanked his hair and he looked into my needy eyes. I was in awe of his beauty and was having an Andrew Hughes moment. He didn't seem real. Yet, I didn't care—his lips seemed real when his signature smirk splayed on his face. I attacked it, and I must admit, I attacked it really well.

This time, he let me take control. I placed firm kisses on his perfect lips and then coaxed them open, starting on his top lip before I attacked his bottom. I wanted a taste, and I didn't care that my heart was beating frantically out of my chest. I wanted to taste him, and taste him I did.

It seemed as if we were making out forever before I heard him say, "Bedroom." Actually, he growled it. Lips still locked, he sat me up and placed his hand in mine. We broke for air as he pulled me up off of the couch. We stood and kissed for a while longer before he started walking me to his room.

I thought, this was finally it, yet my mind and body decided this was a perfect time to start a civil war. My body wanted him, but my mind was saying slow down, it's too soon. Yet I didn't care. Andrew was walking me to his bedroom. Then my legs stopped moving. "What's wrong?" he whispered as his lips trailed behind my ear.

"I'm not sure?" Came out puzzled.

He stopped to look at me funny before smiling, "You ready?"

Well, I thought I was, but I couldn't move. I wasn't sure if it was fear or that I liked Andrew way too much.

"Andrew, maybe we should wait—" Involuntarily came out of my mouth.

Then the next thing I knew he had me pushed up against a wall, and his body pinned mine. He vigorously placed kisses up and down my neck as he pressed harder against me. I could feel exactly how much he wanted to do this when his legs bent lower, and he pushed firmly as he started to move up and down my denim jeans.

I had officially lost my mind. "Andrew. I...oh. .I...can't."

He grabbed my hands and placed them firmly above my head, causing my back to arch. My sensitive nubs rubbed along his chest as his lips brushed over my outer ear. My entire body shivered as he whispered, "I want you."

"I want you too," I breathlessly admitted.

He groaned in response and kissed me harder. His tongue slid along my bottom lip before his teeth pulled it into his awaiting mouth. The room filled with moans as our tongues explored each other. I tried several times to pull away, but Andrew was very good at pleading his case. His hands seared my flesh as they began to lift my blouse, exploring every inch as they slid up my body. When they reached my breasts, I panicked, and breathed out, "Stop."

He placed his forehead against mine as we both gasped for air. "Andria, I'm not going to make you do anything you're not comfortable with."

"I'm not saying that I don't want to do this. I just don't think I'm ready to do this now. Damn it! You're going to hate me!" I buried my face in his chest.

He placed his hands on each side of my face, lifting me to look at him. "I would never hate you, and definitely not because you want to wait. I am not going to pressure you." I couldn't look at him. "Hey! No hiding."

When I looked up, I saw the most sincere expression. "Andrew, I really didn't mean for it to get this far. I know it's hard for guys to—you know."

"Not going to lie to you, it's hard," he said with a grin. "But, I believe you're worth the wait."

"Are you for real?"

"That's what I thought the first time I saw you."

He was killing me.

"Why don't we take it slow, okay? We can play it by ear. We have plenty of time, and it's a good change."

I raised a brow at him. "You don't have to lie."

"I would never lie to you. I have women throwing themselves at me daily—"

"Not helping, Andrew!"

"Not what I meant. When you're ready, I'm ready."

"Until then, the thousands of women can have a go." The thought made me angry, and possessive. "Come on!" I grabbed at him to continue where we left off.

"Andria," he stopped me. "You have nothing to worry about. I want to get to know you better. *You*."

I heard him, but could I trust that he wasn't saying it just to appease me?

"LA and Dallas aren't that far away. You said you'd be in LA. for meetings, and I can come to Dallas. I want to try. And most of all, I want to see where this goes, all right? Don't worry. Now, I better take you back to Erin's before I really lose control." He gave me a chaste kiss, and I watched as he grabbed his things.

All I could think about was did I make the right decision and could this really work?

CHAPTER SIX

Sitting on the flight back home, my head was flooded with thoughts of last night. Erin had stayed up with me until I left for the airport. After the initial shock had worn off, she understood why I stopped things from going too far. She knew I wanted my first time to be special, and was proud that I was able to abstain. More liked amazed that I didn't chuck it all out the window.

I did have my doubts. Several times during our talk, I told her I had made a huge mistake, and was going to call Andrew and tell him to come and take me. Erin stopped me of course, stating how proud she was of me. If it were anyone else, I would have been proud of myself, but it was Andrew. How many chances do you get with a movie star? *Zero* and that was when I sobbed uncontrollably. Erin said it will all work out, and that she had a good feeling about him. I hoped so because I had gone over last night several times in my head, and the thought that I was a fool kept popping up.

Andrew was the perfect gentleman. The whole redo of our first meeting was a surprise. Although, to see him act like a normal guy *really* surprised me. Andrew was easy to talk to, and more than just a beautiful face.

Still, I hoped I didn't mess things up too badly, and he did say that he wanted us to work. I desperately would like to try. But the thoughts of "that may be impossible" and "what happens when he returns home to his life?" Flooded my mind.

Would he forget me? Go back to the multitudes of women who wanted him? What about Brittney? I didn't approach that subject again after he said they weren't together. I took him at his word, but....

For the entire flight home, I continued to go over all of the "what ifs."

It was warm, and I welcomed the heat. The air condition had been turned off while I was away. I checked my messages and emails before unpacking my bags. I hadn't heard from Andrew, and wondered when or if he would call.

He said he would call Andria, I reminded myself.

I spent the rest of the day in front of the television vegging out. A feeling of sadness hovered over me that I couldn't shake off. I missed Andrew, and that scared me.

The next morning I went to my publisher's office for a meeting. Elena had started her own publishing company ten years ago. She had purposely kept it small, calling it a boutique publishing agency. She usually focused on works from Hispanic women or those focused on the Southwest culture. Yet, she took me on, and I was neither Hispanic nor was my book set in the Southwest. In fact, it was set in London. Elena said she wanted to broaden the agency's work. Elena was greatly respected in her field, and she knew her stuff. I was very happy to have her and her team behind me.

"How was Thanksgiving, Andria?" she asked behind the huge glass desk.

"Good. I had dinner with my dad and his girlfriend's family."

"Was that awkward?" She started to type something on her laptop.

"Not at all. I've known them for a long time."

"Good. Don said you met Frank?"

I was surprised she knew him. "Yeah."

She stopped what she was doing and looked at me. "Isn't he hot? We've done some business together in the past."

The way she said it, I knew she was referring to more than business. Not only was Elena smart, but she was drop dead gorgeous. Her body was compact, but she had curves in all of the right places, and her silky brown curls were always perfect. She was a shrewd businesswoman, and a freak in the bedroom, and proud of it. She often mixed business with pleasure.

"Frank gave me tickets to Andrew Hughes's premier." Saying his name out loud hurt.

"He's been Andrew's manager ever since his first one died of a heart attack."

The way she said Andrew as if she knew him made me want to leap over her desk and pull her hair out. I wasn't normally a violent person, but like I said, Elena got around. The thought of her with Andrew...well....

"Now *that* is a hot piece of ass," she added leaning back in her chair. "What I would do for one night with Andrew Hughes..."

First, I felt relieved, and then a bit enraged. By the look on her face, she was imagining exactly what she would do. Then the feeling of panic struck me again. I kept thinking that I needed to call Andrew and tell him I was a fool to have stopped our intimacy from going further, and I needed to rectify that right away.

I called Erin after my meeting, who laughed at me, and said to get a grip. "Of course women are going to want him. He's a celebrity. But he wants *you* remember? You did something right."

"But he didn't call."

"Then call him. You have his number. But, please don't sound desperate."

"Whatever. I'll be in LA the end of the week. If I don't hear from him before then, I'll call. I'll have an excuse, right? I'm coming into town."

"Do what you feel, but he *will* call."

She was wrong; he didn't call. He did, however, leave a bouquet of flowers on my doorstep:

Andria,

I had an incredible time the other night. Thank you for indulging me in a do over.

   I will see you soon,

   Andrew

My heart sighed, and I breathed for the first time since I had left him. I put the flowers in water and placed the attached desert plants on my kitchen table. I stared at them until I realized I should call and thank him.

"You have reached Andrew Hughes's line." Okay? I used the same number he called me from, but why was some girl answering it. "Hello?"

"Is Andrew available?"

"He's in a meeting, may I take a message?"

"Yeah...yes, can you tell him Andria Moore called?"

"Does he have your number?"

I thought if he didn't, he could find out. "Yes, he does. Thank you," I said and hung up.

I did some work in my home office and sent Erin my schedule for the week. She knew my closet inside and out and even had a computerized inventory of it. It was cool actually. She would send me an email, and all I would have to do is open it up, and there was a virtual picture of the outfit she had picked out.

Keira arrived later that afternoon and helped me pack before we went over my schedule for LA. I had a couple of meetings at the studio, and then a book event my last day.

As I finished up some edits, Keira walked into my office with a blank stare on her face and the phone in her hand. "Keira, are you all right?"

Her dark brown eyes were wide under her glasses; before she placed them into her hair, pushing back the fine bob cut strands out of her face. "Andria, do you know Andrew Hughes?" I apparently gave her a blank look myself. "I thought so." She held the phone to her ear. "Sorry, Ms. Moore does not know an Andrew Hughes."

I snapped out of it and ran to grab the phone out of her hand, "Andrew!"

"You don't know an Andrew Hughes? We can rectify that immediately. Because I have it on good authority that he would like to know you very much," he said.

I gushed. Ummm, I meant...ugh, you know what I meant. "I'm sorry, it wasn't like that..." I stared at Keira.

He started to laugh. "How is it possible to miss you so damn much?'

My heart stopped. "I miss you, too."

By then, Keira had a look of shock on her face and stood there gawking at me. I shooed her away, and she left bitterly as I closed the door behind her.

"I heard you called?'

"I did. I wasn't sure how I got your office?" I said as I sat back down at my desk.

"I forward my phone to my assistant, Amy."

I wondered if she was the same Amy I had met with Frank. "The flowers are beautiful."

"Glad you liked them. I picked them out myself. You would have had them sooner, but the ones Amy had ordered didn't arrive to Erin's in time."

"How do you know that?"

"I called Erin, and she said nothing had arrived. I had words with Amy and did it myself. She's usually on top of things, but that was unacceptable."

"That's okay. But should I be surprised that you called Erin?"

"No. *She* wasn't. We had a nice talk."

I was going to kill her. She never mentioned anything, and I can only imagine what she had said.

"She's actually going to send me some samples. I didn't know she was a stylist. Even though I told her I already had one, she wouldn't take no for an answer. She has already emailed me her ideas, and they're actually good. I wouldn't have thought to put some of the clothes together, but they worked."

"You don't have a clue what you may have gotten yourself into. I love my best friend, but when it comes to fashion, she becomes a dictator. Hey, you don't have to do that for me."

"I'm not. She really is good."

"And please don't be mad at Amy. I think I met her with Frank."

"Is that so?"

"At the meeting I had the day of your premier."

"She went with him because I had to do a couple of appearances for the junket. Grant's people needed to go over some details."

"His studio is bidding for my book."

He was quiet for a moment too long. "Make sure you go over everything carefully. You need to have a say in what happens. If you want my people to—"

"Thank you, but my publisher's attorney is helping me."

"I'm sure you have the right people brokering this deal. But if you would allow me to say if it were *me*, I would let my own personal attorney look it over as well."

"Great advice and I was planning on having someone look over the final contract. Thanks for looking out for me. You have been in the business for a while."

"How are you?"

"Missing you." Not sure where that came from, but it shocked the heck out of me.

I could hear that smile over the phone. "I miss you too. When will you be in LA?"

"Oh, I forgot to tell you. I'll be there at the end of the week."

"Great! Can you send Amy your schedule?"

"I'll have Keira email that right away."

It was weird coordinating schedules with Andrew. It was weird that I had a schedule.

"I have to go, but can we talk later?"

"I would like that."

"Is this your landline? People still have them?"

"Funny. Yes, this is my 'landline' it's private—*was* private. No one has it except close friends and family. That's kinda why Keira said what she did."

"Ah-huh. Can I be placed on the list?"

"You already are."

"I really have to go, but I'll call you later this evening, okay?"

He hung up and as soon as I walked out of my office, Keira attacked. "Please tell me that was not Andrew—the—Hughes?"

"Andrew the Hughes?"

"Andria!" she drawled out. Keira would never admit it, but she had a bit of a twang. When her relatives came to visit from Japan, they mentioned she sounded like a cowgirl, and I thought she was going to kick them out of the office.

Not able to contain the gigantic grin on my face, we both giggled like schoolgirls. I told her everything. Well, not everything.

Andrew and I spoke every day for the remainder of the week. We talked about everything and nothing. We spoke a lot about our childhood as well as our families. He was very close to his family, and I loved that about him.

He also had a tight knit group of friends. The number may have been few, but they were very loyal. If they weren't working for him, they were involved in some way in his life. Except for Frank; he was an outsider.

The manager that discovered Andrew was like a godfather to him. He was up in age and had health problems. When he died, it had affected Andrew deeply. He didn't want to get close to anyone again at that time, so he picked Frank. Andrew said he was a prick, but he knows the business.

Frank was the one that brought on Amy, along with a favor he mumbled about. Andrew never wanted an assistant, but Frank felt it would make his life easier. I couldn't agree more. I never thought I needed Keira, but she made everything seamless.

Andrew invited me to stay at his place, but I knew that wouldn't be a great idea. If I was going to stay strong, the last thing I needed was Andrew in the next room.

Naked.

Maybe not naked, but I would imagine him naked, and then everything would be thrown out the window, and yet, why did I care?

CHAPTER SEVEN

The moment the plane hit the ground, I was sick from the butterflies that had been fluttering in my stomach for the entire flight. I didn't want to drink, but I had two screwdrivers to take the edge off, and I was still a mess. Andrew was picking me up.

Both excited to see him and nervous at the same time, it had only been a week and yet it seemed like forever. I thought talking to him on the phone would make the ache disappear, but it only made it worse. Then, I had the bright idea to watch some of his films with Keira, which only made our separation even more excruciating.

The pain of seeing his face kissing and touching someone else was unbearable. Last night, I asked Andrew how he was able to "act" a love scene without feeling something; breasts were everywhere, in his face, in his hands, all over his body. He said it wasn't as simple as I thought. He explained that the end result of what we see in the movies was far from what was actually going on while on set. I missed seeing the production crew standing around, as well as the director and their assistants placing arms and legs in proper positions.

Andrew actually sounded as if it were a pain in the neck. I told him I wasn't falling for it. He became suspiciously quiet before saying that I sounded jealous. *Of course, I was jealous!* He reminded me I could have him anytime that I wanted. I couldn't take it anymore, and my body said 'enough!' My girly bits furiously protested. I wasn't sure how much longer I would be able to hold out before I gave in.

Needing to freshen up before seeing Andrew, I headed straight to the bathroom upon deplaning. I hated airplane bathrooms, which was ironic since I had written about a mile high scene in *Deception*.

When I arrived at baggage claim, I was surprised to see Wade. "Andria!" He bolted towards me, opened his arms and gripped me into a bear hug.

I couldn't breathe. "Hi, Wade. Great to see you, too."

"Andrew is going to flip his lid. You have that hot librarian thing going on," he said and nodded.

I laughed at the fact that I had forgotten to take off my reading glasses. Although, I did have a suit on, and my hair was in a messy bun because I had overslept. I had a meeting this morning and didn't think I would have time to change. "Thanks, I think."

"Which one's yours?"

I pointed to the matching set of designer bags. "Those four."

"Why do women insist on over packing?" he asked to himself. "You may have beaten my wife Taylor, and that's saying a lot."

I grabbed the duffel. "It's my stylist. She always says I should be prepared for anything and everything."

Wade stacked the bags and escorted me through the exit doors. "Drew's in that silver SUV," he said and walked behind it to open the trunk.

The back door opened up, and I couldn't understand how the man could look better every time I saw him.

Andrew looked as if he had rolled out of bed and hadn't shaved in a couple of days. But, that paired with the ripped denim jeans that sat low on his hips and the rolled up oxford shirt, which showcased his toned forearms, made him look like walking sex.

I gawked as he swaggered up to me with a cheeky grin that fell as he looked behind me. "What are you looking at?"

That wasn't what I expected.

I turned to see a guy staring and starting to scowl back at Andrew. He had taken a step forward in our direction before Wade blocked his path. The man grumbled something under his breath like "just looking," and walked away.

The Andrew that stood in front of me wasn't the sweet, charismatic, gentleman I thought I was getting to know. This man was raw, primitive and agitated. He didn't say anything as he wrapped his large hand around my arm, leading me to the backseat of the SUV. He closed my door and helped Wade with the luggage before entering the opposite door. "Andrew?"

He looked straight ahead as Wade sat in the passenger seat, and the driver took off. Andrew started to wipe his hands nervously on his jeans as the black privacy partition came up. The moment I saw and heard it lock, Andrew pounced.

My head flew back against the window while my body slid down on the leather seat as he pressed his chest against mine. Andrew's mouth was claiming dominance, and I submitted willingly. His scruff was scratching deliciously along my face as I tried to find a breath of air. It didn't matter that I could have a concussion from the impact of the glass; Andrew wanted me.

The small space filled with our moans, which they kept getting louder and deeper, the more we kissed. Andrew abruptly stopped just in time, as I felt light-headed from the lack of oxygen. "Did I hurt you?" he breathed out.

"No."

We lay there panting and staring into each other's eyes. "Those glasses. It's been too long...*pant*...need control...*pant*...slow," he rambled on.

Wade was right; he liked the glasses. He *really* liked the glasses. I made a mental note to wear them more. Then I thought better. I couldn't handle another attack like that one and keep my panties on.

Andrew placed soft kisses all around my mouth as he sat us back up. "Are you sure I didn't hurt you?"

"I was just thinking about wearing my glasses more often, so I'm good."

He chuckled. "Not sure if I could handle that. I'm not usually a glasses man, but you look...incredibly sexy. And they make me want to lift up that skirt and bury my face between those long legs."

OMG! I died.

My heart stopped. All blood flow was being directed to my throbbing core, and the aching was causing me to see stars. I was revived when Andrew placed a gentle kiss on my lips as he sat back unaffected by the shocked turned on woman sitting next to him.

"Okay," he said as he answered the cell that I hadn't heard ring. "We're here."

I looked out the window and saw that we were parked in front of a tall building. Still in a daze, Andrew handed me water and told me to drink it.

What he didn't realize was that, at that moment, he could have told me to do anything, and I would have. Thankfully, the car door opened and Wade stared at me, smiling. "You okay there, Andria?" he winked.

I nodded embarrassed by what he could have heard and looked at Andrew. "We'll pick you up after the meeting. If it ends earlier, call my cell."

"Okay," was all I could say in reply.

"I'll drop your things at the hotel, and Andria, you may want to stop by the restroom. It looks as if someone got carried away," Andrew said and pursed his lips smugly.

"Ready?" Wade asked still grinning.

Andrew had squeezed my hand before I exited the car.

When I looked at myself in the mirror on my way to the elevators, I saw that my lipstick was smeared, and my hair was all over the place. I didn't want to think about what the people in the lobby had assumed.

The meetings seemed to go on and on. I found it hard to stay focused, but since it was a million dollar deal, I needed to have a clear head. Maybe I should have told Andrew that before he made me lose my mind, and my thoughts drifted elsewhere.

I thought of his eyes, for one as they burned hungrily into mine. When he said what he was hungry for, I wanted to throw caution to the wind and tell him to feast on me. Literally—on—me.

"Andria?" All eyes were now on me.

I was embarrassed that I had been interrupted from daydreaming, and caught by Elena's attorney when he asked me a question. I decided to push Andrew to the back of my mind until business was resolved.

By six o'clock, we were days away from an agreement. It would have been completed that day, but I heeded good advice and asked for more control of casting and to work more closely with the scriptwriter.

Even though Don was caught off guard by the sudden change, he held his own. He did ask that next time I could give him some warning, but I told him he worked better on his toes. He didn't find that humorous as we walked out of the meeting. I mentioned that I placed a call to my personal attorney who didn't get back to me until that morning. I had planned to brief him on my way there, but Andrew distracted me—I left that out. After I had explained that I wanted my attorney to look over the contract once it was written, he understood and promised to send all the paperwork over as soon as possible.

Don was a little surprised by Wade's presence when he walked up to us as we exited the building's doors. "Are you done?"

"For today. Don, this is Wade..."

"Robinson," he finished after noticing that I was at a loss.

"It's nice to meet you. Don't you work for Andrew Hughes?"

"Yeah." He smiled at me. "Andria," he said as he opened up the back door of the silver SUV.

"Hey beautiful," Andrew said as he smiled looking incredible in a dark gray suit.

I turned back toward Don. "I'll see you tomorrow."

He stood in shock looking at Andrew and me before the car door shut.

Andrew leaned over and placed the sweetest kiss on my lips. It was gentle yet warm, and he lingered on them for a brief moment. *That* Andrew was totally different from the Andrew that had picked me up at the airport.

"I thought you could do a quick change at the hotel before we went to dinner."

I smiled. "That's why you look so good. Where are you taking me?"

"Somewhere private."

"Private sounds nice. Although, it's hard for any woman to get dressed *quickly*."

"If you want, I could help." He looked like a kid wanting to stick his hand in a cookie jar.

I wasn't sure what he saw on my face, but he looked as if that kid was going to eat said cookie. "Not tonight, but I'll try to hurry."

And with that, he kissed me again.

We arrived an hour later to my hotel. Traffic was horrible, but I enjoyed talking to Andrew even though we didn't say much. We listened to jazz and had wine from his collection to unwind. He had a couple of meetings himself and was pretty wiped out.

It took me about thirty minutes to get ready, and Andrew had another drink in my suite. The agency was always generous when it came to my hotels, and I greatly appreciated it. Even though I would be happy with a standard room, having a suite was a luxury I enjoyed. It was nice being able to come back from a long day and plop on a sofa.

When I came out of the bedroom, Andrew's eyes glided over my dark blue dress. It was a short and simple long sleeve v-neck cotton dress, which hit every curve of my ample bottom that I had inherited from my mother.

Andrew smiled as I walked to him. "Ready?"

"You look amazing, Andria. Your blue eyes are radiant in that dress." I could feel a blush coming over my entire body.

He reached out for my hand, and we walked out the door to the awaiting car.

Twenty minutes later, we arrived at a small restaurant that had high tapestry greenery around the front. It was well hidden, and if you walked by, you probably wouldn't notice it. As soon as we entered, Andrew was greeted by the male host who immediately walked us to a private table with two chairs. Actually, every table was private. The restaurant didn't have more than ten tables at most, all separated by decorative glass walls. The lighting was low, and the red candles flickering off the tables enhanced the romantic atmosphere.

"Mr. Hughes. Your usual, sir?" the woman server asked.

"Could you bring any bottle of red and a bottle of white from my reserved collection?"

"My pleasure, sir."

I gaped at him.

"What?"

"You have your own private collection?"

"I like wine, and some of the cases I bring back with me from Europe are stored in their wine cellar. It's hard to find wines in the US without sulfates."

"I see." I had no clue what he was talking about. I drank white wine. The sweeter, the better. That's all I cared about.

Andrew reached over and started playing with my fingers. "I wanted to apologize for this morning."

My heart sank. I didn't understand, and he looked remorseful. "You don't have to do that."

"It was wrong of me to advance on you like that. I hope you don't think I do that often. I'm usually better in control of myself, and I did not mean to put you in a situation that wasn't warranted."

I looked at him dumbfounded. "Andrew. I would tell you if I were uncomfortable, and trust me when I say *nothing* about this morning made me uncomfortable."

He squeezed my hand. "I promised you I would take it slow. This morning, I lost control."

The server placed two glasses of wine on the table and left.

"Andrew. Ummm...I actually liked your losing control." I took a sip of wine, diverting my eyes away from his.

"Andria," he waited until I looked at him. "I enjoyed losing control. But that doesn't excuse the fact that I promised I would behave *until* you're ready."

I picked up my wine and downed the whole thing as I watched Andrew watch me. He said nothing else but had that smirk on his face.

"Mr. Hughes, are you ready to order?" He nodded towards me, and I placed my order for the butternut squash risotto in Bordeaux sauce. Andrew ordered the pan-seared sole with wild mushrooms and butter sauce.

Our conversation fell away from the morning activities, and we talked business. I told him about the requests I had made, and he was very glad to hear that. He told me he would be shooting his next film in four weeks. Washington D.C. was the last press junket for his new film opening in theaters this week. Andrew was currently under contract for two more films and was in negotiation for another one to start filming in eighteen months.

It was fascinating to hear all that he had to do before even meeting with a director or producer. I told him I had been doing a lot of research, but still had so many questions. He said it would take time, and if I had any questions to ask him and if he didn't know the answers, he would find out. Something about that made me happy inside. He was thinking about the future and having a future with Andrew was worth smiling over.

The food was amazing, and I was surprised that I was full. The portion had been small, and I could guess, expensive. The restaurant's menu didn't have prices. Andrew asked if I wanted dessert and I couldn't say no. I loved chocolate, and I wasn't sure what was in theirs, but it was so good Andrew gave me his too. Maybe I should have been embarrassed, but when he said he loved watching me eat, I wanted to eat more.

By the time we finished, it was extremely late, and I had an early breakfast meeting the next morning. When I mentioned that I needed to pick up my rental car, he insisted that his driver could take me anywhere I wanted while I was here. When he said that he wouldn't be able to join me in the morning. I was a little saddened that he couldn't meet me. More so that he didn't tell me why, but I brushed it off. I reminded myself that he was not my boyfriend, and I had no right to pry, but it still bothered me. Yet, Andrew was still going to meet me at my book event tomorrow night. I hadn't done a lot of them, but I was excited about this one. The bookstore had invited a few celebrities, and it would be the official launch for my world tour.

Since I had written about Hollywood, my public relations team wanted to make it the theme for the tour, starting in Hollywood, California. Each event would have a red carpet and everyone would be treated as a VIP. The only thing I fought for were the ticket costs. These events weren't free, and the prices were outrageous. I told them I wouldn't do them if they didn't bring the prices down. In exchange for lowering the ticket price, I had agreed to free bookstore signings in each city.

After dinner, Andrew had taken me back to my hotel, and we said goodnight in the car. He didn't want to take a chance of "losing control" again and was afraid if he walked me to my room, the temptation would be too great to resist. He did walk me to the elevator.

On the way to my room, the thought came to me that Andrew had never kissed me in public while I was here. It was always in the car away from other's eyes. I played with that thought as I got ready for bed.

It had to be a coincidence, yet he didn't kiss me at the elevator. He kissed me goodnight in the car before coming in. I was making a big deal out of nothing, I thought. But if that were the case, why did it bother me?

You know when you think your day is going to go in one direction, and instead it ends up going in one you never had imagined?

My day had started out normal enough. I had a quick breakfast at the hotel restaurant and people watched as I finished my eggs. Los Angeles had a diverse mix of people, and they all seemed to be in my hotel lobby. The hotel was eclectically decorated for the holidays. Instead of the typical red and green color scheme, they used blue and purple with silver thrown in for added flair.

Andrew's driver arrived early, leaving me plenty of time to get settled. We were meeting outside of the studio at an office building close by. The last time I had come here, they had taken me on a studio tour. Mom and Bob took me on one when I was a teenager, but it paled in comparison.

I walked into the room full of men and grimaced as they all perused my body. Being the only woman in the meeting was disappointing, but having to be looked over like some kind of prime beef was disgusting and unprofessional. My disdain showed as the meeting went on. I had been short-tempered, and my patience ran thin.

I was anxious to get back to my hotel to unwind. Andrew texted me that afternoon which only made my attitude worse. He couldn't join me for the pre-dinner but would meet me at the event. After the meeting had adjourned, I had gone straight to the hotel and soaked in the bath for over an hour.

I wasn't on edge due to the filthy men or because I didn't sleep well. It was because of Andrew. I hated that he affected me so much, and his avoidance of kissing me in public still hung over my head. I didn't want to think about it, but I couldn't shake the feeling that he was keeping something from me.

To help relax, I ordered a bottle of wine, and then began to get ready for the evening festivities. I decided I needed to get a grip after going over everything that had happened between Andrew and me. He said he wanted to try. To me, that meant wanting to see where our relationship could go, and he's kissed me many times before. How many women could say that? That last thought actually didn't make me feel better, but I was on a roll.

The tour launch looked like a movie premier but on a much smaller scale. There was press everywhere, and celebrities were being interviewed along the red carpet. The sponsors had backdrops with pictures of my cover placed sporadically on them. I watched as Elena spoke to a reporter while Owen, one of her assistants, stood by her side. That was when Keira spotted me. "Andria, you're late!"

"You told me eight o'clock."

She rolled her eyes. "I told you it started at eight. You were supposed to be here at seven. Why didn't you answer your cell?"

I didn't want to tell her I had turned it off as I wallowed in a cold, bubbleless bathtub, and had forgotten to turn it back on. "Sorry, I didn't hear it ring."

"Well, we *are* behind schedule—they said it happens a lot here—half the guests haven't arrived yet."

I nodded knowingly and took a moment for a couple of deep breaths as I tried to shake the nerves away. It was my first big appearance.

"Are you ready to answer some questions?"

I wanted to say no, but I answered with, "Let's do this."

Keira guided me to a mini stage, and I waited as the announcer said my name. I waved and walked out. It was overwhelming, and cameras flashed everywhere. I shook Elena's hand, as well as those from our subsidiary agency in New York before approaching the podium. It was a surreal moment. I could feel my heartbeat pick up, and I prayed that no one could see how much I was sweating. "I would like to thank my editor and Elena for supporting me and seeing *Deception* come to fruition. I want to thank my best friend, Erin Scott for encouraging me to find my voice. I also would like to thank my family for always supporting me, and the slew of people behind the scenes that make things easier for me—Keira in particular. Most importantly, I would not be here if it were not for my fans; not only for reading my book, but also for sharing it with others. I wouldn't be standing here today if it weren't for them. I want to thank my fans most of all."

I stepped down, took a boatload of pictures and then headed inside. Keira had had me pre-sign books, and I was very thankful for that. No one had to wait in a long line, and everyone could eat and do whatever they wanted. For me, I spent time talking and meeting people before Keira came and gave me a drink. "Your life is going to change."

I shrugged. "I don't think so."

"No one knew what you looked like before."

She had me there. I used an avatar on my book cover. I didn't want my picture on anything. I knew it was unusual, but I liked remaining anonymous. Even though

I did a few public appearances, nothing previously had been done on a scale like tonight. Now there was no turning back.

As people came up to speak, I found myself scanning the room for Andrew. He said he would be here, but it was getting late and the D.J. started spinning dance music. The place changed from a Hollywood premier to a nightclub. The food was moved out, and more bars were moved in.

Elena cut in on some guy trying to hit on me. I laughed when she said she had seen the agony on my face and knew I needed saving. "Come and dance. You did good girl. You need to relax."

She pulled me onto the dance floor, and we began to move to the beat. Keira and Owen soon joined us, and we really let loose. Dancing was something I hadn't done for a while, not since going out with Erin last summer. As we moved to the beat, I felt a chill suddenly come over me. I ignored it at first until the chill turned to tingling all over my body. It was the strangest feeling, and I knew why the moment I caught his hazel eyes. He held a drink up to his pursed lips. I watched in anticipation as he took a sip, before one corner of his mouth tilted up. It wasn't the same look he had given me at the airport, but it was in the same family. The way he stared at me caused goosebumps, everywhere. My chest became heavy, yet I kept on dancing as he watched. He stared into my eyes before they traveled meticulously down my body. His hooded eyes lingered on my hips as they moved to the beat of the music.

Andrew's eyes took their time drifting back up to mine before he mouthed, "Come here."

I obeyed his command willingly as I walked up to him. "Hi."

He smiled. "Hi, beautiful. I'm sorry I was late."

"I was late myself." I grinned stepping closer to him. I needed to feel his touch.

"It's your party. You're supposed to be late." He moved closer.

"Tell that to my assistant."

Andrew chuckled lowly as he brushed his hand down mine as we looked intently at one another.

Startled by a cough, I turned; surprised that it had come from Wade. I didn't even see him, and he's not hard to miss. "I'm glad you were both able to come."

"I wouldn't have missed it," he said with a dimpled smile.

"I have a special copy for you. Although, you said Taylor had already read it, I thought you might like to give it to her anyway."

He smiled widely before giving me a tight squeeze. "I like you."

"Ummm, I like you too."

"I was telling Drew to get a move on before you're snatched up."

I looked at Andrew who was shaking his head at him and said, "I think you have it turned around Wade."

"He's right, Andria. I need to hurry this up," Andrew said with an edge to his voice.

I looked at him puzzled, not sure how to take that. Then I saw a server walk by with a tray of food. "Did you eat?"

"We ate before we came. How long do you have to stay?"

I looked at Elena and Keira who were now getting low on the dance floor as Owen watched. "I think I'm good to go."

He finished his drink, and placed his hand along the small of my back as he guided us out of the room.

Photographers shouted Andrew's name as Wade led us to the front door. He had to remove several hands off of Andrew as he told them, no touching. Almost to the door, we got sidetracked as people Andrew knew stopped him to speak. I kept looking to the door wishing we could gravitate towards it as he talked to them.

A few women approached him offering their business cards and phone numbers. I had to take deep breaths to control the monster that was stirring inside of me. Did they not see him with me? Did it not matter that I was shooting daggers with my eyes at them? One had the nerve to smile and wink at me before whispering in his ear! Even though Andrew backed away signaling Wade to haul her ass away, I was quickly losing my patience.

What bothered me the most was that not once did Andrew introduce me. I knew they knew who I was since my face was plastered everywhere, but they and most importantly Andrew could have acknowledged me.

It was taking too long to leave, and one of my best nights was quickly becoming one of my angriest. I looked at Wade who seemed to understand— thankfully—and he quickly moved us out the door and into the car.

What was I doing?

I couldn't do this!

Andrew and I have totally different lives, I thought. I wasn't the type of person who could stand back and watch women throw themselves at him and not say anything. He was friendly with them; I understand that he had to be, but he gave the ones he knew kisses on the cheek. Why did that bother me? That was more than I received!

We sat in silence. Feeling the tension around us, I knew that if I spoke, I would say something I would regret. I wasn't thinking rationally. Also feeling things I hadn't felt before, and I couldn't breathe with Andrew's scent all around me. I wanted to scream and cry at the same time. When Andrew reached for my hand, I automatically pulled away. "I'm sorry. I didn't..."

"Tell me what's wrong, Andria?"

Not able to look at him, I continued to stare out the window. "I think...I'm just tired. It's been a long day."

"Did I do something to upset you?" The seat dipped as he moved closer.

I looked down at his feet. "It's been a really long day. I didn't get much sleep last night."

He wrapped his arm around my shoulder. "Are you sure that's it?"

I wanted to tell him no, but I couldn't. I was falling hard for the guy, and we really hadn't known each other for that long, even though it seemed as if I had known him my entire life. That thought alone made me nervous.

We pulled up to my hotel, and before he could get out of the car I told him that I was fine and he didn't have to get out; that I had to stop at the hotel convenience store for a minute. He protested, but I got out and shut the door behind me. He rolled down the window looking concerned yet cautious.

He should be.

Andrew reminded me that he had meetings until the afternoon, but he would pick me up for a quick lunch before taking me to the airport. He mentioned how much he was going to miss me and that he wasn't going to let me leave.

Placing on a fake smile, I said my goodbyes. Even though he leaned out for a kiss, it was different. It was chaste, and my heart ached being that close to him. I quickly said another goodbye and told him I would see him tomorrow.

Grabbing a bag of chips from the store, I headed to my room, got undressed, and curled up in front of the TV. I was physically and mentally exhausted, and wanted to hurt Erin for making me wear those ridiculously high-heeled shoes.

I zoned out for a while before realizing the movie that was playing was one of Andrew's. How ironic, I thought as I turned the channel before lying down on the couch. I stayed there until morning.

CHAPTER EIGHT

I woke up lying on last night's bag of chips with crumbs infused to my body. Not exactly how I thought my evening would have ended. Today, I would be heading back home. As I looked at the clock, confirming I had slept through my checkout time, I felt lost. I wasn't sure why. I had the best book launch last night, and by the look of things it was a success, yet I felt blue.

Reaching for my phone, I saw several missed calls from Andrew. Then I dialed a number I knew as well as my own. "Erin, help me."

"What's going on?"

"I'm losing it. Last night was incredible. I should be excited, but I feel depressed."

"I'm here. It's going to be okay, but what's really going on?" She knew me better than anyone, and she knew I needed her.

"It's Andrew. I don't want to see him again." I couldn't believe that came out of my mouth.

"Talk!"

I told Erin everything. I told her how he greeted me at the airport. I told her about our dinner. I told her about how he wouldn't kiss me in public. The book event. The women. I think I hit all the major and minor points. She listened and waited to respond until after I had finished.

"Do you want to hear the truth or would you like me to sugar coat it?"

"Do I want to hear it at all?" I asked as I curled up with a pillow, knowing that I was pouting.

"Not if I'm going to mention the L word."

I sat up. "No way! I am *not* in love with Andrew Hughes. There is no way. I just met him!"

"But you have always had feelings for him. You wrote an entire book based on him."

"She did?" I heard Miles's voice in the background.

"I can't be *in love* with him." I whispered. "That's insane."

"You're not crazy. You're in love. And before you say it, you *can* fall in love with someone that quickly. Some people fall in love at first sight."

"But, I don't—"

"You did. Trust me. Think about it. The butterflies, the revved up hormones, the jealousy, they're all signs. You're in love, sweetie," she giggled in glee.

I felt sick. "What am I going to do?"

"You're going to give Andrew the benefit of the doubt. Get out of your head, Andria."

"Easier said than done."

"You can do this. This is Andrew you're talking about. It was destiny."

I smiled for the first time that day. "It is Andrew."

"Now get up, get dressed, and go see that man."

"He has meetings. I won't see him until I go to the airport." My voice was full of disappointment.

"Use borrowed time. Love you."

What did that mean? "Love you too, Erin."

Taking a much-needed shower, I thought about what Erin had said, and the borrowed time reference and an idea popped into my head. I came up with a plan and called the front desk to reserve the suite until the next day. Next, I called Keira and told her to change my flight to tomorrow. I didn't need to be back until Tuesday, and I wanted one more day with Andrew. He said he had meetings until this afternoon and would be free afterwards. I would surprise him by spending the evening with him. If Erin was right, I needed to sort out my feelings for him. Though, if I were being honest, having actually to do it scared me. Yet, what scared me most was that Andrew didn't feel the same.

Several lessons had been learned by the day's end. First lesson learned—make sure Andrew was still available before rearranging my entire schedule to spend time with him. I found this out when I called him after my shower. "Andria, I wish you had told me sooner. I made plans with Brittney."

Yep. Brittney.

My second lesson learned—ask questions. The only reason he told me about Brittney was due to our going back and forth for about five minutes. He was acting odd and finally told me *who* he was seeing. "Maybe I shouldn't have assumed you would still be free this evening, but you said your schedule was open after the meetings. I thought it would be nice to spend a little more time together."

"I *want* to spend more time with you, but you said you would head out at three. If I would have known...I wouldn't have made plans for after you left."

I started pacing around the room. "I just thought we could have a little more time before I have to leave for the tour. I just wanted to spend one more day..."

"I can change my plans with Brittney," he said, sounding frustrated.

I wasn't sure if he was frustrated with me or upset that he had to cancel his plans with her. But, I was trying to hold it together, and gave him the benefit of the doubt. "That's okay. I can see you next time."

"What? I just said I would cancel with Brittney!" Now, he sounded pissed off.

That only unleashed the beast that I had tried to hold in. "No need. I wouldn't want you to cancel your date with Brittney! Maybe next time." And with that, I hung up.

Yes, I know it was wrong. Yes, I know it was childish. Yes, I know it was immature, but I couldn't take it back. It just happened, and I couldn't undo it. Although truthfully, he deserved it.

I arrived back in Dallas by ten that same evening. As soon as I hung up with Andrew, I called Keira and had asked her to change my flight back to my original departure. Of course, that wasn't easy. The only flight available on a Sunday had a three-hour connection in Salt Lake City. Not caring, I took it; I wished I had rethought that decision when I ended up in the middle seat between a talker and a seat hogger. The hogger leaned on me and snored in my ear while the talker continued on until we arrived at the gate.

By the time I came home, I was mentally and physically drained. I couldn't stop thinking about Andrew, and as much as I didn't want to be upset, I was. He didn't call. I wasn't surprised, just disappointed.

That night, I dreamed about him. One minute, we would be laughing, and he would kiss me tenderly. The next scene, he would be with Brittney or some other woman as they flirted with him and ignored me. Needless to say, I tossed and turned all night.

The next morning, I woke up with the worst headache and really needed to get Andrew out of my mind. I needed a mental break desperately, and I thought the best thing would be to find some Zen. For me, that meant either the spa or my pool; I settled for my pool. It was unseasonably warm for December, and I wasn't in the mood to be around anyone at the spa.

My place was small, but one thing I had splurged on was my small private pool. I had it added as my oasis. I also had an outdoor kitchen and fireplace installed. I wanted koi, but I was too busy to take care of fish. I had a pond installed, but it only had rocks and a small stream that led up to the pool. It was tiny, but it was perfect for me.

I turned on the outside music, made myself a pitcher of tea, and sat in the sun all day. Andrew crossed my mind frequently. I chastised myself for being childish, but I realized it showed just how much he affected me. Also, how much I was falling for him.

The thought of not speaking to Andrew again made me upset. I was sick to my stomach. For the first time, tears ran down my face, and I wasn't a crier. I couldn't stop them, and that scared me more than anything else. I wasn't sure how long I cried, but I didn't feel better after I had let it all out.

Deciding I had enough fresh air, I walked back into the house. Checked my cell phone again, and no missed calls from Andrew. Not sure why I had been hopeful. I tossed the phone to the side as I took off my cover up. I was about to take off my bikini when I heard a strong knock at the front door. I ignored it, not expecting anyone, and I didn't want to see anyone anyway.

Whoever it was didn't go away and started to ring my doorbell. I knew it wasn't my Mom. Both she and Bob were in South Carolina, and Keira had a key. So, I walked to the front door and looked out the peephole to a very red-faced Andrew. As I stared in shock, I watched him bang on the door again. Taking a deep breath, I opened the door. "Where the hell have you been?" he hissed as he pushed his way into the house as I backed up.

His tone startled me. "I was at the pool. How...why are you here?"

"I have been standing out there for a while. Why did you hang up on me?" he growled.

I took another pulled breath to soothe the anger that was quickly erupting inside of me. "You obviously wanted to go on your date with Brittney. So, I didn't push it!" I yelled the last part, surprising myself while taking a step back as Andrew stepped closer.

He started talking to me, but it looked as if he were talking to himself, as well. "You are *very* frustrating. I am *trying* to keep in control, but you are making me..."

Boldly, I stepped toward him. "What Andrew? Obviously you want to be with everyone but me—"

Before I could finish that thought, I found myself flying against the wall. I heard the picture on the table next to me fall as Andrew's face came to within an inch from mine. I stared breathless as his eyes bore into my own.

Before I could ask him what the hell he was doing, he kissed me. No. I wouldn't say kiss. He devoured me, and I let him. I let Andrew's lips dominate every inch of mine while it kept getting harder to breathe.

The tiny sands in the wall scratched my back as he lifted me upward. I grabbed his hair as my legs wrapped around his waist. He let out a growl as he kissed down my neck until he reached the top of my bikini. I watched as the most sinful smile spread across his face. His breath was warm and erratic as he looked up before he hissed, "Tell me to stop, Andria." My eyes widened in confusion as his words contradicted his actions. "You better tell me to stop, or I'm going to claim you as mine."

I squeezed my legs tighter around his waist as my head fell back at his words. I thought I was going to explode from them alone. I looked back into his hungry eyes and said, "I'm yours."

We left a trail of destruction as I tried to lead Andrew to my bedroom. Several times, I thought we weren't going to make it. I couldn't imagine how many bruises we had from stubbed toes to bumped knees, and a fall—that was me. Andrew finally said, "Screw it" and picked me up.

He laid me on the bed as I crawled back onto the pillows. It looked as if Andrew was internally fighting with himself. "Andria, I'm trying to gain some control here, but if you keep looking at me like that while biting your lip, I'm not going to be able to be gentle, baby."

I became a wanton mess, and I couldn't take my eyes off of him. I watched as he began to take off his shirt, and in one swoop, his jeans and boxers. My mouth watered as the glory of Andrew Hughes stood in front of me—naked—before crawling up to me. It seemed unreal. I couldn't speak. Everything about that was hot, and writing it and seeing it were two *completely* different things.

My hands became clammy, and my breath picked up as Andrew centered himself between my legs. He didn't say much, which surprised me. When we had previously made our way to my bedroom, he had *a lot* to say. Mostly cuss words with occasional, "Andria's," "I'm losing control," and "I'm going to have you." My favorite was hearing his repeated chanting, "Mine." But Andrew now let his lips and hands do the talking.

He placed firm kisses along the inside of my thigh before switching to the other. I watched in anticipation as he kissed down my calf before resuming upward until he hit my bikini bottoms. My heart stopped as he looked up with that smirk and slowly scooted the bottoms off. His hands and fingers felt like fire as they trailed up and down my flesh. Andrew took one long adoring look in my eyes before they lingered down my body.

The heightened sensations were becoming too much, and I could feel the anticipation that was to follow. I stared at Andrew in awe, overloaded by vision and sensation at what he was doing. I couldn't take my eyes off of his glorious body, and I didn't want him to stop. I held on as long as I could until I heard him say, "Are you sure, Andria?"

I reached up to his face and kissed his lips tenderly as I answered, "Yes."

He reached for something on the nightstand. In the midst of it all, I didn't realize he had placed a condom there. I thought now wasn't a good time to tell him I had gotten a shot.

I watched the muscles in Andrew's arms flex on each side of me as he lowered himself in slowly. I closed my eyes, breathing erratically at the fullness of him. When Andrew reached what I knew was going to be a big surprise, I opened my eyes as he squeaked, "Andria?"

He had an expression of horror mixed in with a little pleasure as he searched my eyes. I placed my hands on both sides of his face. "Andrew please. Can I explain...*after*?"

Andrew's face clearly showed that he was conflicted. "But...how? I...this is not...how?" and then he started cursing under his breath.

"I want you," I pleaded. "That is all that matters. Please, Andrew. I need you."

"But...and we haven't—"

"Later." I knew we had to talk, but at that moment, Andrew was all that I could see. "I want you."

And with those words his eyes darkened. "Mine?"

"Yours."

I was afraid he was going to halt all activity as I watched his mind spin as his body shifted upward. I was thrilled when his lips started to linger behind my ear as my entire body began to tingle. Then I heard a grumble as Andrew's kisses became something more.

After, when I opened my eyes, I could see the passion in his, and I knew right then that I was indeed in love with Andrew Hughes. I didn't care about the aching burn or that it may not have been my ideal scenario to lose my virginity. He was my ideal man. His expression of gentleness, caring and concern, made the moment perfect.

We said nothing as we lay there in each other's arms. I didn't want that moment to end, and I hoped he felt the same. He kissed my forehead and wrapped his arms tighter around me as we sighed in content.

We fell asleep in that position, and having Andrew's arms around me felt like a dream. I was unclear about what tomorrow would bring. One thing I knew with utmost certainty, though, was that I loved Andrew Hughes.

CHAPTER NINE

I lay still, and tried not to wake Andrew, as I internally freaked the hell out! I was in bed with Andrew. No, I had sex with Andrew. I had lain there awake wondering what the hell happened.

I always heard about the awkward morning after from friends, and thinking about it didn't help my building anxiety. What if I had made a huge mistake? What if it's a one-time thing? Or what if Andrew doesn't have feelings for me? What if he wakes and says he made a mistake? Every "what if" ran through my mind, and I felt sick.

Slowly easing out of Andrew's arms, I fell to the floor. It wasn't the most graceful exit, but he didn't wake. I crawled to the door and made my way out of the bedroom, and shut the door as quietly as possible, I ran outside. I needed air. Questions flooded my mind as I stood there pondering over everything. There were *so many* questions, and I chastised myself for letting my heart rule over my head. But for the first time this felt right, even though he could break my heart.

Sadly, I was too distracted, freaking out, to realize I was bare-naked. The brisk wind that hit all of my girly parts got my attention and I ran back into the house. Running straight into the guest bathroom, I grabbed a robe. I was thankful that Keira had left clothes here to have when she stays over after a late night work session.

As I walked past the mirror hanging on the wall over the dresser, I stopped. I wanted to see if I looked any different—how cliché was that—knowing that I didn't. I *did* look like a hot mess. My hair was all over the place, my lips and eyes were swollen and red, and I could see some bruises forming—all self-inflicted.

I searched the guest bathroom for one of my brushes, and I ran it through my hair. I cleaned up a bit before looking at myself again. But this time, I couldn't help the growing grin on my face as I felt my anxiety slowly ease away.

I had lost my virginity to Andrew Hughes!

I wanted to shout it out and vomit at the same time. It was like nothing I could have ever imagined. He had been incredible and sexy and...everything. It *was* everything I had ever wanted and fantasized about. No matter what happened from here, I would never regret it. And, I hoped Andrew wouldn't either.

Looking at the clock, it was a little past eight, and I thought Andrew would be hungry. I went to the kitchen, and stared in the refrigerator as I tried to figure out what to make for breakfast. What does one cook for someone after a night like last night? Protein, I thought. I always had my heroine fix eggs and bacon. So, I went with that but added cut up fruit and toast to the meal.

The bacon was almost done when I heard bare footsteps enter the kitchen. I froze. This was it, the moment of truth. Yet, I couldn't turn around. I stood still holding my breath as I heard the steps come up behind me. The moment I felt the back of his hand lightly brush my neck as he moved my hair to place a kiss on my shoulder, I exhaled.

"So beautiful," he whispered.

I stood still as his mouth gently trailed soft kisses from one shoulder to the other as Andrew showered me with his warm lips. As I leaned into him, he wrapped his arms around me, and we stood there for an amazing moment. He had placed his head on my shoulder, and I finally looked over at him. "I thought you might be hungry. Are eggs okay?"

"Whatever you make is fine with me. How are you feeling?"

He had a look of concern. "I'm...great."

He raised my head, gently pushing up my chin. "Really, are you okay? Are you in pain?"

Embarrassed, I looked away from him. "I'm fine. Have a seat and I'll get you something to drink. Is orange juice okay?"

He looked as if he wanted to say something else. But, he nodded his head as I directed him to the bar stool with the placemat. I couldn't help paying attention to every muscle that moved as Andrew walked to sit down. I had a clear view of his naked chest and studied his fit form. He wore only boxers and even the sight of his bare feet made me tingly.

I pushed down those thoughts as I plated our food and poured two glasses of juice. I stood across the counter, and watched him eat in an uncomfortable silence. I, on the other hand was unable to eat. I swept my eggs back and forth on my plate as I tried to figure out what to say. I didn't have to ruminate long. "Andria, can we talk?" Andrew was staring at me, and it was hard to look directly into his eyes. "I'll go first. I need to apologize."

My eyes fell as his words felt like a jagged knife stabbing me. I wasn't sure what Andrew saw on my face, but I was sure it was the pain that those words caused.

"Andria? No! I'm not apologizing for last night. Last night was *amazing*." I looked up in shock. "It was incredible," he assured me and smiled. "I'm apologizing for barging in yesterday. Not for only yesterday, but the other day as well I should have said or handled things differently. When you hung up before I could explain, I was shocked and honestly...saw red. You made me feel things I haven't felt before," he said mainly to himself.

"Andrew, I was frustrated, and not just at that. Yes, maybe I shouldn't have expected that you would have dropped everything because I wanted to spend more time with you. But making plans with—"

"I *wanted* to spend more time with you," he interrupted with a clipped tone.

The suppressed anger I had buried deep inside was crawling its way to the surface. "Like I was saying, Andrew-I was thrown off by the fact that you made plans the second I had left. But really, what do I know—"

"Please, let me explain. Brittney..." I glared at him. "Hear me out, please? The morning of your event I received a call from Brittney. Her mother had died."

I gasped and covered my mouth. "Oh my gosh! I am *so* sorry."

I had acted like a jerk.

"It was her biological mother. She didn't really know her. Brittney didn't even know she existed until a few years ago when the mother she knew had passed away. It's a long story, but she had problems dealing with the truth about being adopted in the first place, and now with her birth mother dying, she needed a friend."

I placed my hands on top of Andrew's and squeezed. "I understand that you needed to be there for her. I hope you don't think I would want you to not..."

"I should have explained things more. And that night...and when you got angry and insinuated I wanted to be with other women—"

"I have no right to ask you to be exclusive this soon—"

Andrew quickly got up and stood in front of me. "I need you to understand that I *do not* want other women. *I only want you.*"

I gaped at him before he placed a gentle kiss on my lips; and saw the sincerity in his eyes.

"Andrew, I need to apologize for hanging up. It was childish—"

"It was." He smiled slightly.

"Thanks." I rolled my eyes but continued, "I just wanted to make the most of our time together, and the other night, you were preoccupied...with those people..."

He stepped in closer, this time pinning my body against the kitchen island. "Those people are exactly that, *those people*. I have no interest in other women. When I'm at events like that I play my part, but it's only that, a part."

"But you never even acknowledged me."

"That's what you're mad at?" he laughed. I didn't appreciate that and started to push him away. He grabbed on to my wrists. "They knew who you were Andria. It was *your* event." I struggled to get out of his hold, but he held on tighter. "I wanted to keep my private life private as long as possible. Any whiff that we are together and the vultures would start to circle."

I eased up, and he let go of my wrists. "What do you mean?"

"In my line of work, it's hard to keep anything personal as private. I was hoping that I could keep us private for as long as possible. Once it gets out that we are a couple, your life will change more than I think you're ready for at the moment. It's not going to be easy maintaining any type of normalcy in our relationship. You're going to long for the day when no one is lurking about."

"I never thought about that."

Andrew pushed into me as he said, "Well you should. I'm a very private person. The more I try to keep things that way, the more interesting I seem to become. The paparazzi feed off of anything and everything they can. Any new or little thing they can find on me either explodes into a mess of lies or becomes an issue."

"That's a horrible way to live."

"Unfortunately, it comes with the job. Oh, and I just happen to like my job." He smirked.

My eyes followed as his hand trailed up my arm, to my shoulder, and back down to the center of my robe. I watched as he loosened the tie. My flesh shivered and burned when his other hand cupped my face as he leaned in to kiss me. It was gentle at first until I wrapped my arms around his neck, causing my robe to open. It became more passionate as Andrew lifted me onto the counter and stepped in-between my dangling legs. I sat bare in front of him feeling exposed and a little self-conscious. "I love that you were jealous," he huskily whispered in my ear while he continued trailing kisses down my neck.

"I wasn't jealous," I breathed out, consumed by the feathery feel of his lips.

He looked at me with furrowed brows. "Yes, you were."

"Okay, maybe I was. But can you blame me? The way you acted and all those women throwing themselves at you," I said flailing my arms.

"But I was with *you*, Andria."

"It just made me feel..."

"Territorial?"

Yes.

I looked into his knowing eyes. "Not sure if that's it."

Andrew's fingers trailed between my breasts. "Well, seeing that guy looking at your ass at the airport, made me *very* territorial."

I forgot about that. "Is that why?" I started to laugh. "The whole car thing was because of some guy looking at my behind?"

He reached around and firmly squeezed my bottom. "That and I missed you."

I smiled widely at his words. "You have absolutely nothing to worry about, Andrew."

"Yet, I keep telling you the same thing."

He had me. So, I kissed him. I kissed him good.

Andrew's hands pushed my robe further open as they trailed downward. I winced, shocked at how sensitive I was. Andrew noticed and stopped in his tracks. "There's something else we need to talk about."

I knew, but I was hoping that he didn't remember. "There was never a right moment to mention the whole virgin thing."

He laughed. "What I don't understand is how could *you* have been a virgin? I am honored and giving me...that...gift was incredible, but you are a beautiful woman..."

"It's not like I never had the chance," he growled. I laughed. "There was never a time that felt right."

His face dropped. "How many times, Andria?"

"How many times for you?" That shut him up. "All I'm saying is that I wanted it to be...well...incredible in every way. And it was."

He placed his forehead against mine. "It was?"

"You know it was."

"I thought so, but..."

"Andrew Hughes, do you doubt your skills in bed?"

"Umm, no. But I wanted it to be special with you, even more so after knowing this was your first time. I was too rough."

"I like it rough."

"I noticed." He pulled back with a proud glare.

I was so embarrassed, and he had the cheesiest grin on his face.

"Next time, I promise a little more romance."

As I blinked a couple of times gaping at him, I asked, "Next time?"

"Did you think I could sleep with you once and have my fill?"

"Umm, well..."

Andrew's hands started to explore my body. "I may never get my fill of you."

I moaned, "I hope not," as he kissed me.

"Damn!"

Our heads turned as I looked in the eyes of a very shocked Keira.

Andrew half laughed as he turned back to me. "Blocked again."

While Andrew got dressed, I quickly explained to Keira why he was here. She walked into the house, and saw that it looked as if I had been robbed. She was about to dial 911 when she stepped into the kitchen.

It actually took me a while to get through the story. We giggled, laughed, and clapped—oh, and did a little jig—before I finally got to the end. Keira didn't know I was a virgin, but she did know I hadn't spent a lot of evenings dating. I was either writing or with her.

I had forgotten that she was coming over to discuss edits for the new book. She had a spare key since she worked from my home and looked after things while I was away. But, maybe not so great, since Andrew and I had been interrupted. My mind kept drifting to what we could have been doing if she hadn't interrupted.

Keira almost choked on the bacon she was eating when Andrew walked in freshly showered. Hell, I almost choked as I watched a very wet, very hot, Andrew walk towards me and place a wet kiss on my greedy little lips.

I looked over at a very red Keira as she grinned from ear-to-ear, and excused herself before Andrew said, "It's nice to meet you, Keira."

She waved her hands behind her. "Andria, I'll be in the office," and she was out of the kitchen.

I smacked Andrew on the chest and laughed, "You made her feel uncomfortable."

He wrapped his arms around me. "How did I make her feel uncomfortable? She was the one who walked in on me grinding up on you."

I shook my head. "You smell nice." I love bar soap, and even though I knew he took a shower in my bathroom, somehow he still smelled like Andrew. The yummy, clean, musky scent was all him alone.

"I was hoping you would join me."

The huge grin on my face was unavoidable. "I would have loved to, but it would have been, umm...hard with Keira here." He leaned in for a kiss before stepping away to grab a piece of bacon. "Are you still hungry? I can make us something else. Your food is cold."

"I need to leave for a while, but if you're not busy later, could we have dinner?"

"All right, that sounds nice."

He grabbed both of my hands. "I have to take care of some things while I'm here. Wade found me a hotel and—"

"You don't have to stay in a hotel."

I shocked myself at what had come out of my mouth. Was it too soon?

Andrew smiled pleasantly as he asked, "Are you asking me to stay here, Andria?"

I bit my lip contemplating. "Umm, you don't have to stay in a hotel. I mean, you did come all this way, and...yes, I am asking you if you want to stay here."

His face lit up. "I would love to. The only thing I need to do is take some conference calls. The studio didn't know I was gone until this morning, so I need to do some damage control."

"Are you going to get in trouble?"

"With whom, Andria? I think I can be spontaneous when I want to."

"I guess." Then the doorbell rang. "I need to get that."

I heard Andrew's steps behind me as I opened the door surprised by Wade's smiling face.

"Andria, I see you survived," he said with a knowing grin.

"Wade," Andrew's voice warned.

"Drew, come on. By all the noise you two were making—"

"What? Were you here?" I stared at them both horrified at the thought.

Wade looked embarrassed. "Ah, yeah. I thought you noticed me when Andrew was at the door. I wouldn't let him come alone. He was *not* himself, and I didn't trust him."

"You wanted an excuse to get away from Taylor," Andrew stated.

"Yeah, that too. We're trying to have a baby, and I needed a break," he laughed to himself.

"I'm sure Andria doesn't want to hear how my sister is wearing you out. *I* for sure don't want to hear it. Did you pick up those things I asked for?"

"Yeah." He handed Andrew a couple of shopping bags. "Just the necessities."

I turned toward Andrew. "You came with no clothes?"

He shrugged. "Like I said, I was spontaneous."

"And enraged," Wade muttered.

"Wade!" Andrew snarled out.

"But in a good way. Drew doesn't like to be hung up on," he said and winked at me.

I turned back to a very red-faced Andrew. "I see that now. Wade, would you like to come in?"

"No thanks, I need to be heading out soon. But, you should have seen him. Drew couldn't focus. When you called, he was in a meeting, and he couldn't get out of it. Afterwards, he kept saying he was going to call you, but I told him to cool off first. But, he never did. Then all of a sudden he tells me to take him to the airport and get your information."

"What? How?" I asked.

Wade had a look of guilt plastered on his face along with Andrew's. "Oh yeah, you probably didn't know. I was on the police force before accepting the job as Andrew's head of security. Taylor wanted to start a family, and the stress of me being on the force wasn't helping us conceive. She felt more at ease knowing I would be in a safer environment. No one wants to hurt Drew's scrawny ass."

I stared at Andrew dumbfounded. "*That's* how you always found me?" He slyly grinned admitting to nothing.

Wade continued. "Yeah, I still have my contacts and ask for a few favors now and then under the radar. How did you think he found you?" he laughed. "Anyway, I told him he wasn't seeing little Andria in his current state."

"Little Andria?"

He smiled. "I thought while Drew and I were on the plane, getting a couple of drinks in him would calm him down. But, he only got worse."

"Wade..." Andrew warned again.

"It's true! And it's not like things didn't work out. I stayed behind to make sure all was well, and that I didn't have to pick his ass up from your throwing him out. Though, after I heard the yelling stop, there was a crash, so I peeked through the window before leaving."

Now I was red. "I see."

He grinned wider. "And I see you guys are good, right?"

Andrew answered, "We're good, and thanks for bringing the stuff."

"No problem, bro. Andria, it was nice seeing you again. We'll be seeing each other in the future."

He gave me a bear hug. "I hope so."

Andrew rolled his eyes. "You will."

"You sure you're good without me, bro?" he joked.

"Yes, and thanks for...looking out. I'm going to be staying here as planned."

Wade gave Andrew a fist pump. "Nice. See you in a couple of days then."

We said good-bye to Wade and then I turned to face Andrew. "You were that confident that I would ask you to stay over?"

He opened my robe and wrapped his arms around my naked body. "Not *that* confident. I *was* hopeful that we could spend some quality time together getting to know each other more."

"Quality time sounds nice," I whispered in Andrew's ear as I bit his earlobe.

He moaned. "It does."

"Geez, do I need to announce when I'm coming into a room?" Keira asked, smiling and half covering her eyes with her hands.

"Sorry. Andrew is going to be staying for..." I looked to him for an answer.

"Two days."

I smiled. "Can you set up a make shift office for him in the guest room?" I looked at Andrew. "If you need anything, you have free rein."

"I like the sound of that."

CHAPTER TEN

I worked as fast as I could to finalize the edits with Keira. We did enough to keep her busy for a couple of days, and I asked her to clear my schedule as much as possible until after Andrew left. There were several meetings the following day that couldn't be rescheduled, but I thought it would give Andrew time to take care of whatever he needed to do.

It was hard to focus on anything while we worked. Visions of last night kept popping up in my head as thoughts of him in the next room clouded my mind. It seemed like the last couple of hours were all a blur. The last three weeks had been a complete dream. If anyone had told me then that Andrew and I would meet, let alone have sex, I would have called them crazy.

Images of Andrew's eyes, his expression as he kissed me, the way his hands felt on my body, and the way he felt were too much. All I could think about was touching him again. "Keira, do you mind if we end this early?"

"If you're going to make deadline—"

"I will. I just need–umm, want to spend some time with Andrew." She gave me a knowing smile. "He's leaving in a couple of days."

"Andria, this has to be finished by New York, and you're going with your family to Florida."

"I promise to work on these twenty-four-seven after Andrew leaves, and if I have to work while I'm with my mom and Bob for Christmas, I will. But right now, I need you to leave."

"Andria!" She looked hurt.

"Sorry. I didn't mean it like that," I said sympathetically. Then, I thought about it and emphasized, "Andrew Hughes is next door in my guest room, and I'm in here with you. Do I need to say more?"

Keira hostilely looked at me before a sly grin graced her face, and she nodded in understanding. "See you in a couple of days." Then she packed her things and left.

After putting away my work, I ran to my room to get freshened up. I was on a mission, and my body was craving Andrew. I had never felt anything like it. I was buzzing with excitement, and my body was begging to be touched. I sensed a burning deep inside and I felt as if I would attack his glorious body when I saw him. Unfortunately, when I entered the guest room, he was on a call. "Look. I will be there, I promise. Something came up." He ran his hands through his hair, frustrated, unaware that I was watching him from the doorway. "Brittney, I do care. This is important—no I'm not saying the death of your—this couldn't wait."

Hearing her name was just as effective as dumping cold water over me; the fire was extinguished. I didn't want to acknowledge the tug in my gut, or thoughts of why he was speaking to her. Then, I chastised myself; her biological mother just died and I needed to be more sympathetic. I told myself I would trust Andrew, and not jump to any more conclusions that weren't warranted. Andrew had made it clear that nothing was going on between them, so I was going to swallow my concerns, and take his word for it.

For now. The dark thought crossed my mind.

As I watched Andrew, he started to pace around the room. "I will be back in a couple of days—in Dallas—it's personal. Brittney! I will be back in a couple of days, and *promise* to be back in time for the funeral, okay? Try to get some rest—" He then turned around and saw me at the door. "Hey, I gotta go. Please take care of yourself." He snapped his phone shut.

All of the frustration on Andrew's face instantly went away, making my heart melt as he stood leering at me while wearing a grin. I leaned back against the doorway. "I didn't mean to eavesdrop. I wanted to let you know that I was done working."

He crossed his arms. "I needed to wrap up that call anyway."

"Is Brittney all right? Is she going to be okay?"

Andrew took a couple of steps towards me. "She's having a hard time, but she's tough," he answered, stepping closer. "I missed you."

"I missed you, too. I cleared my calendar, except for a few meetings in the morning; I'm free for the next couple of days."

Andrew stepped directly in front of me. "Perfect. Amy was unable to reschedule a couple of things. I need to take a few calls in the morning and then *I'm* all yours."

"I like the sound of that." My eyes fell immediately to the floor.

What the heck? I couldn't believe I said that out loud. Andrew chuckled and then started to run his hand up and down my arm. "You always look so beautiful, Andria." My heart smiled. "Are you hungry?" he asked.

"Yes..." We stood there smiling at each other until I felt the burn deep inside of me turn back on and I wanted him. No. I wanted him, *desperately*. "...just not for food."

Andrew's eyes danced with delight as he leaned in to kiss me. The kiss was incredible and he took his time. It normally would have been better received if the urges I was experiencing weren't screaming for more.

You know that side of you that not everyone sees; the more seductive, naughty side that only comes out on special occasions? That's when it hit me; Andrew Hughes brought out that side of me. That's how I was able to write *Deception*. Thinking about him doing incredible things to me was both enlightening and freeing. All I could think about was experiencing every last fantasy with him. With that thought, I bit his bottom lip.

I heard the pained moan come from Andrew as he paused. I didn't mean to bite so hard. We opened our eyes at the same time and he had a look of shock at first. But, when I squinted at him, his eyes turned dark.

Never taking my eyes off of his, I started to walk backwards as he followed. I fumbled with my shirt buttons as Andrew watched each button pop open. I loved seeing his eyes yearn in tune to my fingers. I slowly unbuttoned my pants and prayed that I wouldn't fall. It wasn't easy walking backwards while trying to be seductive.

Shimmying out of my jeans, I left my bra and panties on, focusing only on Andrew's eyes burning through my body as he took all of me in. Entering my bedroom, my legs hit the bed as I watched Andrew pull his t-shirt over his head. I started crawling back towards the padded headboard as he took off his jeans one leg at a time, before he crawled towards me. "Are you sure?" I was tempted to respond, "Are you crazy?" Instead, I smirked at him, earning one right back.

It was taking too long, and my body cried out for him to touch me all ready! I unhooked my bra and swung it to the side, while I watched Andrew's mouth drop. I couldn't help being pleased with myself. A little self-doubt tried to creep in, so I kicked it to the curb. Not now, I told myself. I wanted this man. I boldly ran my hand up and down his chest as he hovered over me. I watched as he closed his eyes at the feel of my nails scraping over his chest.

I leaned up and started placing hungry, wet kisses up and down his neck. Andrew trembled as my hands outlined his defined abs. Then I thought of a wonderful idea. It scared the hell out of me, but I was on a roll.

Sitting up, I pushed him over until he laid on his back, staring up questionably at me. Then, I straddled him, reclaiming his full lips before proceeding down his chest. I took *my* time, memorizing every mole and mark as I nuzzled through his fine chest hairs. I continued gravitating downward until I reached his very happy trail, and I both felt and saw his breath catch. "Andria...you don't—"

"Andrew." I nodded my head trying to smile, and hide how truly scared to death I was. If I was going to do this, I wasn't going to hold back. His eyes spoke loud and clear that he wanted this as much as I wanted to do this for him.

I was a girl on a mission. And I was trying to put on a good show, but I was dying to know if I was doing it right. He was my first, and something about that made me even more excited. I finally admitted to him that it was my first time doing *that*, and then he brushed my cheek gently before saying, "You're doing incredibly well."

My entire body was tingling. I never understood how doing that could turn someone on, but right then, I was on fire, and Andrew was fanning the flames. Every time I looked up at Andrew, his face was distorted, yet his eyes stayed on mine. Seeing him lose control made me want to never stop. When he suddenly pulled me up and turned me on my back, I was thrilled for what was yet to come.

Andrew's expression was dark, as he reached over to the nightstand. I looked over and saw a box of condoms. I looked back to him with an arched brow as he said, "Wade got them."

"I see. I was just curious about the *size* of the box."

He smirked, "He thought we would be busy." I laughed, and then mentally reminded myself to *again* let him know about the shot. "Are you sore?" he asked.

I was, but I shook my head. "I want you."

That was all Andrew needed to hear.

I finally understood that "fullness" feeling that people say happens. It wasn't just the mere size of Andrew; he was a very good size—above average—but it was also the connection between us. I had craved Andrew all day, and was afraid I was going to become a sex-starved whore. Then, I thought: how was that a problem, again?

When he would look into my eyes adoringly, we would have these...moments. Yet, I was afraid my heart couldn't take much more of them.

The pace was different from before. It was slower and relaxed. We would look at each other and smile with each movement. It felt like time stopped just for us. Andrew slowly and gently made love to me. That's what I wished he was doing, and the look in his eyes gave me hope. As the rhythmic rocking increased, pulsating pleasure exploded between us. I saw stars underneath my eyes as he placed warm, wet kisses along my face.

What started out as carnal lust ended up as one of the sweetest moments in my life. We had lain in each other's arms for a while before Andrew got up to take care of things. When he returned, he wrapped his arms around me before saying, "That's how your first time should have been."

I looked at him, torn. I loved how our first time was and maybe I hadn't made myself clear. "Andrew, last night was the most incredible night of my life. I would not change *anything* about it." He looked doubtful. "I'm serious. I know, guys think we girls all want our first time to be the same way, but you forget that we're all different. Last night was perfect for *me*...I hope it was all right for you?"

"It was more than all right," he chuckled. "It was...yeah. But if I had known, I would have been gentler."

"Like I told you, I wouldn't change a thing. I'm not saying today wasn't incredible, I'm just saying, I like variety."

"Oh. Well, I can provide variety." He grabbed the blanket placing it over our heads as he started to tickle me mercilessly.

After round two—or maybe three—Andrew and I both thought it was time to feed our hunger; we had worked up a pretty good appetite. "I have some Tilapia in the fridge. I can cook up something quick."

He looked back to me while fastening his jeans. "You don't have to do that."

"I want to. You can talk to me while I cook." I slid out of bed and threw on some clothes.

Andrew hugged and kissed me all the way to the kitchen. My head was still swimming, and as much as I wanted to float in his arms, I knew we both needed to eat. "Why don't you open a bottle of wine?"

I handed Andrew the bottle and opener as he sat down on a stool. Then, I placed two glasses in front of him as he poured the wine. "You have a nice place, by the way."

After walking around the kitchen, grabbing the pans and ingredients I needed, I looked back at him. "Thanks. It's my little oasis."

"It's bright and cheery."

"Growing up in Arlington made me want to bathe in as much sun as possible. I bought this place because of all the windows." My home had floor to ceiling windows in every room. I kept the décor natural with a bit of blue and green as accents. The interior was a mix of the cottage look of my grandparent's home in South Carolina, and the southwest warmth I loved about Dallas.

Andrew took a sip of the white wine, and he said, "Not bad. I have never spent much time in Texas. I drove through it on my way to Louisiana, but never really saw anything."

Turning off the water, I drained the lettuce and walked to the stove. "If you want, I can show you around."

"Maybe next time, when I'll have more time."

I paused and faced him. "You're planning on coming back?"

His brows arched. "Yes, if that's okay?"

"It's fine with me." I smiled to myself as I turned back to continue preparing dinner.

I placed the Parmesan encrusted fish on our plates along with an endive salad. Andrew took a bite of the fish, as my eyes stayed fixed on his plate for a moment. "Umm, is it okay? If you don't like it, I can make something else."

Andrew's face had a somewhat quizzical expression. "If I didn't watch you make this, I would have thought you purchased it from a restaurant."

"Why?" I asked, concerned.

Andrew took another bite before answering, "This is delicious. I knew you could cook, the seafood boil at your dad's proved that, but *this* is unbelievable."

I sighed in relief. "It's something I just threw together one day. I liked it."

"Andria, this isn't something you just throw together."

We both laughed. "Well, my Buppi—that is what I used to call my grandmother—would let me help her with meals when we would visit them in South Carolina. She always said my mother never got the hang of it, but I was a natural like her. It was our thing, and I found that I enjoyed it. I try to cook as much as I can, but lately, it's been hard."

Andrew took several large bites, and said with a full mouth, "Well, you can cook as much as you want for me."

I smiled at his enthusiasm. "Flattery will get you everywhere, mister."

"I sure hope so." He winked as he dived in.

Our conversation was light while Andrew polished off his plate. "I don't have any dessert made, but I could whip us up something if you wanted."

"I bet you can." He smirked. "I'm fine. Thank you."

Getting up, I grabbed our plates and was hit with some discomfort—down there. I paused and thought for a minute before saying, "How about I clean up, and you go find us something to watch?"

"I'll help you." Andrew stood up, taking the plates from my hands, and placed them in the sink.

"Thanks for the offer, but I have something to do, and I can do this fast. Go and get comfortable and I'll be there soon."

Andrew wouldn't budge. "Andria, you cooked. I clean. Besides, I want to help."

Placing my hand on his forearm, I smiled at his chivalry. "I appreciate that, but you're my guest. I insist." I stood on my toes and gave him a peck on the cheek. "Go find something to watch. It'll only take me a few minutes."

He hesitated for a moment before leaning over to place a kiss on my forehead. I couldn't help ogle his behind as he walked away, thinking about how very firm and toned Andrew's butt was. And to think: I had the pleasure of seeing and feeling that ass. I got the giggles just thinking about it.

I cleaned as fast as I could before I grabbed my cell and ran to the bathroom. I prayed she would pick up as I locked the door and sat down on the closed lid. "Hello."

"Erin, listen, I don't have much time."

"Why are you whispering?"

"I don't have time to explain. Listen. Andrew and I had sex—"

"What! How? When?" I held the phone away from my ear.

The moment I heard the screams stop, I continued. "Erin, I don't have time. He's here—"

"Andrew is in Dallas?"

"Erin! I promise I will give you a blow by blow, but I have a question."

"You had better, Alexandria," she huffed out in frustration.

No one could blame her, but I didn't have the time, and I needed her help. "Okay, look. We had sex, umm, several times and it was good, freaking *fantastic* actually, but I think I may have broken my... you know..."

"What?"

"Down there. It hurt a little the first time, but then I wanted him again. At first, Andrew was slow, and then I wanted him *a lot,* and he was rough and hard and...well, yeah. Umm, anyway, I think I did something. It's throbbing and really sore." Erin started to laugh. "It's not funny!"

"Only you would think you broke your hoo-hah."

"Thanks. I know I didn't *break* it," saying frustrated.

"Ahh honey, please calm down and *of course* it's sore. You used it. And it sounds like you used it good," she laughed out.

"Erin, *please.*"

"All right. Take an anti-inflammatory. Oh, and a heating pad may help."

"Thanks. I just needed to know how to help it...for later."

"Geez, girl! You want more?"

"Did I mention that Andrew was here and we had sex?"

She laughed. "Take some pain meds and take care of yourself. I would say you need to take it easy but..."

"Thanks Erin. I'll call you later." I hung up.

I took some medicine and placed a warm cloth between my legs. It felt soothing, but I knew that it might not be enough. How did I go from dedicated virgin to wanton sex fiend?

Oh yeah.

Andrew Hughes.

Eventually, I walked out and entered the living room to find Andrew spread out on the couch with his eyes closed. He was so beautiful. I stilled, trying to be as quiet as possible. I wanted to take a few moments to appreciate the sight in front of me. Andrew was breathtaking and he was on my couch. Nothing about that felt real, but my throbbing girly bits reminded me it was.

I grabbed the blanket on the adjacent lounge and spread it over him. Andrew scared the crap out of me when he grabbed my wrist. "Sorry, I didn't mean to doze off. It's been a long week."

"You need to rest."

"Come, lay with me." Andrew scooted over, opening his arms. I climbed in, my back to his chest, as he took the blanket and wrapped it around us.

I lay in his arms in perfect peace, feeling his chest rise up and down. I felt the warmth of his breath through my hair before he placed his sensual lips along the back of my neck. He squeezed me harder when I hummed in pleasure from his caress. "This is nice."

"It is. I can't imagine a better place to be. Well actually..." Andrew's hand slid down to my pants before reaching a very sore place. I winced. "Andria, are you okay?"

I lied, "I'm fine."

He turned me to face him. "You're in pain?" He didn't wait for a response; it was evident on my face. "How long have you been in pain? And we...I should have given you time."

I cupped his face. "I'm fine. Yes, I'm sore, but I wanted to...I wanted more."

He gave me a timid grin. "I know, but I wasn't thinking. All I thought about was—I have an idea."

He sat us up, taking my hand and led me to my bedroom. I was about to say I wasn't sure if more sex would help, but who was I to argue? I was a little surprised when he walked us to the bathroom and turned on the tub's faucet. "Take your clothes off."

I couldn't help standing there with a shocked grin plastered on my face. Having Andrew act so demanding towards me, and telling me to take my clothes off, was sexy and hot. Andrew poured some oil in the water that I had next to my tub. Then began to unbutton his pants as he looked back at me. "You're going to need to take those off, Andria."

Why? I was having too much fun watching him.

As I began to take my shirt off, Andrew stripped down in front of me. I would never get used to seeing him naked. Each time felt like the first time. He took my breath away every time. Andrew turned off the water and looked back at me, laughing. He stepped in front of me, and began to assist with taking off the rest of my clothes. I guess I was too slow. I had more important things to do, like watch Andrew strip.

After we had taken off all of our clothes, he helped me into the tub and stepped in behind me. The water was hot, but soothing where it was needed. I turned to face him. "How did you know this would help?"

"I know how I feel when my muscles are sore, so I thought this could help."

"Oh, I see." I thought about that, which made sense, but then I had another idea. More like a question that came up when we were making love for the first time. "Andrew, when we first, umm...when you entered me."

He chuckled. "Entered? How does A.P. Moore go from being a hot, direct, author, to a timid, shy, and just last night, virgin?"

I shifted, causing water to spill over the tub as I got a better look of Andrew's face. "It's easy. I'm writing a fantasy. So...you read it?" My heart started to race.

He shook his head. "No, but I plan to while I'm filming. Yet, all of that...imagination came from you." He said with a quirky smile.

"I know that—hey—I can be direct when I want to be."

He raised one brow. "Oh, I know. You can be *very* direct when you want to be."

My body turned red and it wasn't from the hot water. "Okay, Andrew. When your glorious manhood claimed me for the first time—"

He choked before laughing. "Glorious manhood...I like the sound of that."

Then I laughed. "You wanted the A.P. version right?"

"I want the Andria version." He kissed my cheek.

"How did you know to bite my...umm...nub?" I forced out, embarrassed.

"What?" Andrew looked confused.

"When you entered—I mean when it happened— whatever, you bit me." Right then I could feel the throbbing between my legs.

Andrew had thought about it for a moment before his eyes widened with understanding. "Well, I have to admit you being a virgin was a *huge* surprise. You knew I wasn't one. And when I lost mine, the girl was already experienced. Actually, you're my first virgin." I didn't want to hear about some other girl, but knowing I was his first kind of helped. "I just didn't want to be the one to hurt you."

"So you bit me?"

A sly grin splayed on his face. "I came up with that at the last minute. I wanted to divert the pain to pleasure."

"I see." I lay back against his chest.

Andrew wrapped his arms around me. "Andria, allowing me to be your first was indescribable. After the initial shock, I wanted to claim you as mine."

Even though the water was getting colder, I was heating up. "I *wanted* you to be my first," I admitted.

Andrew's lips lingered behind my ear before taking my lobe into his mouth. I moaned at the feeling of his hands as they started to roam over my wet body. I began relaxing into the pleasure his fingers provided as my focus turned to what was beneath me while he continued to lavish kisses along my neck.

We lay there caressing each other until the water was cold. "Feel better?" he asked.

"I do. Thank you."

He kissed my forehead. "We need to cool it for tonight at least." I pouted. "What I would love to do with those lips..."

My mouth dropped.

"The water is getting cold," he said as he stepped out reaching for me to come.

Andrew wrapped a towel around himself before grabbing another to dry me off. It took a while as he focused on several places of my body. I thought I was the only one being driven crazy until he said, "That's enough," and splashed cold water over his face. I offered to help make things better again. He said that we could explore that tomorrow.

We decided to watch TV in bed. I finally remembered to tell Andrew that I had had a birth control shot. After explaining why I would get one, even as a virgin, he looked thrilled at the thought of being without a hat in the future. Andrew tested clean at his last physical—which was recently—and offered to show me the results. With that cleared up, we talked about trivial things before drifting to sleep in each other's arms.

The past couple of days had turned out to be surreal. If it was a dream, I didn't want to wake up. Andrew had destroyed me for any other man. The fact that I didn't want anyone else, terrified the hell out of me.

CHAPTER ELEVEN

Normally I would have been woken by an alarm clock, but that morning it was by the buzzer of Erin Young. I thought I had turned off my ringer, but I had been too busy taking a bath with Andrew to be concerned about that. I wish I had been when my cell phone blew up the next morning.

I couldn't say it was all bad. I had slept like a rock and didn't hear it at first. Andrew woke me up with layered kisses down my naked back before handing me my cell. He said it had to be important because it had rung several times in a row. When I looked at the caller ID, I knew better. Even though the last thing I wanted to do was to get out of bed or leave Andrew, I had no choice. I had a meeting to attend. So, I took my cell to the bathroom and called Erin back, explaining that I would fill in the details once Andrew left tomorrow. That appeased her and I got ready to leave.

When I stepped back into the bedroom, a very sleepy Andrew opened his eyes to look at me. "Andria, you look incredible, as always."

I was wearing a gray button down shirt and black pencil skirt with a pair of black heels—nothing out of the ordinary. I had piled my hair into a messy bun and threw on a light coat of make-up. "Thanks, but this is nothing."

"Come here," he said mischievously.

I could see the hunger in his eyes, and that made me want him. I shook my head, knowing if I stepped any closer, I would not make it to my meeting.

"Andria," he purred.

I stepped closer to the door. "Andrew, if I come near you, I won't leave. This is an important meeting."

He pushed himself up to rest on the headboard, and I swallowed hard as I watched his pecs move. "I only wanted to kiss you goodbye," he smirked.

I stood in the doorway, drooling and thinking that he was an evil, evil man. So, I blew him a kiss before his head fell back in laughter. "If I kiss you, no hands."

Andrew raised his hands. "I promise."

I walked over leaning in for a kiss before he grabbed hold of my shirt and pulled me onto him while slobbering wet kisses all over my face and neck. "Andrew!"

His hand slid up my thigh bringing my skirt with it. "Always ready," he growled in my neck. "I love how you feel."

"Andrew..."

"Let me make you feel good."

His fingers started to move upward. "Andrew...Oh gaaa...I want...ahh...I...caa...can't."

Andrew's touch suddenly caused me to scream, causing him to abruptly stop. "Are you still sore?"

I used that moment to flee. "I have to go. I'm sorry." I wiggled out of his arm. "I wouldn't go if this weren't important."

He nodded. "Sorry. Seeing you dressed like that..." He was killing me as he paused, lingering eyes perusing my body. "I know it's important. Why don't I meet you after your meeting?"

I pushed down my skirt and straightened up my clothes. "Okay. I can meet you—"

"I'll meet you. We can go to lunch."

Looking at him cautiously, I asked, "Is that going to work?"

"Why not?" Andrew placed his hands behind his head.

"What if you're seen?"

"Not worried. I'll meet you."

I blinked at him a couple of times before smiling. "I can leave you the keys to the SUV."

"I'll take a cab and then we can ride together."

"All right." I gave him a quick kiss goodbye. "I'll leave the information on the counter. If you need anything, call me. You have free rein of the place...but no snooping around."

"Afraid I'll find your toy stash?" I was horrified. How did he know? "Andria?" Andrew started laughing. "Andria has toys," he sung out.

I threw a pillow at him. "I don't...have that many."

I was truly horrified.

He grabbed my hand. "Maybe later we can play with a few."

Frozen and now very needy, I looked into his wishful eyes and a cocky smile. As embarrassed as I was, something about Andrew and my toys started an internal inferno, and I needed to quickly get the heck out.

I rushed out, telling him I would call as I wrote down the information, grabbed my keys, and sped out the door. That man was going to kill me.

Staying focused, knowing Andrew was lying in my bed was excruciating, but I needed my head in the game. I was in re-negotiation for royalties and with the offer of the movie, I was asking for more money for book two. Elena and I underestimated the first book's potential and I was thankful that I had only signed on for the one.

When I decided to write book two, she wanted to publish it, but I wanted more control and better royalties. All in all, I was very happy with the deal made and I signed on for two more, totaling a series of three books.

When Elena's assistant told her someone was waiting for me outside of her office, I knew who it was by her flustered voice. She could barely say that a *gentleman* was waiting for me.

"Andria, are you getting a little action on the side?" Elena winked.

"No Elena." I was thinking more like a lot of action. "Well, if we're done."

As I stood, I hoped Elena wouldn't follow, but I had no such luck. She was a very nosy person. I also knew Keira had kept her mouth shut about Andrew, so this would be a surprise to her. As I walked out the door, we both were in for a surprise.

Andrew had on a gray suit with a white button down shirt that had a couple of buttons undone. His hair was a perfectly sexy mess, and the smile on his sunglass-covered face beamed. Elena took a step back in shock before mumbling, "Is that Andrew Hughes?"

Andrew walked straight toward me and placed a kiss on my cheek. "Sorry, I'm late."

I inhaled in his delicious scent. "I knew you would be," I teased, "but we just finished."

"*This* is who you're doing?"

We both turned to Elena. Andrew was amused, I was peeved. "Elena! This is who I'm having lunch with. Why...Andrew, this is Elena Martinez, my publisher."

Andrew wrapped an arm around me while he reached his other hand out to shake Elena's. "It's nice to meet you."

She took her time shaking his hand. "I'm actually good friends with your manager, Frank."

Andrew's demeanor changed when she said his name. "Is that so? Well, it was still nice meeting you."

Even though he tried to play it off, something seemed weird. Elena laughed and giggled placing her hand on his arm. We both noticed, and Andrew looked down at her hand and moved his arm away, and squeezed me tighter. I wanted to jump him right there and claim *him* as mine.

I told Elena we needed to go and drug Andrew into the elevator, not saying a word until the door closed. Then, I pounced. I ravished Andrew's face with kisses, focusing on his chiseled jaw as I nipped and gnawed at it like a starving puppy. Andrew let me have my way with him until the door opened. I calmly walked out of the elevator, into the lobby, and to my car. Before I had a chance to place the car in reverse, Andrew leaned over and gave me a hard kiss. We both smiled as our foreheads came together. "You missed me," he stated.

"I always miss you. Umm, sorry for attacking you."

"You can do that as much as you want."

"I don't know what came over me. Seeing Elena touch you, and her assistant ogling you, it made me...mad."

One side of Andrew's mouth lifted, "I've been there. And for the record, you have nothing to worry about."

"Really?" I studied his eyes.

Andrew narrowed his. "You were worried?"

"Not worried, just...it's nothing."

I wanted to ask him what these past few weeks meant for us, but I was afraid it might be too soon.

He sat back and examined my face. "Andria, what is it?"

"Can we talk about it at lunch? I'm starving."

He looked into my eyes. "All right, but we *will* talk about this."

I took Andrew to one of my favorite Mexican restaurants. I loved how they heated the patio's adobe fireplaces during colder days and evenings. It was a cooler day, but still warm enough to eat outside. Soft music played in the background as we sipped on sangria.

"This is a nice place," Andrew said as his eyes circled around.

"It's my favorite. I knew the place would be empty after the lunch rush, so you don't have to worry about being seen."

Andrew looked puzzled. "Do you think I don't want to be seen with you?"

"No! No, I was just trying to...I don't know." I took a long sip of my sangria as Andrew cautiously watched.

"Huh, after what we...I still feel flustered talking to you sometimes," saying more to myself than to him.

"I fluster you?" He smirked.

Cocky ass.

"You fluster a lot of women, Andrew. You know this."

Andrew's grin fell. "I think you're exaggerating, and those women I fluster...it's a celebrity they see, not me, Andria. You never answered my question. Why are you worried about us being seen here? I thought I explained this the other night?"

I looked down, occupied with my napkin. "You said you wanted to keep us private for as long as possible."

"Oh. I do. But I didn't think there were any paparazzi hanging around your place. I could be wrong, since you *are* A.P. Moore—"

I looked up not amused. "Andrew, there are no paps hanging around my place, nor would they be interested in my daily activities."

His smile wavered. "I hope so; for at least a little while longer. Anyway, no one knows I'm here, so I think we're good for now."

"You told Brittney, and didn't mention you were with me." Why did that pop out so fast?

His brows furrowed. "Yeah, I did tell her. *And* Amy, as well as Frank, but none of them know I'm with you. It's none of their business." Just hearing that creep's name turned my stomach. "Hey, is there something I need to know about them?"

My eyes grew wide as I stared at Andrew. "No! There's just something about him..."

"Frank?" Andrew's face turned hard. "Should I be worried?"

I shook my head. "No! Sorry, I mean...well, he rubs me the wrong way, that's all."

"Uh huh," Andrew pondered before asking, "Did he do something to you Andria?" His tone was clipped.

"It isn't anything like that. It's just, I can't explain it. It's me, forget it, I don't know what came over me. He's fine. If it weren't for him, I wouldn't have gone to your premiere."

Andrew's expression remained tight. "Well, at least he's good for one thing."

I looked curiously at Andrew regarding his comment. He wasn't going to volunteer anything further, so we continued on with lunch.

Andrew scarfed down his enchiladas and ate a few bites of mine. "This is really good."

"I told you."

We spent the rest of our time getting to know more about each other. I told him about my life in Dallas, which really was not much to tell. I was a pretty boring person. If I wasn't writing, I was watching television or reading books. Saying that out loud sounded pretty disparaging, but I enjoyed my life. I travelled as much as I could, and I visited Erin frequently. So, I wasn't all *that* boring. We spoke about us both growing up in the east. I had grown up in Arlington, Virginia with my parents before my dad moved to Baltimore after their divorce. Andrew grew up in horse country, Middleburg, Virginia. We were in the same state, but far from the same experiences and lifestyles. We also discussed our travels and my upcoming trips. As I finished up the last of my sangria, I said, "It must have been great traveling abroad."

"It was. I loved Italy, and I spent a lot of time in England."

"I am scheduled to spend two weeks there," I said, thrilled.

"When?" He sounded grim.

"Umm, remember I told you I was going on tour? I'm in England during *that* time."

Recollection came. "I must admit, I pushed that information aside to deal with at a later date. The reality that I won't be seeing you for six weeks..."

My heart melted. "Trust me. I wanted to change the schedule after our first date."

"As selfish as I would like to be, *this* is your big break. And no one, including myself, should stand in your way. At least, I'm here during the beginning."

"I kind of hoped you would be around for much longer than the beginning, Andrew."

He grinned, "I plan on being around for as long as you'll have me."

"I'll always have you."

Where the heck did that come from? I felt my flesh heat up.

Andrew chuckled. "I love how your entire body blushes. In fact, I think we need to get the check so I can examine it more closely."

Inhaling, I stared into darkened green eyes, as I felt my pulse speed up. The server came over at that moment. "Check, please."

"That was amazing," I said, catching my breath as Andrew fell back on the bed.

I lay beside him as he turned his body towards me. "I can think of a few other words to describe that, Andria."

I blushed as Andrew's finger drew circles on my bare stomach during our post-coitus bliss. Glancing around the room, I noticed the only thing that had survived on my bed was the bottom sheet. Both my duvet and pillows were thrown haphazardly across the room. We laid there, limbs entwined, soaking in the last rays of the sun as dusk started to fall.

I couldn't get enough of Andrew. The feel of his hand softly brushing over my stomach caused me to shiver. He noticed, reaching down to grab the comforter, and placed it over us. "As much as I love studying your naked form, I can't have you catch a cold."

A shy grin graced my face as I pecked his nose with a kiss. "That was thoughtful of you. I must admit having you stare at my body was making me self-conscious."

"Your body is breathtaking," he stated obviously.

"Andrew..." I said, doubtful.

He sat up. "It is. I'm becoming an expert at understanding your body."

I looked up seeing his trademark smirk. "I can't argue with that."

"You're an incredible woman, Andria Moore."

Andrew could make me feel so beautiful and wanted from only his words. And, what I saw in his eyes made me believe them.

"I love the feel of you," Andrew crooned as his fingers slid between my breasts.

Did I say the man also made me feel sexy? When I was with Andrew, he made me feel...alive. When he touched me, everything was more heightened, in a new way.

We kissed for a while before Andrew settled me into his arms. "Andria, you're making it hard to leave."

The joy I was feeling was instantly sucked out. Andrew was leaving in the morning, and that realization made my chest hurt.

Andrew reached over and lifted my face towards him. I refused to look in his eyes. "Hey, this isn't going to be easy for me either," he said, as I finally looked up. "It's going to be hell. But, *we will* make it work."

I buried my head into his chest. "Do you think so? Do you really think this can work?"

He pushed me back as he stated confidently, "I know this can work."

"Oh, Andrew..."

I kissed him and he pulled back. "Are you crying?"

I didn't realize that I was. With everything that had happened, I was feeling overwhelmed. "I just...I wanted to stay in this cocoon for a little while longer. I don't want this to end. It's only been a few weeks..."

He sat up with his back against the headboard. "Andria, look at me." I shook my head. "Please look at me."

He had a pained expression on his face. "Andrew, I'm okay."

"*This*," he pointed between him and me, "will work. I know it's only been a few weeks, but I have wanted us to work from the beginning. Andria, I will do everything in my power to make this work, but I can't do it alone."

"I want it to work too, but—"

"No buts. *This* is going to work. We'll call, video chat, visit, whatever we have to do."

Andrew sounded determined, and for the first time, I thought maybe he could have the same feelings as me.

Saying goodbye to Andrew was insufferable. To not see or feel him anytime soon was unbearably painful to think about. It was much easier leaving him in LA. Although, being mad as hell at him when I left could have helped. We said our goodbyes in the car. Even though he knew no paps were around, there were a lot of people in the airport, and he didn't want any pictures "popping" up unexpectedly. Our little bubble would remain intact for as long as possible.

I drove back on autopilot, and didn't realize I was home until I pulled into the garage. Keira had arrived that morning and was working on the edits until I returned from the airport. I called Erin, and finally filled her in on all the details. She let me cry out my sadness in-between telling her about my exploits. I didn't realize how long we were on the phone until I had received a text from Andrew stating that he had arrived safely, and would call me later that night.

Andrew had a lot of work to catch up on, and since he was about to shoot another movie, he had many things to do before he left. Filming was scheduled to start after New Year's. Andrew was going to Virginia to spend Christmas with his family, and then he would leave to go to Vancouver, Canada to start shooting. I wished it was my Christmas with Dad. But, I would be spending it with my Mom and Bob in Florida before flying to New York.

Keira and I worked late into the night. I did get to speak to Andrew for a little while. I could tell he was tired, and that he still had a lot to do before he left. We said our goodnights and went back to work. It was after midnight when I finally crawled into bed. Even with fresh linens on the bed, I could still smell Andrew on my pillows. I hugged one as the memories of the last two days flashed across my mind. I could feel every touch, every kiss. My skin heated up at the thought of Andrew's fingers. Picking up my cell, I looked at the picture I had taken while Andrew was sleeping. Yes. I knew that was creepy, but he looked like an angel when he slept. My angel, and with that thought, I fell asleep.

Trying, at first, was easier said than done. Even though both Andrew and I knew that our schedules would eventually slow down, currently it wasn't helping. We spoke to each other twice a day. Usually, it was the first thing in the morning and then at night when we would fall asleep on the phone. But, recently, we had had problems connecting. When we did catch each other, it started to feel that Andrew and I were in a normal relationship. One where he wasn't a busy movie star and I wasn't an up-and-coming author with a full schedule. Yet, the bubble would always pop when I had to go because of a meeting or edits, or when he had to take an important call or do an interview. Reality always interrupted.

Andrew and I had decided to video chat as much as we could. So, if I was driving somewhere, I would place the cell on the dashboard and talk, or when he was in-between takes or appointments, he would call. It actually seemed to add to our closeness—being in each other's daily activities. It also gave me a glimpse into the craziness of Andrew's life.

Video chatting came in very handy at night. We would flirt—a lot. I always made sure that I had on something sexy, and Andrew would only wear boxers or pajama pants. A few times, he caught me touching the monitor as I ran my fingers down his screened chest. I just wanted a touch. That's when our discussions would turn more towards the *900 talk* type of conversations.

Sometimes, listening to dirty talking Andrew was too much. By seeing him as flustered as I was, made me feel better. The fact that it was *me* that made him frustrated was a *huge* turn-on.

The moment I arrived in Florida, my mom looked at me with her wide brown eyes, and she knew. How? I hadn't quite figured that out, but she knew her little girl wasn't a virgin anymore. Maybe it was a Mom thing. "Who is he?" she asked, as soon as I entered the kitchen.

I shook my head as I sat down next to her at the table. I noticed Mom's aged skin was darker, and her curly red hair was highlighted by the sun. "Mom, why would you assume-"

"Andria, you're glowing," she said studying my face.

"It's the sun." She gave me an evil eye. "All right—I met someone."

She clapped her hands. "I knew it! Was it good?"

"Mom!" I looked around embarrassed. Bob was somewhere in the house.

"Oh Andria, your secret is always safe with me. I just hope he treated you special."

I never told my mom that I was a virgin. It's something I never mentioned or wanted to discuss; just like I never wanted to hear about her sex life, even though she felt like always sharing. I wasn't as free-spirited as my mother. "Why would you assume..."

"A mother knows. And by the look on your face—" She smirked as she walked to the microwave after hearing the ding.

"It was several weeks ago, how can you see—" *What was I saying?*

"Again, a Mother knows. Now, tell me all about it."

"*That* is never going to happen. Is dinner ready?" I asked to deter her from the line of questions.

"Hearing you speak, I would think you were a prude like your father, but I read your book."

I shook my head, not wanting to listen to anymore and started to get up. "What time is church?"

Yes, even the perverts can go to church on Christmas Eve. "Seven."

"I need to make a call before we eat."

"Well hurry up, I want to hear all about this young man. Or is he an older man? I'll be fine with that." I rolled my eyes and went to my room.

Mom and Bob had recently bought a house in South Carolina and this trip to Florida was planned as a celebration. Bob had accepted a new contractor position with a large construction company and they would be relocating in January. They were still keeping the house in Dallas to use in the off-season. But, I think they were keeping it to have if they got tired of Carolina, or annoyed by my mom's relatives who lived there.

I was sad at first when Mom told me they were moving, but I was considering a move back to Virginia. As much as I hated the winters, I missed Erin, and I wanted to be closer to Dad. My mom's move to South Carolina helped push me to ask Erin to start looking for condos, and I was going to keep my place in Dallas as an investment.

After getting ready, I had an urge to call Andrew, but looking at the time confirmed that he might not be alone yet. We had been video chatting more, which helped—a lot. Seeing him made such a difference, and I think it made one for him too.

After attending the long-awaited funeral with Brittney—the family had quarreled about arrangements—Andrew had called that night drained. He had done everything he could to support Brittney and her family. He said that Brittney was in bad shape, but she had friends and family around to help her. Looking at Andrew, you could see that he was wiped out and needed a mental break.

So, I flashed my breasts at him. Yes. I, Andria Moore, flashed my breasts. Something I had never been comfortable with. I always wondered if someone could hack into the video feed, but I did it. It may have been for a split second, and I was beet red from embarrassment, but the look on Andrew's face made it all worth it. Andrew went from Mr. Gloomy Face to Mr. Ray of Sunshine. Of course, he wanted to see more, and I had to explain why I wasn't going there. But, he did appreciate me trying to make him smile, and it had done the job.

Andrew was in Virginia for Christmas, and he had brought Brittney with him. Evidently, she had some issues with her family after the funeral, and was going to spend the holidays alone. *Again*, Andrew came to the rescue—which I loved him for—but I'm not going to lie and say I wasn't upset. I tried to be sympathetic, and asked Andrew why she couldn't spend the holidays with her *girl* friends or someone *other* than him. Andrew explained that she didn't have many girlfriends, and she was comfortable with his family.

Of course, she was comfortable—they dated and his family knew her. Yet, *I* was still an unknown. It took several deep breaths, as I spoke to him, to compose the turmoil that was stirring in my gut. Yeah, I knew he was trying to "protect" me from his crazy lifestyle, but it also made it seem as if Andrew had no one in his life *other* than Brittney.

It didn't help that every time we talked, Brittney somehow interrupted our conversation. I started calling Andrew late at night in order to get him alone. I hated waking him up, but I wanted uninterrupted time. And, if I was honest with myself, I was really bothered that Andrew and I hadn't spoken about the terms of our relationship. I only had myself to blame for that.

I didn't want to push at first, and our relationship was still new. Andrew and I hadn't known each other that long—it had only been a month, and I wanted to see where things led naturally. If I only had some confirmation that we were exclusive or that he was my boyfriend, I would feel at ease. But, until then, I felt like I was in limbo. I told myself as soon as I came off of the tour, we would sort this all out. Even though Andrew told me time and time again that Brittney and he were only friends, I hated that she made me doubt him. But most of all, I hated doubting us.

Andrew had said that his family celebrated on Christmas Eve, so I knew I wouldn't be speaking to him until later that evening. I wanted to confirm that he had received my gift, so I thought a quick call would be in order. Andrew answered on the first ring. "Andria!" He sounded joyful.

"Merry Christmas, Andrew." I stopped just outside my door.

"Merry Christmas to you. How's your Mom?"

I quietly laughed. "Funny. Good. Can you believe she figured out we had sex by looking at me."

"I'm *that* good," he confidently stated.

I giggled. "Did you get my gift?"

"I did. I was going to open it."

"No! Can you wait until tomorrow? And when you're alone?"

"Now, I'm really going to open it," he said, quizzically.

I peered down the hallway, hearing my mom's voice. "It's not like that. I just wanted you to open it, *alone*."

Andrew hesitated before saying, "Okay. I had planned on it. Hey, is everything all right?"

"Great, and you?"

"Well, it would be a lot better if you were here."

I spoke softly. "I wish that I could be."

Then *her* voice came through loud and clear in the background. "Andy, you're missing the game," Brittney whined.

"I'll be there in a minute. Well, enjoy your time with your Mom."

I wanted to say something to Andrew about Brittney, but I held my tongue. Later, I thought. It's Christmas. "I will, and enjoy the time with your family."

I was about to hang up when I heard, "Oh, Andria, my mom says Merry Christmas."

"What?" I paused in shock. I had never met his Mother.

"Like your Mom, my mom noticed a difference too. She hounded me until I conceded. I told her everything about you and she can't wait to meet you." I didn't know what to say. I was in shock. "Andria?"

"I would love to meet your mom," I smiled at the phone.

"As soon as we're both back in the states, I told her I would plan something. If not, she threatened to come find you on your book tour," he chuckled.

"If she's anything like you, I think she would."

"Where do you think I get my detective skills from? Oh, and Wade says the same. He wants you to meet Taylor. That meeting can wait a bit. She's a little harder to take."

My mom's voice got closer. "Okay. Well, I have to go. I wanted to wish you a Merry Christmas." I wanted to add "I love you" but that wasn't going to happen.

"I'll call you tomorrow."

I felt a little lighter after our phone call. Andrew had told someone about me, and *that someone* was his mother. My heart grew a bit larger thinking about that. It also cringed at the thought of Brittney being there with him. I couldn't shake the feeling that something was up with her.

Walking down the hallway, I bumped into my mother. "You look better. Talk to that man of yours."

I smiled. "Yes, Mother. I spoke to him."

"Thought so." She winked walking past.

Mothers always know.

CHAPTER TWELVE

I loved spending Christmas in Virginia as a child with all the snow, but spending it at the beach house in Florida wasn't bad at all. We woke up, opened gifts, and made a huge brunch before we headed to the resort. I had booked rooms at one of the luxury beach hotels in the area since we were going there for dinner. I wasn't going to eat my mom's cooking, and I thought we could enjoy the resort's amenities for the day.

Bob golfed while my mom and I lay at the relaxation pool. I love kids, but this pool was for adults only. They also played spa music while people waited on you hand and foot. Merry Christmas to me.

Andrew called in the late morning when he opened up the watch I had given him. I had no clue what to get him, and since he was always late, it seemed apropos. I had it engraved on the back with a picture of a beer pilsner and my initials. He loved it.

Andrew didn't mention anything for me, but I didn't expect it. I wouldn't say that I was overjoyed that he hadn't had time to buy me anything. Lately, everything that Amy was supposed to do fell through the cracks. This frustrated Andrew so much that he had started to handle personal matters himself—he was getting good at ordering flowers. Andrew's been busy lately, and his hands have been full with Brittney stuff. So, I didn't say anything, just happy that he had liked my gift.

During our conversation, Andrew had expressed several times that he was freezing his ass off; it had snowed in Virginia. I bragged how it was eighty-five degrees and sunny as I sipped frozen drinks and relaxed in the Jacuzzi. He didn't find that funny, but I did. My mom kept looking over at me with a knowing smile—I had told her few things about Andrew. I also ignored her while I told Andrew I would call him when I arrived in New York in the morning.

Christmas day was relaxing, and dinner was incredible. I ate so much my belly swelled up and looked as if I had a baby pump. I had chills thinking about a baby, and then Andrew came to mind. I had to shake that thought away. It was *way* too early, and I wasn't nearly ready to entertain that idea.

When we arrived back to the house later that evening, there was a package on the doorstep along with a bouquet of flowers. Mom read the card, and said with a goofy smile that it was for me. She handed it to me to open. As I looked at the perfectly scripted card, I knew it was from Andrew. He had remembered. Even funnier was what the card said:

> Andria,
>
>   I remembered.
>
>   Merry Christmas
>
>   Andrew

"Are you going to open it?"

"Yes, Mom. But, in private. Can you put these in water?"

She smelled the red roses, smiling as she went into the kitchen. I went into my room and locked the door. I knew my mother, and she was a very nosy person. I unwrapped the small box that contained a red jewelry box and I knew this box well. I *was* friends with Erin, and she had expensive taste. It was a platinum bracelet with a very delicate chain. In the center were three circles intertwined: pink, gold, and silver with a diamond attached at the end. It was magnificent, expensive, and too much. I called Andrew. "O.M.G. Andrew! Cartier?"

"Do you like it?" You could hear his smile through the phone.

"I love it! It's too much," I said and sat on the edge of my bed.

"Nothing is too much for you."

"But..."

"All I want to hear is that you love it. When I saw it, it reminded me of you."

My heart ached for him so much right then. "I love it, Andrew."

"Good. You thought I forgot."

I giggled. "I didn't."

"You did."

I lay back on my bed. "Well, I know you've been busy, and I didn't want you to feel obligated to give me something."

"I have said a thousand times, I will never be too busy for you. It's Christmas. How could you think I would forget to buy you a gift? I love my watch. Maybe I'll start to be on time."

We both laughed as tears dropped from my eyes. I was an emotional sap, and I knew that I loved this man. I wanted so much to tell him right then, but I knew it had to be done in person.

I was scheduled to leave for New York early the next morning to arrive at a store signing by one. I had called Erin yesterday to see if she liked the earrings I had bought her, but she didn't answer. Usually, I would be concerned not to hear from her, but with Miles in her life, things had changed. It was just weird that she hadn't called me back on Christmas or answered her cell. I sent her a couple of urgent texts, and knew she would respond as soon as she could.

I also checked on Andrew who had a couple of days off before heading back home. He planned on spending some quality time with his family before he and Brittney returned to LA. I promised we would have some time later that evening to talk. We ended up planning a phone date for nine.

There was something magical about being in New York in the winter. Erin and I would fly in for a weekend of shopping during the month of December. I loved to look at the Christmas store window displays while Erin just loved to shop.

Keira had arrived before me and checked us into the hotel. The driver pulled up to a very beautiful and elegant boutique hotel. My keys were waiting for me at the front desk, and I had a few moments to take a shower and relax before taking off. I tried Erin again and nothing, which made me start to worry. This in turn made me regret that I had never asked for Miles's cell phone number. I knew his email address and sent him a happy holiday's greeting and have you seen Erin email.

I wanted to lay down for a bit. But, as soon as I got out of the shower, Keira was at my door. "Andria, how was your Christmas?"

She had on a cute sweater dress that was a perfect fit for her petit little body. Her short black hair was pulled back by the cutest headband. But, it was the glowing smile and twinkling dark eyes that showed through her glasses that caught my attention. That was something new. Keira Tanaka was a very beautiful girl with great full features, but her brown eyes were beaming more than normal. "Good and yours?"

She smiled. "I brought a friend to my parents' house."

That explained the glow. "Ah-hah. Was this a special friend?"

"Maybe?" She grinned with a slight giggle.

"Do I know him?"

"Andria, it's in the beginning stages," she warned.

Keira had always been a very private person, and I respected that. "All right, I won't press it. How was the flight?" I asked as I finished brushing my hair.

She placed a folder on the vanity desk in front of me. "Long, but at least they added lie-flat seats in first class. I have your schedule for today."

I looked it over and saw that I would be done around seven tonight. I had a couple of meetings the next morning, and a tour of our affiliate's publishing house that Elena worked with. She wanted me to meet their creative team.

Keira and I decided to get something to eat before heading to the bookstore. I wanted a slice of cheese pizza and a potato knish. The best thing about traveling was the local food. I was a foodie at heart, and I loved to try new things. But that wasn't new. Every time I came to the city, I had to get a slice of pizza from a stand and a knish from a deli. I had Keira take a picture of me eating the dripping cheese from the pizza, and I sent it to Andrew. I knew he wouldn't see it until he woke up, and I was surprised when he sent a response back.

I want to lick that cheese off MY lips~ A.

"That good?" Keira asked and smiled as she looked at me grinning at my cell phone. I nodded. "So, it's serious?"

I wasn't quite sure how to answer that question. It was for me, but we hadn't discussed everything yet. "I hope so."

She gave me a warm smile before my cell rang.

"Are you having fun?" Andrew's raspy voice spoke directly to my girly bits.

"It would be better if you were here."

I could hear Andrew's sheets shuffling. "We'll plan a trip for just the two of us."

"That sounds great. Did I wake you?"

"I like being woken up by you. Too bad it wasn't under other circumstances." You could hear his smirk through the phone.

"Maybe we need to plan on that soon," I said, lowering my voice.

"Don't tease. I can barely stand it as it is."

"You said you would try to visit me."

"I did, but my schedule keeps filling up. They keep adding earlier times to the production."

The joy of eating the pizza was wiped away in an instant. The thought of not seeing Andrew for a longer time.... "Andrew, I need to go. I'll call you tonight."

"Okay...I miss you."

"Miss you too, talk to you tonight."

"Can't wait."

I hung up staring out the window. "Is everything all right?"

"It's fine. Andrew's schedule is getting busier."

She placed her hand on top of mine. "Hey, it will work out. If I need to rearrange some things, give me the word."

I smiled at her. "Thanks, but you know how jam-packed things are. It'll be fine. Hey, can you do me a favor?"

"Name it."

"Can you keep trying Erin for me? I haven't heard from her."

She looked concerned. "I'll get on it. We had better head out, or you'll be late."

I threw out the last bites of my food. Between missing Andrew and not hearing from Erin, I had lost my appetite.

The line of fans formed around the block. I was shocked at the amount of people who were waiting, and the response my book was getting always surprised me. The book signing was being held at an independent bookstore, and it could barely hold the fifty people allowed inside at a time. It reminded me of the bookstores I would find in Virginia. They were the best places to explore. There was something about the whimsy of old books, and obscure stores with friendly shop owners that kept me coming back. I would love for all of my signings to be at places like that.

I was halfway done with the line when I saw Keira walking toward me with a concerned face. I thanked the person in front of me for her support and excused myself. "What's wrong?"

"I have Erin on the phone, and she sounds as if she's upset."

Taking the phone out of her hand, I walked into a private corner. "Erin!"

"I'm sorry I didn't call," she sniffed. "I love the earrings."

"What's wrong?"

Erin cried out, "Miles and I broke up."

"What?"

"It was horrible. We were driving back from my parents, and I mentioned that I wanted kids. He froze and started spitting out things like, 'I'm not ready', and 'we're young', and he had a bad childhood, and 'isn't it too soon'?" She started to sob harder.

"Please calm down. You *are* young, and the two of you have plenty of time for that."

"I didn't say that I wanted kid's right then. I was trying to hint about a commitment."

"You two *are* committed."

"It's my fault. I thought he was going to ask me to marry him."

"What? When?" I asked a little too loud. I hunched further in the corner, lowering my voice.

"I thought he was going to do it on Christmas. He's been acting funny. Suspicious and weird, Andria. I thought if I brought up the subject, he would feel more comfortable."

"So you mentioned having kids?"

She started bawling. "I know! Ugg, I don't know. And I was hormonal. We met my parents!"

Sadly, Erin being hormonal explained some of it. She can get pretty nasty. "Did that go well?"

"As well as expected. Mom was drunk, and Dad kept asking what his intentions were with his little girl."

I couldn't help chuckling. He sounded like my Dad. "I'm sure things will calm down in a couple of days."

"I broke up with him!" she yelled before sobbing.

"Erin..."

"I was mad, Andria. I broke up with the love of my life."

"Did you try to call him, maybe if you talk—"

"That's it. He won't talk to me! In fact, he wasn't even at home. I went over late last night, and he wasn't even home. I have a key. I went over again this morning, and it looked as if he never came home." She sobbed harder.

"I'm sure he's just at a friend's."

She blew her nose and her voice started quivering. "He was with *her*."

"Excuse me?"

"There's a girl at his firm. She works with him, and I know she likes him, but he never showed interest until..."

I felt myself getting heated. "What, Erin? Tell me."

"I saw them walking down the street a few days ago. I thought they bumped into each other, but then he opened his car door for her, and she got in."

"Hell, no! I swear, I will come there and cut his balls off! *No one* cheats on my friend!"

I said that a little too loud forgetting where I was. Keira cleared her voice, and I saw a couple of women stopped in their tracks. *My bad.*

"It gets worse. When I called his friend Pete to find Miles, he said he saw Miles at the bar. They were performing last night, and he mentioned that Jocelyn—that's the whore's name from his work—was there. But after their set, Miles disappeared. I am such a fool. And it's Christmas, and I'm alone."

She was breaking my heart. I couldn't take it. "It's going to be all right. Try to get some sleep, and I will call you later, okay?"

"What am I going to do? I loved him so much. He was the one."

"I know. Please get some rest. I will call you as soon as I'm done here, okay? I love you."

Erin hung up, and I had to take a couple of deep breaths before I could face these women. I turned my head signaling to Keira. "Is everything okay?"

"No. I need you to get me on a flight tonight to DC, Erin needs me. Do *whatever* you have to." I walked back to the table and put my game face on.

Keira was unable to find any flights for tonight. When I told her I would drive, she worked a few miracles. Keira was able to find a rental car that needed to go back to the DC area. She arranged for me to take the scheduled meetings I had tomorrow as a conference call instead. Then she was able to push back the other meeting with the creative team out a couple of days in-between personal appearances that were scheduled. I had two days to be back in time for the network interviews and talk show appearances. I was worried about those, but now I had no time to focus on them. Keira said she gave them my standard questions, and I already knew the answers, so I was set. Keira was getting a raise. I don't know what I would have done without her.

I called Erin and told her I would be there late that evening. I drove four hours and arrived at her brownstone around midnight. I had known Erin for most of my life, and I had never seen her look this bad. She was a wreck, and I knew I had made the right decision. I couldn't stand hearing the pain in her voice and not being there. Erin looked and sounded like a broken woman. Even though I wanted to kill Miles, I knew he loved her and there had to be an explanation.

Miles was still M.I.A., and no one had seen him since his performance Christmas night. I prayed he wasn't with that skank, Jocelyn. Erin was a prize, and he was damn lucky to have her. Erin and I talked the entire night until we fell asleep around 7:00 a.m. I listened to her stories about how wonderful Miles was, and how she was shocked that he would cheat. Erin also outlined why she thought Miles was going to ask her to marry him. It all made sense to me.

As soon as we fell asleep, around 7:15 a.m., there was a loud knock on the door. I stumbled out of her bed and yanked the door open, pissed off that someone had the audacity to knock so loud. To both of our surprises, Miles and I now stood face to face. Once I remembered the situation, I promptly slammed the door in his face. "Andria, please. I need to talk to her."

"You should have talked to her that night, Miles!"

"I know. I was mad and upset."

I pulled the door open. "Are you serious? You were angry that Erin mentioned kids? Hell, some women might have mentioned marriage or kids after one month of dating. You two had six together!"

"I know. It wasn't that. Erin caught me off guard. I was plannin' on asking her and then—"

"Wait, what?" I pulled him in and lowered my voice. "You were going to ask Erin what exactly?"

"I was goin' to ask her to marry me."

My eyes started to water. "Why didn't you?"

He looked embarrassed—timid. "I got scared. Shi—damn it—I even asked her dad."

"You what?" I looked towards Erin's room hoping I wasn't loud enough to wake her.

We both waited a minute, listening for any signs of stirring before Miles continued. "Christmas day, I spoke privately with her dad while Erin and her Mom were in the kitchen. I had it all planned. I was going to sing her a song that night at the club confessing how I felt about her. But I was a bag of nerves. I don't know what happened."

"Why did it escalate to this?" I waved my arm towards Erin's room.

"Erin started gettin' upset in the car, and everything that came out of my mouth was wrong. She got mad and said she never wanted to see me again. Andria, it broke me. I was mad at myself for ruining everything, and losing the love of my life." His southern accent grew stronger as he became more and more upset.

"Where the hell were you then? Erin came over to your place several times. And who's this Jocelyn whore? What the hell, Miles? You were going to have a wife and some side action?" I punched him in the arm.

"No! What? What does Jocelyn have to do with this?"

"Everything!" I spit out. "Erin saw you one day with her, and she was in *your* car. Erin also found out she was at the club that night. The last time you were seen was with *her*." I punched him again in the same sore spot on purpose.

"Crap! I would *never* cheat on Erin. I love her with every fiber of my being. Jocelyn has only been in my car once, and that was when I needed help picking out Erin's ring. I would have asked you, but you weren't here. Also that night, Jocelyn wanted to see it happen. *That's all.* She was there with her girlfriend! This is all messed up."

I stared at Miles, and you could see he was a broken man. "Let me talk to Erin first, stay here."

"Thanks. Hey, weren't you supposed to be in New York?"

I glared at him and walked into Erin's bedroom. It took a lot to wake her; she had more to drink than I did. It wasn't the best idea to cry over wine, but it had calmed her down. I ended up pouring cold water on her face in order to get her to open her eyes. Then, I had to hold her back when I told her Miles was in the other room. After the long and overdramatic fit she had, Erin calmed down and listened.

First, I explained that Miles wasn't with Jocelyn. I knew that was the first thing that needed to be said. Then, I told her that he loved her, that I believed him, and to hear him out. Erin agreed and took another half an hour to get ready to see Miles. As soon as Erin closed the bedroom door behind her, I was out. I couldn't keep my eyes open, and I knew they would be fine.

I woke up to Erin jumping on the bed, waking me up at around 1:00 p.m. She had the biggest smile on her face, and her hair was a mess. I kind of knew why by the freshly made-up look on her face. Erin told me the story—*again*—but I noticed she omitted the proposal plan. I wasn't surprised; I knew Miles would eventually try again. He was very creative with Erin's version for why he got mad, but it worked. She seemed to have no clue about his plans.

Miles was going to come back later that evening to take Erin on a date, but she wanted to thank me by taking me shopping. I wanted to sleep, but I was there and I could take the time left to spend with Erin. Keira was able to book a flight back to New York that didn't leave until later that evening.

After getting ready, we headed to an affluent part of the city, and she insisted on buying me something. That wasn't going to happen, but I was in the mood to shop. I was starting to like the shoes she had selected. Even though they hurt like hell, they were sexy and Andrew— oh, my, Andrew! I asked Erin to hold on a minute before entering the shoe store. I pulled out my cell and saw six missed calls and numerous texts. I had left in such a hurry that I had forgotten to let him know I was coming to DC.

Andrew picked up on the first ring. "Andria, where the hell were you? I called all night," he asked, indignantly.

My cell phone reception was bad when I was driving last night. Frustrated, I had turned it off, and never turned it back on. I turned toward the display window trying to be discreet. "I am *so* sorry. Erin was upset, and she needed me—"

"I needed you! Damn Andria, it's hard enough being apart. We only have so much time, and I rearranged things to make sure I was available."

I wasn't sure if it was Andrew's tone or the fact that he wasn't letting me explain, but how dare he! "Are you joking? I rearrange my schedule too, Andrew! If it's so damn hard to pick up the phone to call me then why do we do it?" At that point, I didn't care who heard me as shoppers passed by.

"I'm not saying that, it's just Brittney—"

"It's *always* Brittney! Did *she* need you? You had to put her on hold to call me for a minute? *So* sorry for keeping you away from Brittney. Didn't she get enough of your time at Christmas?"

He was quiet for a moment, and then cussed under his breath before saying, "Are you upset that Brittney was here for Christmas? Because if memory serves me right, you spent Thanksgiving with your ex. should I be upset about that?"

I had forgotten about Brandon. "That's different."

"I'd say. I told you there's nothing going on between Brittney and myself, yet its obvious Brandon still harbors feelings for you."

Okay, what? I didn't know what to say, so I hung up.

I remembered what had happened the last time I had hung up on him, but I shrugged it off. Well...I did smile a little at the thought of how it did work out, but he pissed me off. I was tired of hearing him say Brittney's name, and he's questioning *my* friendship with Brandon?

"Should I ask what just happened?" I had forgotten Erin was there.

"Andrew and I had a phone date last night, and I forgot to let him know I was coming here. I mean it was last-minute, and then I saw you, and I was *so* tired. I should have called, but I just remembered. He's an ass, Erin."

She looked sympathetic. "It will be okay."

I shook my head. "I want to believe that. He's pushing me over the ledge. And Brittney...I hung up on him...again." I wasn't making any sense.

"It's all right. Hey, why don't we take a seat on the bench over there and you can explain to me what's up with Brittney?"

We sat on the bench in front of the shoe store as I filled Erin in. I told her how Andrew had been there for Brittney after the death of her biological mother, and that he invited her to his home for Christmas. I understood that they were friends. I stayed friends with Brandon, but they had been lovers. How would he feel if I spent that much time with my past lovers—look how he reacted to Brandon, and we never even got that far.

"Andrew is a cluelessman, Andria. I have my theories, but as you know, I can jump to some conclusions pretty quick. You need to tell him how you really feel. It's time for you both to define your relationship. From everything you have told me, it does seem as if he cares for you, and you *are* in love with him. It's hard having a long distance relationship. Yet, I know you can do it. But first, you need to get your man's head out of his ass."

We both laughed. "My toes are numb. We need to get coffee. Oh, and thanks. After I calm down, I'll call Andrew and try to hash this mess out."

She draped her arm around my shoulder. "I'm sorry that I was the one to have caused all of this."

"Please. You would have been there for me."

"Damn right I would have." We both laughed and headed straight to the coffee shop before returning to the shoe store.

We had spent a good hour shoe shopping before I decided on a studded black pair. Sadly, as I shopped, I kept asking myself what Andrew would like. He seemed to have a thing for heels, and I bought shoes that I knew we both would like. I only hoped there was still a 'we'. Things had been going well for the past several weeks, and we *were* getting closer. Even though I was still pissed at him, deep inside I had already forgiven his insensitive ass.

When Erin and I walked out the store heading down the sidewalk, Erin looked across the street, and then pulled me into a nook pointing. "O.M.G. Andria! Is that Andrew?"

I looked over and saw the tall man wearing a baseball hat and sunglasses walking to a car. As much as Andrew tried to be incognito, it was his walk and hair sticking out of the hat that gave him away. Then, I noticed the tall beautiful blonde, who was *not* Brittney. I watched as they laughed, and then she touched his face as he opened his car trunk to place bags in it.

Everything turned red.

One minute I was hovered in the corner with Erin, and the next I was crossing the street heading straight toward Andrew. He looked up with an expression of shock and excitement as I stepped in front of him. "Andria?"

"How *dare* you get mad at me and your with *her*?" I bawled my fists up.

"Andria, calm down." Erin said behind me as she placed a hand on my shoulder.

I glared at Andrew. "How dare you!"

He looked like a deer caught in headlights before his face turned hard. "Andria, I can explain."

"You wouldn't let *me* explain. Now *you* want to explain? I think it's a little too late for that. What, Brittney's busy so you had to find another heifer!"

"Hey, bitch! Who are you calling a cow?" Blondie stepped in my face.

"Andria." Erin pulled me back in warning.

"What's going on here?" We all turned—except Andrew kept his eyes on me—to see a very well dressed woman who had Andrew's green eyes. "Taylor, Andrew, what's going on?"

And that's when I wanted to die.

"Mom, this is Andria. The woman I was telling you about." Andrew said as he continued to stare at me.

I couldn't look at him.

"Oh, well, Andria, it's a pleasure meeting you. Andrew didn't tell us you would be in town."

"She's not supposed to be in town, Mother." I could hear the agitation in his voice.

I spoke softly to the ground. "Andrew, I am..."

"Kids, why don't we leave these two alone for a moment, huh? I need to pick-up one more thing. Sweetie, why don't you come with us?" She looked at Erin. "Maybe you can shed some light on...this," she whispered the last part.

Andrew and I now stood face to face, and I still couldn't look up at him. He was close, and his height shadowed my entire body. I missed that man so much, and I had the chance to see him in person. But, I couldn't raise my head. Not to mention that I humiliated myself in front of his family. "Andria..."

I could hear the agitation in his voice clearly. "Andrew, please let me explain." I forced myself to look up at his glowering features, but his eyes had a touch of sadness in them as he nodded for me to continue.

As fast as one could, I explained everything from the beginning. Not being able to reach Erin. Worrying. Erin crying and her break-up. The last-minute drive and the morning discoveries. How I realized hanging up on him may not have helped things, but he wouldn't listen, and I was still a bit mad at him. Finally, I told him how I missed him so much, and that I didn't want this to be the end of us.

Andrew stood and listened to the entire rant without saying a word. After I had finished, he stood staring at me. I couldn't read him, and I was praying he would give us another chance. Nothing prepared me for what happened next.

Andrew took a step closer, leaned in, and took me into his arms before placing a passionate kiss on my lips. I could feel the weight leave my body as he squeezed harder. I couldn't breathe, but I didn't want him to let go. We kissed for a while before having to take a breath, and then we started again.

I loved that man, and I would never forget to call him again. I felt him smile before releasing my lips. "I was very angry."

I kissed him again before saying, "So was I. And we need to talk! But, I'm sorry."

Andrew placed his forehead against mine. "I am, too. I was angrier more with myself than you. I made the same mistake, twice."

"We both did."

He hugged me tight. "I don't care about any of it. I'm just happy you're here."

My stomach turned. "I called your sister a heifer."

He chuckled. "She'll get over it."

"I made a complete fool of myself in front of your Mother."

He smiled. "No, you didn't."

I squinted my eyes at his. "Yes, I did. I can never take away that first impression."

"Andria. Trust me. My family is going to love you."

I hoped so, but how could I make up for my behavior? I heard Erin laughing behind us as they approached. "Well, I see you two made up?"

We turned to the three women and then me to his Mom who had a huge smile on her face. "Dr. Hughes. I apologize for my behavior." I looked at his sister. "I didn't mean to call you a...umm, name."

"Oh Andria, Taylor's been called worse," his Mother added.

"Mom!"

She gave Taylor a knowing eye. "You have darling." She winked at me before looking at Andrew. "From what I hear, Andrew wasn't an innocent party in this."

He gawked at his Mom. "What?"

She gave *him* a knowing look and then winked at Erin. "Well kids, why don't we get to know each other better over an early dinner? I'm sure all this excitement has made everyone hungry."

I wasn't ready for all of this. "Dr. Hughes, we wouldn't want to impose."

"You're not, Andria. And Erin said you don't have to be at the airport until later this evening. Andrew can take you to get your things after dinner. Besides, I have wanted to meet the girl who has made my Andrew look like that." She pointed at a now beaming Andrew.

I admitted, "He does the same to me."

She smiled before squeezing my hand. "Follow us dear. We can have dinner at our home, and Nelson wants to meet you as well."

And with that, Dr. Hughes gave Andrew a kiss on the cheek, and he opened up the car door as she got in. He walked over and kissed me on the forehead before opening the other side door for Taylor. "I'll wait until you're behind me," he said with a smirk.

Erin entwined her arms with mine and led me to her car.

I was about to meet the Hughes.

CHAPTER THIRTEEN

We crossed over a bridge to a private gate that entered into a very affluent neighborhood in Middleburg, Virginia. The homes were gigantic and sat back off the beaten path onto acres of land. We followed Andrew's sports car to a long driveway that rounded to a gorgeous colonial home.

"What do they do for a living again?" Erin asked.

"His mom's an Oncologist and his dad owns a small automobile tech company."

"By the look of this, it might not be as small as you thought." Erin said as she stopped the car behind Andrew's.

Andrew grabbed all the bags from his trunk and walked over towards us. "Welcome to my home," he smiled proudly.

"It's gorgeous, Andrew."

"My mom fell in love with it at first sight," he said as we walked up the stairs.

We entered into a grand foyer. "You grew up here?"

Curiously smiling, he answered, "Yes, why?"

I shook my head. "Just wondering."

The interior was grand and beautiful, yet...welcoming. The colors were rich warm tones, and the space was impeccably clean. I saw where Andrew got his cleanliness.

"Please, make yourself at home. And Andrew, show them around, please," Dr. Hughes said as she grabbed the bags from Andrew and headed up the staircase.

Andrew took my hand and began to give both Erin and me a tour. We saw the two living areas and both the formal and informal dining rooms. We also saw a study with a library, and the largest most incredibly stocked kitchen ever. It was my dream kitchen. It had every state of the art appliance and it was the size of half my home. I noticed Andrew studying my reaction as I swept my hand along the countertop. "I wish you looked at me like that."

I playfully hit him on the shoulder and he captured my hand. "I love this kitchen."

He kissed my wrist. "I can tell."

Andrew walked us out to the back patio that overlooked a very large lake. Even though it was winter, the garden looked well maintained. There was also a large pool with cabanas in the corner of the property.

Next, Andrew showed us the upstairs. When we approached his room, Erin said she needed to use the restroom and left us alone. He paused, and it looked as if he wanted to say something. I gave him a smile of encouragement to say whatever it was. "Andria, the whole Christmas thing with Brittney...honestly, I didn't think you would mind." I narrowed my brows. "You and Brandon managed to stay friends, and I thought you would understand that Brittney and I could be friends as well."

Damn! I *was* still friends with my ex and for the first time, I could understand why it bothered Jaimie so much. "Andrew, I never really thought of Brandon..." I didn't know how to explain it. Yes, Brandon and I dated, but I never had the same feelings for him as I did for Andrew.

"All I want is for you to trust me."

I knew it was definitely time for Andrew and me to have *the talk*. But, I heard Rebeca and a man's voice from down the hall, and it was something that we needed to do in private, and this was not the time. So, I nodded my head in agreement.

Andrew opened his door to a very telling space. One section still looked as if a teenager lived there, while the other half was obviously unused and updated. There was an iron frame king size bed with a gray comforter, and two black leather loungers along the wall positioned near the balcony. "I bet you had a fun time with that." I pointed to the balcony and he laughed.

"I had several scrapes and bruises from climbing up and down that," Andrew chuckled.

"I bet you did."

"So, this was my room growing up," Andrew said from behind me. I could feel his eyes on my body.

I walked around, looking at the posters of indie and grunge bands. There was an electrical keyboard and guitar in a corner. "You play guitar as well?" He nodded. Andrew was full of surprises.

Again, one part of the room looked as if a teenage boy lived there, but then the expensive art work on the walls told another story. Andrew spoke about studying art abroad and the pieces on his wall looked like the real deal. I wouldn't be surprised if they were. The artwork in his condo was incredible.

"Well, what do you think?" he asked from across the room.

"It tells a story."

"A good one?"

I glanced over at his bed. "I wonder how many girls have seen this room."

Andrew walked over wrapping his arms around me. "Not many. The bed is new. You can be the first one to try it out." As I pushed out of his arms, he held on tighter. "Are you jealous?"

There was nothing humorous about his comment of me being the first one to try out his new bed. Then he had the audacity to ask me if I were jealous? "You were jealous of Brandon."

He scowled. "I wasn't jealous of that—"

"Andrew," I warned.

He huffed. "Well, I can't say much. You've been fair about Brittney."

I almost choked. Biting my lip trying to refrain from saying something snarky. Then I thought, "Well, I better get a new bed in *my* bedroom in Maryland then."

Andrew looked down scowling at me. "How many, Andria?"

"Oh no, mister. You started this."

How does it feel Andrew, I thought to myself.

"I was only joking. No one has been in my bed."

"No one?" I found that hard to believe.

He looked me square in the eyes. "Only you." I took a hard gulp as thoughts of Andrew and me on his bed flashed in my mind. He must have had similar thoughts

185

as he continued to ask, "Why don't I lock the door and we can discuss this further?"

Andrew's hands slowly dropped down to my behind, and he firmly squeezed it. His mouth dropped to my ear as he whispered, "I was thinking that we should make-up properly."

I closed my eyes at the thought of having Andrew touching me. I quivered when his lips touched the sensitive spot behind my ear as he placed feather light kisses down my neck. My hands automatically reached for his hair and found refuge between the silken bronzed strands.

Andrew's hands traveled up along my body, lifting my dress, until they reached my breasts. I loved the firm grip of his hands as he squeezed and played with them. He had a serious expression on his face when he looked down at me for a moment as if he was studying every feature on my face. He moved in closer about to kiss me until we heard his mother and Erin in the hallway. "Andrew, as much as I want to continue this, we can't do this here."

He leaned back. "I know. My mother will be walking in at any minute. She's excited to get to know you."

"I'm terrified."

He gave me an encouraging smile. "She's harmless."

"Uh huh. We'll see. You *are* her only son."

He laughed before stealing one more kiss that we both didn't want to end. Yet, we did with Andrew sighing before taking my hand and guiding us back downstairs.

When we entered one of the living areas, a very handsome older man who looked a bit like Andrew, except shorter, with darker hair, and brown eyes, joined us. Along with an animated Wade and a curious looking Brittney. Her smile threw me off. I was expecting hostility, but she looked sincere. I had forgotten about meeting her, and I was glad I didn't have the time to think about it, because I was feeling apprehensive. "Andria, it's good to see you," Wade was the first to say something as he gave me one of his bear hugs.

I squeezed out, "It's nice seeing you too."

He released me. "I hear you called my wife a cow?"

"Oh, my gosh, Wade, it wasn't like that! I am so—"

"No worries, little one. Taylor said you had the gonads to speak to her like that, so you're okay. I was glad she didn't rip your hair out."

My eyes grew wide as I turned toward Andrew. "Should I be worried?" He shook his head.

"Next time you speak to me like that I won't be so pleasant." Taylor said walking in drinking a glass a wine. Both Wade and Andrew laughed. I found nothing funny about it.

"You harm a hair on Andria's head and you have to deal with me," Erin stepped in nobly.

"Umm, I think that won't be a problem." I looked between the two women before they comfortably started laughing. "Am I missing something?"

"Taylor has been shopping in my store for a while. I didn't realize she was Andrew's sister. We just figured out how we knew each other."

Dr. Hughes entered walking towards me. "Andria, this is my husband Nelson."

We shook hands and he gave me a warm smile. "Mr. Hughes, it's a pleasure to meet you."

"Please call me Nelson."

"And you have to call me Rebeca. Have you met Brittney?" We all looked over at the Swedish beauty. She was even more stunning up close and in person.

Andrew's arm tightened as I turned to her. What did he expect? For me to claw her blue eyes out in front of his family? "It's good to finally meet you, Brittney. I never had a chance to give you my condolences."

She cupped my hand in hers. "Thank you. How sweet of you. I don't know what I would have done if it weren't for Andy taking me in during this time. I hear he is quite smitten with you," she teased.

Andrew huffed. "Smitten, Brittney?"

"Oh, Andy, you know I'm right," she smiled.

"I think she *is* son," Rebeca chimed in.

Brittney turned to Andrew and placed her hand on his arm. "Oh, don't be that way. Andria obviously feels the same way. You have such a good heart."

"I do feel the same way." I said mostly to myself as I noticed Brittney's hand was still on Andrew's arm.

"And, Andria. I'm sure once I get to know you better I'll find that your heart is as good as his." Her words sounded sincere—strange—and her glazed eyes threw me. "Andy and I have always been there for each other. I don't know what I would do without him or the Hughes's."

We stared at each other for a moment before I said, "It's nice having people you can depend on during times like this."

"Well, I think it's time for lunch." Rebeca said as she walked over to me interlocking our arms as we walked to the informal dining room.

The table was large and looked as if it could seat twenty. The fabric-covered chairs were tall with cushioned seats. Andrew sat next to me on one side and Erin sat on the other. Brittney sat across from Andrew and Nelson sat at the head, while Taylor and Wade were across from Erin.

I couldn't help noticing that Brittney kept her eyes on Andrew while he kept his eyes on me. Andrew had been doing so for the entire time we had seen each other. Every time I would look at him, he would be staring at me.

"Andria, do you have any plans for New Years? My wife and I are throwing a party and we would love for you to come," Nelson asked while taking a sip of his cocktail.

"Dad, she'll be in New York," Andrew answered.

"That's right. How is the book tour coming along?"

Nelson actually looked interested. "Good, so far. I have a couple of personal appearances and a few talk shows on Friday I'm nervous about."

"You'll do fine, dear." Rebeca added walking into the room, setting down a tray.

"I would be more than happy to share some tips I have learned. Andy and I do them so much, it's become second nature," Brittney interjected.

I looked a bit stunned by her offer. "Thank you, Brittney. That would be helpful."

"That's a great idea. You two can get to know each other better." I squeezed Andrew's hand. I wasn't sure if that was a *great* idea, but I did ask Andrew to give Brandon a chance so I was backed into a corner. The look on Brittney's face said she wanted to try. Maybe I was wrong about her, I thought. Yet there *was* something, and I wouldn't figure it out unless I got to know her better.

Rebeca asked both Taylor and Brittney to help her bring the rest of the food from the kitchen. Erin and I offered our help, as well. When I started to get up, Andrew pushed my thigh down, and started to speak in my ear. "Did I tell you how wonderful you are?"

"No. But after how I have acted today, I'm surprised you still feel that way."

"Oh, I haven't forgotten earlier, Andria."

The agitation that came out of Andrew's mouth caused my body to liquefy. The man could turn me on like a faucet, and the wicked expression on his face showed he knew exactly what he was doing. "I had better go help your Mom."

His hand squeezed my inner thigh as he said, "Thanks for being nice to Brittney. Not only do I have to work with her, I consider her a good friend. Maybe you two will become friends as well."

I gave him a peck on the cheek before standing up. "Maybe."

When I entered the kitchen, Brittney smiled cheerfully at me. Well, let's do this, I said to myself as I approached her. "Hey, Brittney. If you have time later, I would love to get a few pointers for my interviews."

I saw Erin turn, and look at me suspiciously. I gave her the '*I'll explain later*' face. But the look of surprise on Taylor's face threw me as she walked past us.

"Great, I would love too."

We smiled at each other for a moment as Rebeca dished the food into the servers while she spoke to Erin about clothes. Rebeca apparently had a thing for fashion designers.

"I'm glad Andrew has someone like you."

I was shocked by Brittney's confession, but apparently so was everyone else when they all paused what they were doing before continuing on. "Really?"

She stepped closer to me. "I'm not sure what Andy has told you about us. Knowing him, he was kind. But I wasn't always the best girlfriend. It was hard dating on and off-screen. Our personal lives were scrutinized all the time. It became too much."

You would think that I wanted to hear all of this. At least she was telling me more than I knew, but for some reason everything coming from her mouth about Andrew was making me sick. I made mental note to ask Andrew what she did exactly that made her feel like she wasn't a good girlfriend..

"Andy really likes you. It's in his eyes," she said nicely, before her eyes narrowed at mine. "Just make sure you don't break his heart. I would hate to have to mess you up if you hurt him."

I gawked at her for a moment before saying humorously, "Wow. I'm being threatened by Brittney Price."

Her scowl eased up as she grinned. "I know, right! I'm a nice gal, but don't mess with the people I love."

There it was. Red flags started waving. But, I'll push it aside for Andrew. I said the same thing to Jaimie about Brandon. Brittney's only protecting Andrew—like he needs that—but I'll let her say her piece. So, I smiled and walked over to Rebeca, grabbed a tray and carried it to the table.

Once we were all seated, lunch was fairly entertaining. Andrew seemed happy when Brittney told him I had asked her for some advice. It didn't go unnoticed that she would look at him often as she ate.

After lunch, we had coffee and dessert in the living area. I sat and talked to Rebeca, while Brittney went to talk to Andrew and Erin. Wade and Taylor had to leave, and Nelson excused himself to his study to complete some urgent business.

Rebeca and I spoke about Taylor's and her London trip. They were planning a girl's weekend and would be there around the same time I would. We made arrangements to meet up for lunch and shopping when they arrived. It gave me another chance to get to know Andrew's family better. It also gave me a chance to make a better impression. I constantly kept apologizing to Rebeca and she would just blow it off.

I loved Andrew's mother. She and Taylor looked more like sisters than mother and daughter. Not only was she beautiful *and* intelligent, but also very witty. You could tell that his parents were still very much in love. When I walked into the kitchen earlier to bring Rebeca more dirty trays, Nelson had her pinned against the island and was kissing her passionately. I hurried out and told Andrew what I saw. Horrified, he explained that they always do that and they all know to make noise before entering the room. He said that had saved him for being severely scarred on many occasions.

As Rebeca and I talked details on where to go in London, I watched as Brittney found reasons to touch Andrew. He had lint on his shoulder or something on his cheek. She would laugh and place her arm on his bicep. Andrew seemed oblivious to it all, but it kept me wondering about Brittney's true feelings. I knew that look very well—the one that was in her eyes.

Every now and then Andrew would look over to me and we would smile at each other. I couldn't take my eyes off him and Rebeca noticed. "You really love my son." I didn't know what to say as I hadn't told Andrew yet. "It's in your eyes, Andria," she said warmly as she placed her hand on top of mine. "I am very happy that we will have a chance to know each other better. I'm looking forward to that."

"I'm glad as well," I said, admitting nothing as Andrew smiled at us.

Rebeca looked at Andrew as well, and Brittney had her hand on his arm again. "You don't have anything to worry about. I think my son feels the same for you." Then she looked at me saying, "But make sure you fully understand what life with Andrew will entail. It's not an easy one," she said absently looking back at Brittney. "But, I believe *you* are going to make it a good one."

We needed to leave if I was going to make it in time for my flight. I loved getting to know Andrew's family better, and surprisingly, I had had a decent conversation with Brittney. She knew her stuff in the business, and she gave me some good pointers on how to answer questions that may be thrown at me without prior knowledge. I was unaware that interviewers did that to regular people. I thought the surprise questions were a celebrity thing, when there's a scoop or something. But, Brittney explained they do it sometimes to spice up an interview for ratings. That was good to know.

Erin had left earlier to meet Miles for dinner, and it gave Andrew and I alone time for a bit longer. The thought of leaving him again was even more painful than the last time. I wondered if it would ever get easy, but I knew the answer was no.

I said my goodbyes and thank you's, and Andrew and I were off. We held hands and listened to classical music as we headed back to DC. Andrew seemed to be heavy in thought, yet I bathed in his presence. It was nice having him close even though little was said between us.

When we entered Erin's home to grab my suitcase, Andrew asked if she was there. I told him that Erin had already left for her date with Miles. That's all I managed to get out before my body was turned face to the wall, and Andrew was pressed firmly to me. He moved my hair off my neck as his lips brushed across it. "I haven't forgotten earlier," his honey coated voice purred. "I hate being hung up on!"

Hearing Andrew's hungry growl caused a waterfall, and my body was lit up with excitement at Andrew's forcefulness and words. I was a hot mess.

"This is going to be quick," he whispered in my ear before biting the lobe.

My heart was pounding out of my chest as we both breathed out an aspirated sigh of content at the feel of each other. I could feel Andrew's breath warmly along my neck as I heard the sound of his zipper. My heart grew with excitement as his body pressed me firmly into the wall. A unified gasp came out as I slid up the wall trying to find something to hold on too. It was sensory overload as he continued to move.

He grabbed my hair harder and growled, "Do you feel that, Andria?"

I couldn't breathe. "Auhh," gasp, "yes!"

"Don't you *ever* forget how this feels!" Andrew's head came done hard on mine. His scattered breath hit the back of my ear as he breathed out, "Every time you move—I want you to feel me—e.v.e.r.y.w.h.e.r.e," Andrew emphasized as he licked the outer shell of my ear. "Mine!" he snarled.

That was all it took for me to explode, speaking incoherent words as waves and waves of pleasure overtook me. I reached behind and grabbed hold of his hair. He showed no mercy, giving me no relief. I couldn't take anymore and my body became limp as Andrew wrapped his arm around my stomach. We both took a step back, as Andrew placed his hands on each side of my hips before we fell to the floor.

We lay there for a while panting and catching our breaths. I turned to look at him. "That was..."

"I know," he breathed out.

We laid a little while longer before I felt him move. "You're going to be late."

My limbs felt like jelly. "I don't know if I can stand after that."

Andrew laughed and helped me up. "I wanted to give you a parting gift."

"I'll take a gift like that anytime." He leaned in to kiss me. "Oh, no. If you touch me again, I will miss my flight. I'm already on thin ice."

"Ah, but one more..." He wrapped his arms tightly around me.

"No, Andrew. I need to change, and quickly." I wiggled out of his arms grabbing my bag.

I threw on a pair of jeans and a sweater and headed back to the front door. Andrew was running his hands through his freshly sexed hair, and I wanted to jump him again. When he turned and looked at me with that smirk, I had to remind myself I had a job to finish. He grabbed my suitcases, kissing me in protest, and we headed to the airport.

CHAPTER FOURTEEN

Andrew and I had had another make out session in the car before we said our goodbyes, again. But, it felt different, as if something had shifted, but I was, still in a post orgasmic funk. He had made it clear to call him upon landing back in New York. The moment I heard his voice, my body was reminded of his incredible skills. My thighs rubbed together, and the soreness started to throb.

It took everything I possessed to not say 'the hell with it all' and fly back to DC. Yet, I couldn't and wouldn't do that, and we both had commitments. Andrew would soon be shooting his new film in Canada, and I had a tour to finish. So, I headed straight to my first meeting with the creative team that Keira had to change twice. Not only did I forget to call Andrew; I missed a conference call yesterday morning. Erin can do that to a person—so can several bottles of wine.

My last-minute detour had filled my calendar for the next couple of days. It looked as if the only sleep I would be getting for a while, was on the flight from which I had just deplaned until the morning. There were several bookstore appearances, and dinner with the team later that night. Tomorrow was my first network interview, and I was starting to feel anxious about it. It was my first television appearance, and all I could think about was Andrew.

The last few days were surprisingly a blur. I had met so many people and had shaken a lot of hands. I was starting to get confused with both my comings and goings. Yet, all of my meetings went well. I was very pleased with how the new book was turning out. It was a prequel to the first one. It provided a more in-depth dimension of my characters and why they were destined to meet. I was given almost a year to finish it, and was very happy with that deadline. It was hard to write while I was on the road, and my schedule was filling up fast.

The television appearances were a learning experience. I had to wake up by 3:00 a.m. to arrive at the studio for 4:00 a.m. for make-up, and to meet the interviewer. The good thing was that I was so tired; I wasn't awake enough to feel anxious. The coffee didn't kick in until shortly after the second interview. I knew the questions ahead of time, and Keira prepped me well. I was thrown a couple of off questions, but they weren't anything I couldn't handle.

"Does A.P. Moore have a special man in her life?" I answered, "yes" and continued with, "it's in the beginning phase." They weren't really that interested; they needed filler for time. "What are your plans for New Years?" I hadn't thought about it, so I answered, "No plans. Maybe my assistant Keira and I will go out on the town," I lied. I had no desire to do that, but I didn't want to sound boring. I most likely would be sitting in my hotel room, and watching the ball drop while talking to Andrew on the phone. Now *that* sounded fun.

Andrew and I tried to speak to each other before going to bed, but we found that hard to do with our schedules. Our conversations were short with a few 'have a nice days' and 'I miss yous' thrown in. All of my meetings were in the mornings, and Andrew was up late reading over script rewrites and such. We did make a point to find the time to connect even if it was at 3:00 a.m. One thing not affected was that I was falling deeply in love with Andrew, and I wasn't sure how to tell him.

Erin and I had wracked our brains. Actually, I had wracked *my* brain; Erin's only input was "Just tell him already." But, the thought scared me. Putting yourself out there to someone was horrifying. But, I kept thinking that this was Andrew, and he was worth taking that risk.

One good thing about returning to DC was that Erin and Andrew's sister were becoming friends. Taylor was a shopaholic, and that made her an honorary friend of Erin's. I was glad they were getting along, and it helped me to obtain some insight into Andrew's family. Who seemed perfect, by the way.

Rebeca had been working with labs to create new cancer treatments, and her practice focused on critical ill children. She also sits on several boards for various charities, and somehow finds time to be a super Mom and loving wife.

Nelson had inherited his company from his maternal grandfather, and it was named after him. Nelson would assist his grandfather, Duke while he worked on cars. It had created a special bond between the two men. Nelson tried to share that bond with Andrew, but he wasn't interested. Surprisingly Taylor was, and now she ran the business with her Dad. Erin was full of information. All I could get from Andrew was that his mother was a great doctor, respected by her peers, and his father liked cars.

Elena insisted we have the holiday off, so she asked Keira to rearrange some meetings until the New Year making my calendar free for two days. The first thing I thought about was seeing Andrew, but then I knew Keira would be alone. I asked her if she wanted me to stay and we could see the city together, but she had other plans. His name was Owen King, one of Elena's assistants, and he was coming to New York for the weekend. I didn't put two and two together—it's been crazy—and Keira's been busier than ever. I guess after the launch party in LA, interests were peaked and they had started dating. I was happy for her, and that meant I was going back to DC to celebrate with Andrew.

Andrew wasn't answering his phone and I figured he was busy helping Rebeca with last-minute details for their annual New Year's Eve gala. I called Erin, who was busy with dress fittings, and said she would call me back, but never did. So, I sat in my hotel room watching old movies and eating potato chips. The only flight I could get was leaving late, and it was only 5:00 p.m. So, I napped on the couch in my suite while waiting for someone to call me back.

It was now 11:30 p.m. and I was on a flight back to Washington. Andrew had called while I was going through security, but I was running late, and barely made it into my seat. I texted him; along with Erin, Rebeca, Taylor and Wade to inform them that I was returning to DC.

Erin, because I needed a dress for the party, ASAP. Taylor, because I couldn't find Erin and she had been with her earlier that day. Wade, because I never texted him, and since he usually knows where I am at all times anyway, I thought I would give *him* the heads up. Rebeca, to change my RSVP—I was glad that I did—she had invited me to stay at her home. Which I gladly accepted. Actually Erin, Miles and I would be staying over and attending the Hughes's New Year's brunch, as well. And Andrew; first, to remind him how awesome I was for flying back to see him. And secondly, to make sure he didn't have any other plans. I had learned my lesson last time.

My flight arrived at 12:30 a.m. and Andrew was personally picking me up—in baggage claim. He was easy to spot with his hair sticking out of his baseball cap and his eyes shaded by dark glasses. I needed to inform him that, *that* disguise only brought more attention to him at night. He did look hot, and the moment he spotted me, even hotter as he graced me with his signature smirk.

"Hey," was all I could get out before Andrew passionately claimed my lips. That was new. I thought, breathlessly saying after, "Maybe I need to leave more often if I get greetings like this."

Andrew kissed me again before saying, "I missed your lips."

"Only my lips?"

"I missed *a lot* of other things but there are kids around." I playfully hit his arm as he grabbed my carry-on.

When we were comfortably seated in his car, I asked him what was up?

Andrew's brow rose as he kept his eyes on the road. "What do you mean?"

"You never pick me up *in* the airport, and you have never kissed me in public before."

He turned his head slightly to look at me. "I *have* kissed you in public before. I usually don't have to worry about the paparazzi here, Andria. Anyway, they think I'm in Canada. Erin read it online."

I wasn't sure where to start first; the change in public display, or the fact that Andrew and Erin were obviously buddying up. "Do you talk to Erin often?"

He looked at me and smiled. "Now I do. It seems that my family has taken her in."

"I see."

He laughed. "Erin dressed my entire family for tonight. My mom has her on the books for the rest of the New Year."

I shook my head. "I warned you."

He chuckled, "You did. How was your flight?"

"Crowded. How's the script?"

"Boring."

"No." I turned toward him.

"Yes. It's usually easy for me to learn lines, but for some reason I'm not into it. There has been changes trying to improve it, but nothing is working. I knew I should have never let Frank push this movie on me. It was my agent, Tom that eventually helped me weigh the pros and cons. But it's different from what I usually do— which is good—but my heart isn't in it. The director, Christopher Bryant, is the only good thing about it."

"I have heard a lot of good things about him. I believe he's on the list for directing my film. I'm sorry, Andrew. Hopefully things will get better."

"Don't be sorry, and they already are. The contract that Brittney and I had with the studio is over at the end of this year. And, I think after I'm done with these last two projects that Frank signed, I'm getting a new manager."

I didn't know what to be happier about. That Brittney and Andrew would no longer be working together, or that Frank was going to be out of the picture soon. Even though I didn't know Frank well, the man gave me the creeps, and I wouldn't have to see him anymore. Except, I was told that he and Amy would be attending the Hughes's party tonight.

Andrew and I held hands and talked the entire way to his parent's estate. That's what it was, a very large estate, and at night it looked even grander with the lights illuminating the house.

What I wasn't prepared for was the greeting that waited for me. The entire Hughes clan, except Taylor and Brittney, were up. I was told Taylor wasn't feeling well, and Brittney had had a sudden headache before I arrived. Yeah, Brittney had come back for the Hughes's party. I guess it's a huge deal.

The moment I walked through the door, Rebecca gave me a hug and told me how much she had missed me. I hadn't been gone for a week, but I appreciated the sentiment. She showed me to the guest room, and made it clear that she didn't want to assume I would be sleeping with her son. She hadn't wanted to ask Andrew. He always thought she was prying, but my room was across the hall from his. I thanked Rebecca for her hospitality, and wanted to tell her I didn't plan on sleeping with Andrew in her house; I didn't think it was appropriate. Then I thought maybe I should let Andrew know there was no way I was having sex in his parent's home.

Fifteen minutes later, I found Andrew at my door as he yanked at my clothes, and pushed me toward the bed. I felt badly breaking the news, and it was very hard to say no to him. He tried many things to get me to change my mind. But, I stood my ground. I had just met his parent's last week, and I wanted to make a good impression.

Andrew relented, and we found ourselves downstairs drinking hot cider the cook had brewed. Yes, they have a cook, and several housekeepers, and a slew of other employees but who's counting. Rebeca told me that she enjoyed cooking now and then, but with her schedule, it was hard to find the time. I found out Nelson actually did a lot of the cooking on his days off. He had a thing for his grill.

Everyone was dressed in their pajamas, and we sat around the kitchen table talking to around three in the morning. Rebeca and Nelson called it a night, and Wade wanted Andrew to play some video game with him. I said my good nights as I kissed Andrew, and told him to have at it. I was beat, and tomorrow/today was going to be a busy day.

I sank into the plush soft bed enjoying the feel of the silky cotton sheets. The mattress was so soft it felt like I was floating on a cloud. I fell asleep quickly and dreamed of Andrew. Although knowing he was across the hall did little to help my girly bits from protesting.

It was nice sleeping in, but it was even more so, being cradled up in Andrew's arms. Around five in the morning, Andrew had startled me as he climbed into my bed and wanted to cuddle. I wasn't going to argue as long as there wasn't any funny business. When Andrew pressed himself into my backside and began to say, "I want to feel you," it became a full on groping session.

When the burn became too much to bear, I halted all activities—it wasn't easy, *trust me*—but, I reminded Andrew that his parents were in the house. He conceded defeat, but told me we would check into a hotel later if we had to, because he was *not* going one more day without being inside of me.

I choked.

Actually, I coughed violently as I tried to get my breath back. The bastard had the nerve to chuckle before he settled in, and fell immediately asleep. I was now wide-awake and aching. All coherent thought was gone as I started to visualize exactly what Andrew would do in that hotel room.

There was a knock on my door. Rebeca told Andrew to hurry up or they'd be late for the golf clinic. The Hughes men and a few invited guests were going to a golf clinic where they practiced their swing with some virtual thingy at the country club. That's how much I knew about golf, and they would do this while we women folk go to the spa. That's Andrew's way of being funny.

I sat up staring at a smug Andrew as he pushed back the sheets. "So, now your mother assumes we slept together in her house."

Andrew smiled and pecked me on the cheek. "My mom assumed that we would when she asked you to stay."

"I'm trying to be respectful."

"And you are. Trust me. They love you already." He shifted out of bed and put on his pajama bottoms.

I ogled him and watched every curve of his firm dimpled ass as it flexed. Oh, didn't I mention the man climbed into bed naked? *Now* you understand? It took everything to not climb on top of him while he was sleeping.

I crawled out of bed as he opened the door, and kissed him goodbye. "How long are you going to be gone?"

He gave me another kiss before answering, "We'll be finished around 2:00 p.m."

"Then, are you all mine?"

Andrew leaned in and bit my lower lip as he growled. "I'll be all yours, Baby."

Suddenly, we were interrupted by an, "Ah hum."

We both looked at Brittney who had stopped in front of us in the hallway. She had a calm expression, but there was something about her eyes that seemed to be telling another story. I thought maybe it was an expression of grief, and she was trying to hide it by smiling, but there was something dark behind them.

I turned back to Andrew who was giving her a hopeful looking grin. "Good morning, Brittney. Did you have a good night?"

"Hello, Andria." She turned to Andrew and said, "I had problems sleeping Andy, but apparently you slept well."

"Yes, I did," he said while kissing my forehead.

I smiled inside. More like jumped for joy. Andrew was different. I don't know why, but he was.

"Sorry ladies, but I need to go before my dad starts yelling. He hates to be late."

Andrew said goodbye to Brittney before placing a passionate kiss on my lips. It took a moment to catch my breath as Andrew walked to his room, humming. Brittney and I watched as his door closed.

"You and Andy seem to be getting closer."

"We are," I said turning into my room.

"Andy trusts you." I stopped, looking back at her cautiously. "It would be a shame if your intentions weren't honorable," she grinned bleakly before walking downstairs.

What kind of cryptic crap was that, I thought as I closed the door behind me.

Brittney did not join us at the spa, and I would be lying if I said I was disappointed. Rebeca said she had her moments of grief, but she seemed to be doing better.

She also explained that it was a tradition of sort for the women in the family to pamper themselves at the spa while the men hit little balls. Erin and I were honorary guests, and Rebeca welcomed us both. It was nice getting to know Andrew's mother and sister better, and she made sure to tell all of Andrew's embarrassing childhood moments.

While Erin and Taylor were finishing up their manicures, Rebeca and I had a chance to speak alone while we relaxed by the sauna. As embarrassing as the topic was, I had to apologize for this morning. "Rebeca, I hope you don't think that I would...umm...*do* anything inappropriate with Andrew in your home."

She looked at me strangely before saying, "Are you saying you wouldn't sleep with my son?"

"What? No!" What was I saying? "I meant. I wouldn't want you to think that I would do that with you and Nelson—or...ummm..."

She snickered. "Andria, darling, take a breath. It's all right and I think I get the gist. It's admirable that you want to keep a level of discretion, but honey, my children are grown adults, and they have been for a while," she winked.

I stared at her nodding my head before snapping out of it. "Well, umm, thank you *again* for letting me stay in your home."

"Of course, dear. Andrew was missing you terribly."

"He was?"

She gave me a knowing smile. "He may not have mentioned it, but I know my son. Andrew is a complex man—always has been—but I can read him like a book. Don't let him know though. It's nice having a leg up on him."

We both laughed and took a couple of coconut and cucumber waters from the attendant who passed by.

"For example Andria, take our first meeting. I knew Andrew did something wrong."

I shook my head. "Oh no, it wasn't all Andrew—"

"Did I not say I know my son? And from everything I have heard from him *and* Erin, I do believe he was at fault. I told him so."

That got my attention.

"I may not be around Andrew as often as I would like, but I know the games people play and Andrew...as smart as he is...well, he needs to realize when he's being railroaded."

I gawked at her.

"Not by you dear, close your mouth." I obeyed. "All I'm saying is that when I asked him why you would be that upset with him, he told me the gist of the story. And by the way, he behaved horribly at your book signing. I did not raise him to act that way."

"He told you that?" I said a little too loudly. The attendant glared at me.

"No. Wade did. He's a talker, and when I make him my mother's chocolate chip cookies—the boy has a sweet tooth—He will dish over a plate of cookies and milk," she chuckled.

"That is good to know."

"Well, I'm glad Andrew made up for it in Dallas."

I know I turned red at the thought of Andrew and me, and everything we did in Dallas.

"By the look on your face, I see he did." Rebeca said with a grin.

I guzzled down my water embarrassed that Rebeca could read *me* like that.

"You and Andrew have more in common than you realize. But, I wanted to let you know that I did speak to Andrew, and I understand his concerns for wanting to keep your relationship private. But one thing my son doesn't realize is as long as he stays in his career, his life will always be on display. He tries—very well I may add—to make sure there is some kind of normalcy for the people he loves; not realizing that he sometimes puts them at an arms distance." My breath hitched at the word love, and I think Rebeca noticed but continued on. "But, Andrew *will* eventually realize that as hard as he tries to keep things private, he may push the most important people away."

Rebeca gave me a moment to think about what she was saying as she took a few sips of water.

"Andrew's a smart man, Andria. But remember as most men, he's clueless about love. Andrew will figure it out. Hopefully, sooner rather than later."

I thought about that for a moment. Amazed at how in tune she was with everything. "I think Andrew might have started to figure some things out already. I have noticed a change in him since I arrived."

Her eyes smiled brightly. "Good. All Nelson and I want is for our children to be healthy and happy. It seems as if you make my son very happy."

"I hope so."

"You do dear. Very much. Now, let's ditch these waters, and get some real drinks, shall we?"

And with that, we collected Erin and Taylor, and headed to the bar.

"I see you and Miles are doing well," I said as I washed my hands.

Erin stood in front of the bathroom mirror reapplying her lipstick. "Very. I think he's going to ask the question," she giggled out in glee.

"Again?"

She rolled her eyes. "I think he's going to do it this time."

She was right. Miles had called me a few days ago, and asked me to look over Erin's ring. I saw it this morning when he met the guys for the golf clinic. It was a simple platinum square cut diamond from Harry Winston's, which hurt your eyes from the glare off of the stone. It was perfect. He was going to propose to Erin tonight at midnight. They would first attend the Hughes's party, and then he was going to take her to a quiet restaurant and propose. It was taking everything to not tell her, but I played it as cool as I could.

When we returned to the house, I was disappointed that Andrew wasn't back from his outing. His last text stated he would be back by 2:30 p.m. giving us some time to spend together before the party. It was 3:30 p.m. and they weren't back yet. I received a text from him at 4:00 p.m. apologizing that they had lost track of time, and would be home shortly. The party started at 7:00 p.m., and it didn't leave much time to be together, but any time with Andrew was good.

The men walked through the door a little after 5:00 p.m. and Rebeca started right into Nelson. It was interesting to watch their dynamic. Nelson was the quiet one, while Rebeca was the life of the party. But the look that Nelson gave her, and the fact that she quieted down immediately, made me feel like a voyeur looking at them. Especially when he started sliding his hand up her backside. Nelson had another side to him, and I immediately thought *that's* where Andrew gets it from.

"What are you thinking?" Andrew asked me from behind as he wrapped his arms around me.

I laid my head back on his shoulder. "That your father reminds me of you."

"Huh? People say I'm more like my mother."

"I see that too, but you are definitely your Dad in other ways."

"Is that so? Have you been talking to my mother?"

I paused, not knowing if I should mention our earlier conversation. "She shared wonderful stories about you that I can use."

Andrew laughed in my ear as he placed a kiss through my hair. "I've asked her not too."

I turned my face to the side looking at him. "I really like your mother."

"She really likes you too. Do you want to take a walk?"

"Isn't it cold outside?"

"Yes, but I was going to take you to a warm place."

"Okay? I'll bite."

Andrew led me out the patio door, through the gardens to the pool. In the corner was a roaring fire pit that had two mugs and a bottle next to them.

Facing him, I squeezed his hand, pulling him into me. "This is romantic."

"I wanted to spend some alone time with you. Sorry, I was late."

He wrapped our entwined hands behind my back as he nuzzled through my hair. "Did you forget to wear your watch?"

"I didn't want to bring it. I was afraid it could get lost or damaged."

How cute, I thought. I did the same thing by leaving his bracelet—which I never take off—here. "You're forgiven."

We sat down on the outdoor couch as Andrew poured two mugs of mulled wine, and it tasted divine. We both leaned back, and I crawled into his arms as he placed a blanket over us. "This is nice."

Andrew kissed my forehead. "I thought you would like it."

"How was golf?"

"Great. It's always a good time."

"It's nice that you have traditions. When my mom and dad split up I lost a lot of our traditions."

"Maybe this can be a new one we can share, together?" he sounded hopeful.

I shifted my body so that I could look into his beautiful hazel eyes. "Do you really mean that, Andrew?'

He looked upset at first, and then calmly asked me, "Why would you ask that?"

"Well, I guess..." And then I realized this was it.

It was time to lay all of my cards on the table. There was no better time than the New Year. I couldn't see my future without Andrew and it was time he knew.

Okay, it may have taken a little more time. I watched Andrew's many facial expressions shift as he tried to figure out in his head what was going on. "Andria?"

I placed my wine down, turning back towards him, and his eyes were filled with worry. For some strange reason, that gave me the courage to go on. "Andrew, even though we haven't known each other very long, I feel a special connection with you. Obviously, I feel something more, I gave you a part of me I wasn't able to give to anyone else."

Andrew placed his glass down, curiously searching inside my eyes as he said, "I know, and that meant everything to me."

"Did it?"

"*Of course*! You're my world."

I took a deep breath. "I hope you mean that."

His hand cupped my face as the pad of his thumb began to stroke my lips softly. "I sincerely do, Andria," he answered with assurance and yearning in his eyes.

"What I'm about to say...I have thought about it for a while. I know it's soon but...I can't help my feelings for you..." I closed my eyes and said, "I love you, Andrew. I think I have for a while."

Silence.

Then I heard Andrew pull in a breath, and sensed his eyes on me before I felt him capture my lips. I opened my eyes and stared into his as he passionately deepened the kiss. All types of jumbled thoughts entered my head, but all I could focus on was the love I felt radiating from him. I only wished he would say something.

I swear the man could read my thoughts. When he pulled back, looking into my eyes, he placed lingering kisses along my lips and cupped my face. "I love you too, Andria."

A sheer sense of euphoria came over me as Andrew placed chaste kisses along my face. Hearing those three words caused a state of being that I had never felt before. This was what love felt like, I thought as Andrew continued to express his love for me. My mind became muddled as my heart rate slowed down, and a presence of peace came over me. A feeling of joy consumed me as it wrapped itself around my heart as the realization of Andrew's love hit me.

We stayed wrapped in each other's arms; talking and laughing in our new-found knowledge until Rebeca sent Wade to let us know that it was almost 7:00 p.m., and if we wanted to wear what we had on that was fine. Rebeca was being sarcastic, and Wade made sure to reiterate that.

Wade looked spiffy in a black tuxedo with a red and black vest. It was a style you would see an older gentleman wear, but he was working it.

It felt as if a large weight had been lifted off of me that I didn't even realize was there. Andrew loved me, and as I thought about that giggles would escape from my mouth. Andrew seemed pretty happy himself, which made me even more giggly. Who knew I could giggle, but I did. That's what the man did to me.

We made our way back to the house as the first guest rang the doorbell. Andrew walked me to my room, and gave me the sweetest kiss before saying he'd pick me up at 7:30 p.m. I floated around the room until 7:15 p.m., and texted Andrew that I needed until 8:00 p.m. I texted Erin the news, who came barging in and we hugged, kissed, and giggled like two schoolgirls.

After the love, Erin helped me get dressed. She looked *amazing* in a short sequenced gown. She said Miles was wearing a matching green cummerbund and bow tie. When she took my dress out of the garment bag it was the first time I had seen it. It was a short strapless black dress with an overlay that curved along my body in all the right ways. It was beautiful and very sexy. Erin braided my hair into four sections and created a gorgeous updo that she pinned with rhinestones.

Andrew knocked on the door before entering, and the look on his face said it all. He was very happy with Erin's selection, and I must say, she had done an incredible job on him. His black tux looked amazing and Andrew in a tie was yummy. I could do a lot of things with that tie, I thought.

"Stunning," he said as his hand brushed down my bare arm.

Enjoying the feel of Andrew's fingers on my skin, I stepped closer. "You look very handsome."

Erin wiggled her way in-between us as she started adjusting Andrew's jacket. "I do good work, and Andrew is partial to Tom Ford suits—which I wouldn't change, because he looks so damn good in them. I chose one of his dresses from Gucci for you, and *damn* girl, it works." We all laughed. "Okay, my work is done. I'll leave you two alone." She closed the door behind her. Even in my new Louboutins, I had to stand on my toes to kiss him. I wanted to taste him. Andrew was like the finest piece of chocolate that you wanted to nibble from constantly.

"Are you ready to make our début, Andria?"

I didn't even think about that. "Are you sure?"

He had a guilty expression. "I need to apologize if in any way I have made you feel that I didn't want people to know about us."

I stepped back from him, guilty myself. "I did have some concerns, but now I completely understand. I spoke to Rebeca—"

"Is that so?" His brows furrowed.

"I did, and she said she had spoken to you."

He took my hand. "She did."

"Oh, and I love your Mother. She is a very smart woman."

He laughed to himself. "My mother has always helped me see things...mmm...clearer. And I warned you that I had many flaws. Or did you forget what you said in The Anchor about me being, umm, what was it? Perfect? "He smiled leaning in as he pecked my lips with a warm kiss.

"I'm far from perfect myself, Andrew."

"You're perfect for me." I swooned at Andrew's words and gave him a thorough kiss.

A little too thorough. As our tongues danced, I wanted to strip him out of his tux and show him exactly how perfect he was for me. Hearing the mumbled crowd and music playing downstairs was a subtle reminder that we had a party to attend.

The house was transformed into an elegant affair. Candles flickered everywhere, and thousands of silver and black balloons hovered overhead in preparation for the midnight drop. The house was bustling with people as a small quartet played in the corner. Everyone was in after-five attire, and waiters in white coats served trays of libations and canapés. Andrew took two glasses of champagne from a passing tray and handed one to me, "What should we toast to this time, Andrew?"

He thought for a moment and then a smile graced his face. "How about to new traditions. Here's to us."

I was immersed in Andrew's eyes and lost in his words. My heart now only beats for that man, and everyone around us faded as our kiss lingered before we clinked our glasses.

"You two look happy." Nelson interrupted, smiling. Rebeca beamed next to him as she hugged both of us.

Andrew wrapped his arm around my waist pulling me in tighter. "Mother, you look beautiful tonight."

She placed a hand on his lapel. "You look handsome as ever."

She winked at me as I added, "Rebeca, you've out done yourself."

"She always does. The only credit I can take is deciding what perfume she wears. I can't even say I splurged on this little soiree. It's all my beautiful wife," Nelson said as he placed a kiss on Rebeca's cheek.

"Oh, Honey. You have the most important role. Being the man I love." They embraced each other with another sweet and loving kiss.

You could feel the love they had for each other from just being in their presence. They were high school sweethearts, and I made a wish to myself that Andrew and I could be that in love after thirty years.

"Rebeca, your dress is incredible." She had on a long sleeved black dress with a long folded V that exposed most of her back. Rebeca was in very good shape.

"All Erin." She smiled.

"Hey, guys! Mom, when can I get my jam on?" Wade started to do some sort of funky chicken as Taylor walked up behind him, horrified.

Of course, she looked incredible. She had an off the shoulder, short flowing red dress that looked as if it had been made for her. It was beautiful. Miles and Erin joined the group, and we all mingled and talked.

I nodded at all the right places, and laughed when prompted, but I wasn't truly focused on anything that was being said. I could tell Andrew wasn't either. I was preoccupied with the clasped fingers that drew circles on my back, and the way Andrew would lift our entwined hands to place soft kisses on the inside of my wrist as his eyes bore into mine. When he leaned over and asked me if I wanted to dance, I internally squealed for joy to finally be in his arms. Andrew walked me onto the makeshift dance floor in the living area, and pulled me in close as we swayed to the music.

One could live in Andrew's scent as the clean, crisp, sexy allure of him wrapped around my senses. I laid my head on his chest as we swayed unhurriedly to several songs. I didn't even realize who was dancing next to use until I heard Frank's voice. "May I cut in?"

I felt Andrew's protective hands pull me in tighter as Brittney added, "Come on Andy. We haven't danced in a longtime."

Andrew's eyes showed that he was mulling that over, trying to find some excuse. "Andrew, it's fine. Dance with Brittney." I looked at her slimy dance partner before taking in a breath, "I would love to dance with you, Frank." That was a lie, but the sooner we danced the quicker it would end.

Andrew kept on his game face, but I could tell he wasn't thrilled with me, yet he smiled as he turned me to Frank. "Make sure your hands are at ten and two," he joked. But, I knew he was serious, and so did Frank.

Andrew placed a firm kiss on my forehead as Frank took my hands into his. They were wet and clammy, and felt disgusting. His whole being gave me the willies, but I could play nice. All I thought about was two more films, and he would be out of our lives.

As we danced, Frank stood a little too close, pretending to be unaware when I nudged him back. "Andria, I was a little surprised to see you here."

"Why is that?"

"Andrew never mentioned you two were..."

I looked him square in the eyes. "Dating? Why would Andrew mention that? I would have thought *you* of all people would know that Andrew likes to keep his private life *private*."

He was taken back before a sly grin appeared. "Oh, I do. But Brittney—"

"There *is* no Brittney." I challenged, wiping that grin from his face.

Frank didn't say anything more while we continued to dance to the same slow song. The band seemed to be playing an extended version.

I looked over at Andrew who had his eyes on me the entire time—I couldn't help noticing him in my peripheral vision. Brittney was talking and Andrew nodded, but his focus was entirely on me; which made me want him even more.

The song finally ended, and I couldn't get away from Frank quickly enough. Andrew beat me to it when he popped up in front of me with Brittney trailing behind. "Are you hungry?"

I narrowed my eyes, pinching my lips together in order to not say, "Yes, for you." But instead, I answered, "That sounds good."

Andrew grabbed my hand, and before we could walk away, Grant stepped in front of us looking dapper as always. The man knew how to dress. The shiny specks in his tuxedo complimented his silver hair. He was always one that had flare. His appearance was a surprise to me, since I didn't know he was coming. I had actually never inquired about the guests. I had last seen the studio head when I was signing the final contract of our deal. Andrew kept his hand in mine and shook Grant's with the other. He gave Andrew a genuine smile at first, but it had an edge to it when he saw our clasped hands. "Andria, I didn't know you and Andrew knew each other?"

"Andria's my girlfriend," Andrew said proudly.

Well, alrighty then!

Andrew squeezed my hand, and his statement didn't surprise me. I knew we would talk more about our relationship, but I loved hearing the word *girlfriend* from his mouth.

"When did this happen?" Grant asked harshly, as his shaggy brows furrowed into his creases.

I looked at Andrew, confused as Brittney stood next to him, and Frank followed in with a look as if he had eaten the proverbial canary.

Grant then looked at Frank. "Is the publicist on this?"

Frank's expression fell. "Ah, yeah. I'll see how they can spin it."

Spin what, I thought?

"No!" Andrew said sharply. "The junket is over. There is no need to *spin* anything. We don't need the added attention on us."

"What about video sales, Andy?" Brittney asked.

Obviously, I was missing something, as I looked between the four people.

Andrew looked directly at Grant, ignoring the others around him. "I've done my time."

Okay, now I was at a total loss.

I stared with the rest of them as Grant's face stayed fixed as he thought that over. He finally moved, nodding before directing his attention towards me, "You two make a lovely couple, Andria."

"Thank you?" I couldn't help the surprise in my voice.

Grant took my free hand and placed it between his as he said, "Now, I see why you suddenly renegotiated."

He said it sweetly, but I didn't appreciate what it implied. "It had nothing to do with Andrew. I wanted more involvement."

Andrew wasn't my cash cow, and I wasn't going to exploit our relationship for financial gain.

He pondered that as he patted my hand. "Well, enough shop talk. Andria, Andrew."

The little man floated off as quickly as he had appeared. I turned to Andrew with questions in my eyes. He mouthed *later* and we proceeded to the abundant spread that Rebeca had laid out.

"Why were you dancing with that scary looking perv?" Erin was always direct.

I grabbed an olive off the plate while we stood in a corner watching Miles and Andrew talking. "I didn't want to dance with him, but Brittney asked Andrew, and I didn't want him to think I felt weird about it."

"Ah, huh? You let your man dance with his old flame so you could dance with the creepy guy?"

"No. Well, yes. But that *creepy guy* is Andrew's manager."

"No! Did you know Andrew is having Miles look into his financials?' She grabbed a piece of cheese.

Looking over at Andrew, he winked flirting, and I smiled back as I answered, "No, Andrew never mentioned it."

"I wouldn't worry about it. Miles only told me because he was thrilled that Andrew had asked him."

"I didn't know Miles was a fan?"

"He's not, but he gets excited when he does something new. Bringing Andrew in as a client opened up the door for handling entertainers. He's excited about *that*."

I laughed, watching Wade join Andrew and Miles as they do some hand fist bump. "Andrew like's to have a relationship with the people he does business with, so he must have taken a liking to Miles."

Erin nodded towards our men. "The three of them have some bromance going on."

We continued talking and laughing, finishing up a plate of food we were sharing. Watching the three love birds joined together in the opposite corner talking and laughing about something.

Occasionally, Andrew and I would make eye contact as we flirted across the room. It was liberating to be able to be ourselves in public. To see the weight of whatever Andrew was carrying off him was freeing. It looked as if he didn't have a care in the world.

The party picked up as the DJ came on. Wade was finally able to do his robot as we looked on laughing hysterically. Erin, Taylor, and I danced a while before Erin left for her "surprise." I was bubbling over when they said goodnight and Miles had to give me a warning glare to not ruin his surprise.

Andrew spent the night drinking, socializing with guests, and watching me. He danced a few slow songs with me, but when the music picked up he headed straight to the bar and watched. At first I was upset that he didn't want to dance, but the way he was watching made it up to me. The boy's eyes burned through me as the hunger in them grew. My mouth dried up as I watched his darkened eyes slowly peruse my body as his tongue wet his lips.

My lips, I thought as I swayed my hips slowly, watching his eyes travel along with my hands as they slid up my side stopping as they approached my breasts. That's when his eyes would flicker up to mine as I licked my lips at the smirk that was now present on his face.

We played that cat and mouse game for a bit longer as I seduced him with my moves. Unfortunately, I was very aware of the fact that Brittney *and* Amy—who I didn't see until later—were both in Andrew's line of sight gyrating on each other. My suspicions of Amy grew as I caught her staring at Andrew when she was dancing with Frank. Sadly, Frank thought I was looking at him. I thought Amy had a problem with me because of Frank, but the blatant way she tried to get Andrew's attention...well...you had to be blind not to see who she really wanted. Andrew was in love with me, and he didn't notice them at all. That filled my heart even more than before.

It was almost midnight, and the closer it came, the more I wanted to be alone with Andrew. I soon had an idea, and walked over to an inebriated looking Andrew, who seemed to have forgotten that we weren't alone. He lightly brushed the back of his fingers over my collarbone. "Are you ready to leave? I think there's something upstairs that needs attending to, be it now or later. It's up to you, Andria."

Inhaling a scattered breath, I stared into his darkened eyes. Andrew winked at me smirking before taking a sip of what I discovered was water. He knew exactly what he was doing. I challenged him with my own smirk as I whispered into his ear to meet me in my bedroom in ten minutes before I bit down on his earlobe.

Pleased with the groan that emanated from his lips, I went to find Rebeca. I needed help with confiscating a bottle of champagne and glasses. She was able to aid me with my request, and when I started up the back stairs, she made a comment as she was leaving the room, "It took you long enough to drag Andrew away. I was going to lose my bet with Nelson if you two stayed any longer. Goodnight, dear."

I loved Rebeca Hughes.

CHAPTER FIFTEEN

While Andrew was waiting to join me upstairs, I hurriedly took off my dress, poured two glasses of champagne, and tried to position myself seductively on the bed. Well, as provocatively as I could, trying out different poses I'd seen, but nothing felt natural.

There was a knock on the door, and that's when I remembered to turn on the mood music. I sat up on all fours reaching over to my Ipod on the nightstand when I heard Andrew breathe out, "Damn, Andria."

I swung my head around catching Andrew looking at my very exposed bottom. *That* was *not* how I had planned it. I literally felt my entire body flush red as Andrew's eyes floated across my backside with a wicked expression plastered on his face. I watched as he loosened his tie, and kicked off his shoes while throwing his jacket to the floor. He began to unbutton his shirt as he approached.

Quickly coming back to my senses, I turned around and grabbed the two glasses and handed one to Andrew.

"This is nice," he said, sweetly.

"I wanted to start the New Year alone with you."

Clinking my glass to his, I took a few sips of the champagne as I watched Andrew's tongue taste the liquid on his lips. My girly bits started to squeal in anticipation as I watched him set his glass on the nightstand before dragging his shirt down his arms exposing his beautiful bare chest. I was never a chest girl before, but when it came to Andrew, I was a chest, arm, leg, butt, toes—yes toes—girl.

When I heard the sound of his zipper, I wanted to sing out in glee. It had been too long, and my body was about to take over. I needed to calm down, so I took another sip of champagne while Andrew continued to strip down to his boxers in front of me. Even though I was drinking liquid, my throat was very, very parched. Andrew sat down on the bed as I handed his glass back to him, watching while he finished the bubbly liquid.

That was it! My body had had enough.

I placed my glass down and went for his adam's apple. My lips circled it and the vibration from Andrew's surprise and chuckle made me explode. I leaned firmly into him and really took hold of it before trailing kisses done the center of his neck. I felt and heard the hum from his chest and reveled in the fact that I, Andria Moore, did that to him. Andrew placed his arms behind me leaning back; basking in the enjoyment of my lips showering kisses everywhere. I struggled to my knees and I pushed him back further onto the bed. When he reached the leather-padded headboard, I straddled him.

As I kissed and sucked on his sexy lips, I paused looking into his hooded eyes. Andrew sat up; our chests connected and his arms wound tightly around me as he started kissing and biting down my neck. Each deliciously painful bite went straight to my core causing me to melt.

We kept to the rhythm of our own music, and I could feel the low burn inside increase as he slid his boxer shorts down his legs. Suddenly, hearing the crowd downstairs cheering, he said, "Happy New Year, Andria."

"Happy New Year."

He placed *that* smirk on his face as our eyes locked. "All I needed to do was tell you that I needed you, and you change your mind about having sex in my parents' house?"

"Dirty talk *always* does it Andrew," moaning out before nipping his bottom lip. "But Rebeca was the one who reiterated that we are adults...who do adult things."

"Saying my mother's name while you're gyrating on my junk isn't going to get us anywhere."

I laughed out while Andrew squirmed uncomfortably. "Sorry." I started to kiss down his jaw. "Maybe *this* will help." I slid off of Andrew who groaned in protest and took off my panties.

"Hey, I liked those," he pouted.

I gawked.

Andrew having a pouty lip—I didn't know it could get any better. "Oh, I can put them back on." As I reached over for the thong, he grabbed me around my waist and brought me down on top of him.

I squealed and squirmed trying to get to the panties, but Andrew was strong—thankfully. When I vocalized my surrender, Andrew leaned back on the bed and positioned my legs to straddle him. With hooded lids, he slowly perused my body landing on my breasts. "I really like that bra."

I did an internal happy dance thinking about how long it took for me to pick it out. While I was in New York, I had stopped at one of my favorite lingerie boutiques, *Kiki de Montparnasse*. They specialized on a selective clientele, and I loved their lingerie. The lace demi bra was elegant, yet sexy. I used many of their pieces in my book and my favorite was the one I was wearing. There was a garter belt that went along with the collection, and I bought a long pair of gloves to finish the entire ensemble—unfortunately both the garter and gloves were at home.

I must have been in my head too long. Andrew's lips brushed across my lips returning my attention. "I bought it for you."

His eyes darkened. "Good. You're going to have to buy another one because I'm going to rip that off."

He left me speechless for a few seconds before I protested. "Don't you dare, Andrew Hughes. This cost me a small fortune."

"I'll give you a check. Keep the shoes on. Oh, and put those back on." He pointed to my discarded panties on the floor. "I'll rip those off too." He pinched my side.

"Andrew..." I warned.

"If you're going to wear lingerie like this, it's bound to get destroyed. I thought you women liked having panties and bras ripped from your bodies." He smirked.

Umm...yeah...what could I say?

Andrew's hand came up to touch me, while the other cupped my face, "You're so beautiful, Andria—so sexy," he added as his thumb traced my lips.

"You make me feel beautiful," I breathed in. "And sexy," adding as I pulled his thumb into my mouth and began to suck.

I felt the rumble of pleasure along his torso as it vibrated beneath me. We moved together in perfect harmony, our hips danced to the musical score that our bodies began to create. This time there was no rushed or frenzied movements. Andrew and I took our time slowly feeling every inch of one another as whispers of endearment fell from our lips. Our eyes never left the other's as our rhythm increased. The passion and emotion in Andrew's eyes reflected in mine. I loved this man and he loved me.

The next morning, Andrew and I lay awake in bed talking, and placing lazy kisses on each other. I didn't want to leave the bed, but Rebeca was expecting us at her New Year's Day brunch. Eventually, we got up. Andrew headed to his room to get dressed. I took a long, lazy shower, reviewing the night before in my mind. I was still shocked that I had told him my feelings first. I was so afraid he wouldn't feel the same way, but at that moment, I knew I had to tell him. All that mattered was that he knew how I felt about him, and he could take it from there. I was ecstatic to hear that he loved me. A girl putting her heart on the line shouldn't be kept waiting, and he didn't disappoint.

When I finished dressing and packing up the last of my things, I stared at the bed that Andrew and I had made love in. As much as I wished it were my bed at home, this place would forever hold a special spot in my heart.

When I walked out of my room to meet Andrew downstairs, I thought I heard his voice through his door. I paused at the stairs when I heard Brittney's. "What about me?"

"Everything is going to be fine."

"The fans are going to go crazy."

"They'll understand."

"Andy..." she whined.

"Brittney. I'm in love with Andria. Everyone will have to understand that."

I smiled to myself at his declaration.

"It's that serious?" She sounded appalled.

That got my attention. I turned my head toward the door and saw Taylor a step behind me listening, as well. We both looked into each other's narrowed eyes as we heard, "Andy, you barely know her!"

"Brittney, I know you're concerned, but—"

"She could be using you."

As I turned, about to interrupt them, Taylor shook her head and placed her palm out asking me to wait. I wasn't sure why she wanted me to continue listening, but her eyes were curious.

"Trust me. Andria is *not* using me. You wonder why I didn't want to tell you anything about her. Like always, you'll find something wrong."

"Because there's always something wrong with the women you choose. Andria conveniently meets you when she's finishing up a movie deal? And, coincidentally, one that she's going to need a big name actor for."

"Andria earned her success *before* meeting me. She has *never* asked me for anything, especially not to be in her movie—"

"*Yet.* She hasn't asked for anything, *yet.* But having Andrew Hughes associated in any way would be pay dirt for her. What makes her different from the others? Or did you forget about all the bright-eyed wanna be starlets who were using you to become famous. Didn't you learn anything?"

I couldn't listen to her accuse me of something I never even thought about. Protecting Andrew or not, she doesn't know me! When I stepped passed Taylor and pushed open the door. I was taken aback by a bare-chested Andrew in only slacks. "Andria?"

I heard him, but directed my glare at Brittney, as I quickly stepped towards her before Andrew blocked my path.

"Brittney, I think it would be wise if we left these two alone." Taylor said behind me.

Brittney didn't say anything. She hurried past Taylor as she shut the door behind them.

Andrew stood in front of me. "Andria, it's not what you—"

"Andrew." I tried to keep my voice calm but failed. "I need to make something very clear to you. *I. Don't. Share!*"

"I don't expect you to—"

I shook my head to myself. "Sorry. That wasn't clear enough. I won't be sharing you with Brittney or *any* other women. If you have a problem with that then you had better tell me now." I looked him dead in the eyes.

His eyes showed fear, yet his lip curled up at the corner. "Yes, Andria. I understand. You have made things crystal clear. And that goes for me, also."

"Oh, that's a given. But you will *never* see any of my exes talking to me half-naked. Or..." I thought about that. "Maybe, you should so we can really drive this point home."

He growled as the smirk dropped. "Andria..."

"I heard what Brittney said in the hall."

He heavily inhaled, "She doesn't have a clue—"

"What is she to you?" I stared into his eyes ready for any hint of insincerity.

"What do you mean?"

I took a deep breath, "Are you in love with her?"

His eyes widened. "How could you think that? Last night...did that not mean anything to you?"

"It meant everything, and that's why I need to know. Answer my question, Andrew."

He pulled me in by my arms as he said, "Andria, I am not, nor have I ever been in love with Brittney Price."

My body went limp. "I am so happy to hear that."

"How could you have thought that?"

"How could I *not*? You two have a history, and she's made it pretty clear that she thinks I'm going to hurt or use you."

He kissed the top of my head. "I know you're not."

I looked up at him. "Damn right! Oh, and for the record, you're the *last* person I want cast in the movie."

"Wait. Why?" He had the nerve to look hurt.

"I have my reasons." Then a knot formed in my stomach. Was now the best time to tell him?

"Brittney was only trying to protect me. Along the way, people have had some false pretenses. I'm sure once you two get to know each other—"

I shot daggers at him with my eyes. "Are you kidding me?" I yelled.

He looked at me for a moment before taking my hand, "Please, sit down. We need to talk."

Okay? Usually when someone starts with that statement it's not a good thing, and my heart sped up its pounding pace. I sat down on Andrew's bed as he started pacing in front of me and said, "I'm not proud of what I'm going to tell you, but you need to know. I was an ass when I started in the business."

That was not what I expected. My expression must have shown it because Andrew paused his pacing. "Go on."

"Well, the fame went straight to my head—I'm still embarrassed by how I acted at first. I made a lot of people angry. What was worse, my family was disappointed in me."

"They could never be—"

"They were, Andria." He stopped pacing, standing in front of me. "I gave them every right to be disappointed. My focus was on the next party and spending absorbent amounts of money on nothing. It was all about me, and I pushed my family and true friends away. Brittney was the one who slapped me back to reality."

"You were young and talented..."

"And stupid," saying as he sat next to me.

"That may have been true, but all that attention had to be overwhelming."

I remembered hearing about the new up and coming heartthrob, Andrew Hughes. His picture was plastered everywhere. It was hard not to miss him, but I didn't see his first movie until years later. By then, he was a huge celebrity.

Andrew stood up to continue his pacing as he dragged his hands through his hair. But, it was his guarded expression that puzzled me. "It was very overwhelming and I was a cocky bastard," he chuckled to himself.

"Umm, you kinda still are." He stopped pacing and narrowed his sexy eyes at me. I almost lost my train of thought. "Andrew, you were young. I'm sure the mistakes you made would have been the same ones if you had gone through college instead of going into acting."

He pondered that before sitting back down on the bed as he stared ahead. "The people who surrounded me—at that time—didn't have pure intentions. Honestly, they used both me and my fame to get ahead."

I turned to look at him. "*That's* why Brittney questions my motives?"

He shook his head. "It's not because of you; it's all because of who I used to surround myself with. Brittney and I became friends at one of my lowest points. I thought I had lost everyone I cared about. She was the one that taught me how to live with my reality. Brittney was already a seasoned player. She and her friends showed me the ins and outs of the business that people don't tell you about. They schooled me on what came along with fame and how to juggle it all." Andrew placed his hand over mine, as he looked deeply into my eyes and said, "It was hard to trust anyone for a long time, Andria. You knew I only had a handful of friends, and now you know why. I keep them and my family very close. They are my rock, and now I have you. I trust you. I know that you never have or will use me to gain anything, except my heart." He smiled and placed a lingering kiss on my lips.

My stomach started to turn as I thought about what Andrew's reaction would be once he found out my book *was* based on him. Would he think I pursued him for fame? I wanted to tell him that he was my muse, but something deep inside stopped me. I knew it was the fear of losing Andrew's trust if he thought that I had indeed orchestrated our relationship in some way. As much as I wanted to lose that feeling, and believe that he would be thrilled to know that it was always him...I couldn't.

"Andria, what is it?"

I wanted to shake any and all concern off, but I felt an overwhelming sense of panic come over me. I stood; I couldn't look at him anymore.

"Andria, are you still upset with what Brittney said?"

Brittney. That was one person I needed to deal with. I spun around to look at him. "Brittney can think what she wants. Hey are you hungry? I'm starving."

He stood wrapping his arms around me as I laid my head on his chest. "I love you." I could never get used to him saying that, and at this moment, it stabbed me in my heart. "Andria? You're keeping something from me."

I looked up alarmed. "Why would you think that?"

His brow rose. "You're acting odd."

"I'm fine. I promise, it's really nothing."

"Okay, let's go eat."

Yes, lets. But before we did, I needed to find Brittney.

Everyone was still nursing their hangover while mingling in the large dining room. Brittney stopped Andrew and me before we entered. She apologized for causing any problems, and stressed that her only intentions were to remind Andrew to protect himself. She didn't realize how things could have looked with her being in his room. Andrew reminded her that she barged in unannounced. She had the audacity to look hurt. That's when I asked to speak with Brittney privately.

As soon as I closed the door to the study, Brittney began to speak. "Andrew and I have been friends for a long time, and I've seen many people befriend him looking for a hand out." I said nothing. She walked to one of the bookshelves and turned towards me. "Andria, I'm not saying that you would do such a thing—"

"Didn't you already Brittney, by telling Andrew that he can't trust me? You don't even know me, yet you tell him that I'm using him?" An eerie calmness rang out of my voice.

Her eyes grew wide, but she quickly placed her mask of concern back on her face. "You have to understand that I care for him—"

"Oh, I'm beginning to understand just how much you care. How long have you been in love with my boyfriend?" I asked, brushing my hands along the wall of books looking at the old bindings.

"You know we've dated."

I turned to look at her. "Yes, I know, but you're still in love with him."

Her eyes narrowed. "I will always love Andrew, he's a good friend."

"That he is," saying more to myself. "But...I'm thinking you may want more than his friendship?"

The mask fell slightly. "Andrew will always hold a special place in my heart, Andria."

Brittney's eyes told me everything; she still loved Andrew. Then, I wondered what she was going to do about it?

"Does Andrew know that you're still in love with him?" I stepped closer to her.

Her brow rose. "He told me he's in love with you."

Walking closer. "You told him that I was using him," I snarled out unintentionally, stopping myself from closing in.

"I don't want Andrew hurt."

"I won't be the one hurting him."

She remained quiet and I heard Rebeca calling us for brunch. We glared at each other for a moment before I turned toward the door. But, before opening it, I needed to say one last thing to Brittney. "I've been cordial to you for Andrew's sake because I love him. But if you *ever* try that crap upstairs again, I won't be so nice. Andrew is very capable of protecting himself. "

Andrew and I had a long goodbye at the airport. It was weird having people stare at us as he kissed me. I heard a camera shutter, and turned to see a young girl timidly smile as her smart phone was pointed directly at us. We were officially a couple, and I wanted to shout it from the rooftop. But, I wasn't ready to have our parting exchange plastered on the cover of tabloid magazines, although, I was sure that girl wasn't moonlighting as a paparazzo.

After a tearful goodbye and several long kisses later, I walked through the security line, headed back to New York.

"Why didn't you tell him?"

"Erin, it wasn't the right time. I want it to be special, and dealing with the Brittney thing and everything else right then wasn't the *right* time," I said frustrated through my cell.

"Ah huh..." Erin didn't sound convinced.

I called Erin while I waited to board the plane, and had ended up holding the phone away from my ear most of the time while she joyously and loudly recited how Miles proposed.

Of course, Erin already had a date in mind. She wanted a summer wedding, but I was surprised to find that it was going to be held in Louisiana. This did, however, make sense. Erin was an only child and had a very small family, while Miles came from a large one. She had been told that they were not very accepting regarding Miles dating outside of his race. I wasn't sure how they were going to respond to him marrying an African-American woman. Obviously, Erin had given serious thought as to the type of wedding she wanted before she had received the ring. That was Erin. She had my wedding already planned, as well.

Erin officially asked me to be her maid of honor, and I happily accepted. Miles's older brother was going to be his best man. His immediate family members adored Erin, and I couldn't wait to meet his brother from the stories I had heard. After a brief conversation about Andrew, I continued to listen while Erin talked about colors and themes before Miles caught her attention and she hurried off the phone.

When I arrived back into New York that evening, I had the rest of the night to play catch up on work, and I used that time wisely. I would be heading out in a few days to start the US tour and then I would be off to Europe.

That night, sleep didn't come easy. Every time I closed my eyes, I had nightmares. First, Andrew was angry with me for not telling him that he was my muse. Then, I had one of Brittney hovering over Andrew as her hands explored his body, before flashing to a dark alley where some creature was chasing me. It was going to be a long and strange New Year.

Fourteen days later and I was still on a roll. The tour was going well. I loved talking to my readers, and they had given me a lot to think about for the next book. All of their questions and theories provided some great material.

Keira was on cloud nine. Her relationship with Owen was moving along nicely, and she mentioned he could be the "one" several times a day. Erin was in full wedding planner mode, and we touched base every day. I wondered on several occasions if Miles was going to run away fearful of Erin's pre-wedding demands, but he loved her and showed her every day. Andrew was knee deep in filming. There were a lot of script changes—that I found out bugged the heck out of him. He had to memorize and re-memorize the same scenes over and over.

We tried to talk every day, but texting was the most used form of communication. It was easier for him to text in-between work. I loved hearing the ins and outs of his day and learned a lot about filming. It was nothing like I thought it would be. This caused me to be more excited than ever that my deal was being finalized. I was looking forward to casting the movie.

The final papers were on my lawyer's desk and I sent a copy to Andrew. He kept asking me so many questions about it that having his own copy to look over was easier—surprisingly, he made time to do just that. Andrew would email or text me questions or changes that I would pass over to my lawyer to add. It looked as if everything would be ready and signed by the end of the week. A courier was bringing me the original paperwork to sign and carry back to the studio.

While all that was happening, I never really had the time to process the fact that my book was still on the bestseller list, and about to be made into a movie in the next year with a starting payout of over ten million dollars. That amount of money was unimaginable, and the idea that it was all mine...well, I couldn't fathom it. Andrew asked me about my financial plans. I told him it was all going to my financial adviser, Miles. I wanted someone who I knew and could trust. He worked at a reputable firm that had key people who knew how to handle and invest funds. By the end of the next week, I had a substantial amount of money deposited into my account at the firm.

While working in my hotel room, Andrew called out of the blue exasperated, "Andria, are you okay?"

"Yes. Why do you sound like that?"

"Did you see the picture?"

My heart jumped a bit. "What picture?"

"The picture of us at the airport in DC. Someone took a picture of us as we said our goodbyes."

Then, the thought of the young girl crossed my mind. "I think I saw it being taken."

"What?"

All concerns left his voice and now he sounded angry as I tried to explain. "Andrew, it was one of your fans. I saw her take a picture and thought it was harmless."

"Yet, you didn't tell me?"

Yeah, he was angry.

"Why would I tell you that? Isn't your picture taken daily?"

"That's not the point, Andria."

Now he was pissing me off. "Well, what is then? Every time someone takes out their smart phone, I'm supposed to let you know!" Raising my voice frustrated.

There was a long pause before an exasperated sigh. "Sorry, Baby. I didn't mean to take this out on you. I was enjoying the no attention I've been receiving lately. The dogs are now sniffing around, and I'm worried about how it's going to affect you."

"Please stop worrying about me. We have discussed this, and I need to get used to it. Oh, and where can I find said picture."

He chuckled. "Look online under Hughes and mystery girl."

Mystery girl, I thought, as I typed the key words in the search engine and a picture of Andrew holding me popped up. Yet, my face was buried in-between his neck and shoulder. I missed that neck. "You can't see my face."

"No, but someone may recognize *my* body."

I was at a loss. "Clearly, I can tell it's you Andrew. It's plain as day and they said it was you."

"No Andria. I don't want anyone recognizing *your* body; the one that I consider is mine. The one that I was holding on to as I kissed her berry flavored lips."

Ohhh was all I thought as clarity came. My girly bits squeezed tightly. "Well, umm, I'm sure no one will figure out it was me."

I was wrong.

I received a phone call from my father *and* Brandon. Apparently, Jaimie reads the tabloids and she recognized me right away. The fact that I was in Northern Virginia—so close to Baltimore—and didn't mention it to my dad...well that conversation didn't go well.

After I tried to explain it was last-minute, and I was only there to spend time with my boyfriend, the accusations started flying. When was I going to tell him Andrew was my boyfriend? Why did he have to hear about it from some trash magazine? How serious was it with this boy? And what does all of that have to do with seeing your father when you're in town?

Guilt washed over me as I tried to explain, even after reminding him that I was an adult, *again*. Yes, I was indeed dating an actor, and our picture most likely will be showing up more often. I did state that next time, I would make it a point to tell him when I was in the area. But, since I was planning on moving there, that was pointless. After hanging up with Dad, I was mentally exhausted. I went to bed wondering how Frank was going to "spin" all of this.

It was my final day of the US tour and I was heading to England. I hadn't been there in a while and I missed that country. Last time, I had spent a few days in a small village outside of London, and it was an incredible experience. The people welcomed me openly. Every morning before I started to write, I would run into town, through the brisk fog before picking up my morning scone and newspaper.

On this trip, I would be spending most of my time in London. I had asked Keira to spread out my events so that I could also have a mini vacation at the same time. My heroine's love interest was English and they met in London. I could picture the two of them walking through the streets, holding hands and groping each other down dark corridors.

After the discovery of the "mystery girl" with Andrew, I couldn't help searching online during my downtime. As I waited while Keira finished editing a chapter in the other room, I sat at the desk in our suite and searched anything that related to the picture. I was concerned about the reactions of Andrew's fans, yet surprised that most seemed supportive. Andrew had a strong fan base and he took that very seriously. They hadn't seen him in a romantic embrace with anyone publicly since Brittney.

Even though the majority of his fans seemed unaffected, there were a few who were not happy with Andrew. I read one comment that said he and Brittney were recently seen in their own romantic embrace. That caught my eye, and I clicked on the attached link provided. It was indeed a picture of Andrew and Brittney as they were beginning or finishing up a kiss. But, Andrew's hair was cut short and he hadn't had short hair for many years. It had obviously been taken a while back.

After seeing that picture, I began to search for more of them together. My brain told me to stop, but my fingers kept typing. There were hundreds of pictures that popped up at a time. Seeing the two of them carefree, or embracing one another was literally hell. I couldn't sugar coat, swallow down, or accept it. Seeing another woman in Andrew's arms wasn't easy for me. But, knowing he loved me, and that part of his life was over, helped dull the pain.

A little bit.

My fingers finally stopped typing as I sat back in the chair. My eyes narrowed on one photo that was captioned, Andrew and Brittney "forever." One very peculiar difference I noticed when searching, was that on Andrew's end, his fans seemed okay with his new love interest. There had been confirmed rumors that Andrew and Brittney were no longer dating for a while now. But, on Brittney's end, I was a home wrecker. I wasn't sure how that was possible since they had always lived in different homes, but I was. I sent Andrew a text asking him about just that.

> **Me:** Brittney's fans hate me?

> **Andrew:** No

> **Me:** Online they do

> **Andrew:** Ignore!

> **Me:** Easy for u

> **Andrew:** No it's not. Frank is working on it

> **Me:** ?

> **Andrew:** Brittney's reps are slow

> **Me:** ?

> **Andrew:** I promise it's being handled. No worries trust me

Me: *Okay*

Andrew: *I love U*

Me: *I love U 2*

Andrew: *I miss U*

Me: *I miss U 2*

Andrew: *I want U*

Me: *Now?*

My cell rang immediately after the last text. "How bad do you want me?" I teased.

"Twice this morning, and once this afternoon."

I couldn't help laughing at Andrew's crudeness. "Should I be concerned that it was only once this afternoon?" I would have turned beet red if I had said that to Andrew's face.

"I was waiting to hear your voice before I started round two."

The visual alone made my body tense up, and the anticipation for something that wasn't going to happen for a while. "Andrew, it's not nice to tease."

Andrew had to rearrange his planned trip to see me before I left for England. Production was behind schedule and he couldn't leave. He worked nonstop every day into the late evenings. He also griped nightly about dinners in his hotel room, and not having any free time to visit one of his favorite Japanese restaurants. It looked as if I wouldn't be seeing Andrew until next week when he arrived in London. He was going to fly down for a few days, collect his mom and sister, and then head back.

Taylor recently found out that she and Wade were expecting, and everyone was treating her with kid gloves. Apparently, Taylor had a few medical issues and it was difficult for her to conceive. Both Wade and the Hughes's were worried that she may have a difficult pregnancy, as well. When Taylor found out, all of her fears about conceiving vanished, and transferred to the others. Wade usually stayed with Andrew for an entire production, but had some of his men fill in for him so that he could check on Taylor. I had heard that Wade doted on her—as he should—but his being overbearing drove Taylor insane.

Wade didn't want Taylor traveling, but she insisted since she wouldn't be doing much of it after the baby was born. She agreed that he could come with Andrew when he visited me in London. She and Rebeca would be in-town that same week, and they could all fly home together. I hadn't spoken with Wade to find out how he felt about that compromise, but Andrew said that he was fine.

Andrew brought back my attention when I heard a slow rumble through the phone. "Andria..."

I sat up in my chair. "Andrew?"

"Your voice always makes me want you," he panted out.

My core heated up. "Andrew...I don't think—"

"Oh, Andriaaa," honey coated sex was what that sounded like.

Andrew had started round two, making me light-headed as I slumped in my chair.

CHAPTER SIXTEEN

Five states and twelve cities later, we were on a plane to London. Keira and I had a few glasses of wine to unwind before going to sleep. It seemed at the exact moment that I closed my eyes; a flight attendant who asked if I wanted breakfast was awakening me. I nodded, knowing we had a book signing first thing that morning. After that, I had a date with a bed. Even though it appeared I had a few hours of sleep, I knew that wouldn't be enough.

Going through customs seemed quicker than the last time I had landed at Heathrow. The bags took a while longer, but the driver was prompt, and before long, we were off to the bookstore.

It was a small bookstore in Camden. I had previously spent a lot of time in that part of the city shopping and roaming through the Camden Market. It was one of my favorite places to eat, and I asked Keira if she wanted to come back that night for Indian cuisine. Excitement showed on her face. Even though Keira always showed professionalism, it was great seeing her eyes light up to a new experience. It was her first time in the United Kingdom.

We pulled up to the little Camden bookstore, and while Keira set up, I met the storeowner and greeted the line of readers. When she finished, Keira left me to prepare while she checked us into our hotel. The signing was scheduled for an hour, followed by a read through, with Q&A's at the end.

By the time I was finished signing books, the jet lag started to hit me. I was able to read a few pages of *Deception* without stumbling over the words—which shocked me. Everything I was reading seemed to blur, except for what caught my eye on the magazine stand. In the front of the store, I saw a very familiar looking head of hair. I smiled at the thought of Andrew, and made note to text him that I had arrived before the Q&A started.

We took a five-minute break, and as I came closer to the magazine cover, it was indeed Andrew. But he wasn't alone; Brittney was with him.

Normally, there was nothing unusual about that; tabloids still placed them on the cover to sell magazines. I knew Andrew was in Canada working and Brittney was in LA. Andrew had been so busy shooting that he told me he had no time for anything else, including dining out. But it was the headline that kept my attention. *Reconciliation?*

I looked closer and it was a blurry, blown up picture of the two of them sitting in what looked to be a Japanese restaurant. On the bottom was a small circle, with an even more blown up picture, which looked as if Brittney was whispering something in Andrew's ear. That was what I wanted to call it, because it sure as hell looked as if she was kissing Andrew's neck.

I turned the pages, ripping through it until I reached the article. As I read, it appeared that Brittney *was* indeed in Canada and that she and Andrew had had dinner at what I discovered *was* his favorite Japanese restaurant. I stared at the date on the photo and it was stamped last week. The same week Andrew complained about having no time for anything.

My heart sped rapidly at the final sentence stating that both sides have yet to comment, and the two stars may have decided to give their love one more try.

I felt sick, as my hands and fingers started to tingle with electricity, before my chest caved in with a brute force of weight that could have knocked me over. I stared straight ahead as everything around me went dim, while the inferno inside of me grew. My mind was a total blank. I thought of absolutely nothing as my body started to take over. Keira placed her hand on my shoulder saying something, but I couldn't hear her. I wasn't even aware that she had come back. I just walked back to the group of women and asked if anyone had any questions.

I was on autopilot as dozens of answers spewed from my lips. It wasn't until a woman asked the question "was my character based on anyone in particular," I realized that if I didn't leave soon, my career could be ruined. I was about to express some very unprofessional words, so I dodged the question.

As I looked over towards Keira—who seemed to be staring at me with a wary eye—I mouthed, "I'm done."

She immediately stepped in, wrapping things up, explaining that she needed to carry me away to another appointment—blah, blah, blah—and how glad it was to have everyone come. I said thank you and goodbye to everyone as I shook hands while I made my way to the exit. I stopped to ask the owner if I could buy the tabloid magazine. She gave it to me, and I was grateful when we got into the car. Before Keira could say one scolding word, I gave her the magazine as I dazed out the window.

She read quietly with occasional gasps, growls, and what the hells. After she had folded it closed, she said, "Maybe Brittney's working on the film."

I continued to stare out the window. "Their working contract is up. She wasn't scheduled on that film."

"Okay, umm," she thought about it for a moment. "Maybe the pictures are old."

I grabbed the magazine and flipped to the page. "I thought that at first too." I pointed to the picture where you could see Andrew's arm clearly. "But that's the watch I gave him for Christmas."

Sympathetically, she said. "It's probably all a misunderstanding, Andria."

"Yeah. Brittney's lips—or face—just 'happened' to be on Andrew's neck. I must have misheard Andrew when he told me he was too busy with re-shoots and script re-writes to even eat. Keira, he should have let me know that Brittney was even there. Huh...I actually felt bad leaving the country. All Andrew would say was that he missed me so much and wished we could be together. Yeah, it's all a misunderstanding." I turned to stare out the window saying nothing more.

We pulled up to the hotel and Keira showed me to my room before giving me the keys. We weren't sharing the suite, because of Andrew's arrival next week. The thought of him coming to visit made me sick to my stomach. Before I entered, Keira asked me if I wanted anything else. I told her no, thank you, I just needed to sleep.

You would think that sleep would have been a hard thing for me to do knowing that my boyfriend may have cheated on me with an ex-lover. But I fell asleep as soon as my head hit the pillow. I woke up the next morning to a glass of water and aspirin laid out on my nightstand. Keira always knew what I needed. I took the medicine and headed to the bathroom. They had a large lovely tub, and as much as I wanted to take a bath, for some reason I couldn't. I just stood in the shower until the hot water turned cold.

As I dried my hair, I saw the vibrations of my phone ringing on the nightstand. I went to see if it was Keira checking on me, but I was surprised to see Brandon's name. I wasn't expecting that and then I checked all my missed calls. Erin, Brandon, Dad, Mom, Wade, Rebeca, Taylor and countless ones from Andrew. I wasn't sure why the other's had called, but I quickly realized I never told anyone I had made it safely. I sent Keira a text thanking her for the aspirin and as soon as I pushed send, she was at my door within minutes.

"Do you want something to eat?" she asked, and brushed passed me heading straight to the living room.

I followed behind her. "I'm not sure if I can eat anything."

"Well, try. I ordered some lunch," she flatly stated and plopped down on the couch.

"I forgot to tell everyone we made it safely, could you handle that?"

"I already did the moment we landed."

"Did you text my family?"

"Yes."

Okay then, what was going on? "They have left several messages. I haven't looked at the texts."

She hesitated before answering, "It's because of Andrew."

Hearing his name cut through me. "Why?"

She sighed. "They all saw or heard about the article."

"Oh, I see. And my Dad?"

She turned her body fully towards me. "Jaimie got to him and Brandon. Your mother called as well, along with Erin.

"Uh-huh. Rebeca?"

She smiled warily. "She called wanting to check on you. She also said that she wanted to see you next week."

"Taylor and Wade?"

She chuckled under her breath. "They were checking on you, as well. Taylor did say something like Andrew's an ass and Brittney's a backstabbing whore. I explained to everyone that you haven't spoken to anyone, and I wasn't sure how long it would be until you did. All you said was that you weren't going to speak to Andrew for a while." She grinned timidly. "Now, you're free until tomorrow afternoon. What would you like to do?"

"Stay—"

"*Except*, stay in your room. You have been waiting for this trip for a long time and nothing, and *no one* is going to ruin that for you."

"But Keira—" I felt the tears forming for the first time.

"Until you speak to Andrew, you don't know what really happened. You of all people know that everything you read isn't always true. I have seen the way that man looks at you. He adores you, and before you do anything rash, you're going to take a moment and cool off."

I blinked at her a couple of times. "Well, thanks Dr. Rationale—"

"I'm not saying he won't pay for this. *Or* Brittney..." She coyly grinned, "I'm saying take your time."

After a much needed lunch—I wasn't going to tell Keira she was right about me being hungry—I discovered that my closest friends had been emailing each other on how to handle everything. *Including* Rebeca and Taylor. Wade wanted to get into the action, but Taylor wouldn't let him. She said he would tell Andrew.

Rebeca and Taylor weren't defending Andrew, but they made a comment to Keira that Brittney and Frank had to be behind it somehow. Frank was always quick to refute things or he at least warned the parties involved. This had come out too quickly. They also blamed Andrew for not putting his foot down with Brittney. But they hadn't told him yet; they both weren't speaking to Andrew either.

Every time I thought about Andrew, excruciating pain radiated from my heart. I knew there had to be an explanation, but my eyes and mind weren't seeing 'eye to eye.' I thought it was best to not think about it for a while. The rage steadily consuming me wasn't helping, so *not thinking* about it seemed to slow down the burning, as well as the murderous thoughts that flashed rapidly in my mind. Between Erin threatening to cut off Andrew's balls and both Brandon and Dad threatening to bring a few guys up to Canada; I couldn't hear anymore.

I tried to just relax with Keira in the room, but everything hurt. Tears constantly pooled in my eyes afraid to fall. My heart felt like a concrete brick that was slowly crumbling away. My eyes burned as visions of

Andrew and Brittney together flooded my mind. My chest heaved grasping and forcing out air to breathe.

I looked apologetically at Keira, and I couldn't hold on anymore. She understood. I didn't want to be weak, but my heart couldn't handle this kind of pain. It was suffocating. I slowly drifted into the welcoming darkness of my room, as I floated to the bed, and laid my head on the pillow.

Andrew's voice haunted me as I woke in the darkness. His touch...his eyes...his smell...all penetrated my soul as I clung on to some sort of sanity.

That's what he did to me, and I had every right to be scared of it. Without Andrew, I couldn't breathe, and the thought of him suffocated me back to sleep.

Being awakened by a loud ringing phone didn't help the anger nestled inside. "What?" It was still dark and insanely early.

"Ms. Moore, my apologies, but I have a Mr. Hughes on the line and he said it was an emergency. We usually respect our guest's do not disturb requests, but he said he would contact the coppers."

Andrew was a dumb ass; he thought this was going to make me talk to him. "Please tell Mr. Hughes, that I will call him at a later date." I started to hang up and heard the man calling out my name. "Yes, what is it?"

"Ms. Moore. Again my apologies, but Mr. Hughes threatened that if I did not get you on the telephone, he would indeed contact the coppers. He said something about dragging you out and brute force."

"Put him on," I said, exasperated.

Andrew immediately began to speak. "Andria please let me explain! The first I heard about those pictures was yesterday. Frank dropped the ball! I've been busy with—"

"Andrew, save it! That's not going to change the fact that you're a clueless jackass. Oh and threatening a front desk clerk is not going to make me hear you out."

"You wouldn't answer any of my calls or texts."

"Does that surprise you? When I'm ready to talk to you, I will."

"It's all a misunderstanding. Please, baby—"

"Hell, no! You do not have the right to call me that or even utter my name! I have given you the benefit of the doubt about Brittney so many times, but Andrew, I've had enough!"

"If you would just let me explain."

"What? It's not what it looks like, right? You're going to tell me you weren't out with Brittney? Somehow her lips got stuck on your neck or whatever she was doing."

"It wasn't like that!"

"That may be true, but you are always *so* careful when you're with me. You try awfully hard to keep your 'private life' private—"

"That's because I'm trying to protect you, Andria."

"Yet, you're seen with Brittney in a compromising situation? Maybe, you should have put some of that effort towards her. Or doesn't it matter that you keep me hidden while traipsing across the globe with your ex-girlfriend!"

"Andria..." he sounded defeated.

"Just the fact that you *were* with her shows that she was *somehow* able to manipulate you, again! My patience has run thin."

"There is *nothing* going on between me and Brittney-"

"Does she know that? Do you know that she still loves you, Andrew?"

He huffs. "She doesn't—"

"Ask her. Because I sure did and she never denied it."

He was quiet.

"Have nothing to say? The woman who accused *me* of not having honest intentions played you Andrew. Hell, she played both of us at first. I truly tried to believe that the two of you could only be friends, but I was wrong. I knew she would try something, but I trusted *you*. But no more!"

"I didn't know."

"Right..."

"I wouldn't lie to you. I love you, Andria. Only you."

"I want to believe that."

"It has *only* been you," he choked out. "Without you...I can't breathe..."

I felt my throat closing in. I couldn't do this now. "Andrew. I need time. There is so much going on in my life right now that I need to focus on my tour. I will talk to you when I get back. But until then, please *do not* call me or try anything. I swear Andrew if you do...I will never talk to you again." I hung up.

I rushed out of bed and headed straight for the toilet. I was afraid that I wasn't going to make it as everything inside of me came up. I lay on the cold, hard tile while streams of tears poured out of me.

CHAPTER SEVENTEEN

That was the first time I had woken up wrapped around a toilet bowl. It was Keira's shrieks that got my attention. "Andria, are you sick?"

I opened one eye. "No. Andrew called me this morning."

She squatted down next to me. "I told the hotel you weren't accepting any phone calls and to send all the flower deliveries to me."

Andrew had sent five bouquets yesterday. "Thanks. But when you're Andrew Hughes, apparently you can threaten your way through anything."

"Did he explain?"

I opened both eyes squinting at her. "Do you think I wanted to listen to his explanation?"

"That's my girl." She sat up and started to turn on the tub's faucet. "What are you planning to do?"

"...I plan on working, and told Andrew that I would deal with him when I return. I need to get through this tour."

She grinned. "I'm proud of you, but you're hurting."

I fumbled to my feet. "Keira, I knew Brittney was going to try something, even though I warned the bitch. My stupid mistake was to think Andrew could handle her."

"You know there's more to the story, right?"

I walked to the sink, splashed cold water on my face, before facing myself in the mirror. "That, I am sure of."

Her arched, browed expression reflected behind me. "So, eventually you're going to hear Andrew out?"

I turned to face her. "Eventually..."

Keira added more appearances and signings to fill in every crevice of my schedule. Elena was happy about that; more appearances meant more sales. It seemed to help, and meeting my readers always brought me joy.

There were *a lot* of tough moments; the ones where I had to talk about my characters' relationship and the love they have for each other. Their relationship is an all-consuming one. The last thing I wanted to speak about was *that* topic.

In-between work, Keira and I had time to visit Harrods department store. I loved getting lost there, and I went a little crazy. I never quite understood why shopping could make a girl happy, but buying five pairs of shoes helped.

We had tea at Ladurée, and I stuffed myself with my favorite selections of macaroons. Chocolate helped as well. But, the gaping hole in my heart wasn't easily fixable. Despite my best efforts to plaster, tape, glue and fill in the hole, it grew bigger.

Keira and I returned back to the hotel with a ridiculous amount of shopping bags. She told me we would meet up later for dinner. But, I wasn't prepared for the surprise when I entered her suite for dinner and saw Rebeca, Taylor, and Erin. Rebeca and Taylor were supposed to arrive at the end of the week, but their plans "miraculously" changed, and they had arrived three days early. Erin, on the other hand, never planned to come to London.

Keira took care of all the arrangements and had Erin staying with me, while Rebeca and Taylor were in the adjoining suite next to her. We didn't speak about anything too heavy at first. We were all spread out on the floor in Keira's suite eating ice cream and drinking bottles of liquor we had raided from the mini bar. Rebeca said it helped with jet lag.

Everyone was talking among themselves, and Rebeca scooted beside me. "Andria, I would have been here sooner, but I had to perform a last-minute surgery on one of my kids."

"How can you do that without having your heart wrenched out?"

"Oh, dear. I have my days. But, helping the ones I can makes up for it. Until we find a cure for cancer, we all have to do our part."

I looked at the woman amazed, and honored that she would be concerned with what was going on between her son and me. "Why me?"

She looked confused. "I'm not understanding, dear?"

"Andrew and I haven't been together that long. I'm sure you've seen your fair share of women come and go in his life. Why be so kind to me?"

"You don't give yourself much credit. I haven't seen my son this happy, well...in a very long time. I can't remember exactly." She smiled. "Andrew loves you dear, and that makes me love you. Of all those *girls,* you speak of...he has only asked to bring one home, and it was you."

That's when conversations stopped and all eyes were on me. "What about Brittney?"

She grimaced and Taylor mumbled something under her breath before she said, "He never brought Brittney home until this past Christmas, Andria. And it was my idea."

"What? Why?" Erin and I said at the same time.

Rebeca answered. "When Andrew was going through his 'I'm too famous for the people I love' stage, we gave him space. He thought we all had abandoned him, but he had Buck, his old manager watching over him. Nelson and I let him make his mistakes, but I knew he would find his way. For some reason, he gave Brittney the credit for helping him, even though he did most of it on his own. She may have nudged him along, but I knew Andrew would be the man I knew he could be."

"He still has some room for growth, Mother," Taylor added.

"That's true dear," she looked sympathetically at me. "Brittney seemed to have some hold over him. At first, I thought it was some debt that Andrew owed to her. But, then I saw that she was an expert manipulator, and to do that to my son was a feat in itself. When Andrew came into his own, he was usually on his A-game when reading people. But, when it came to Brittney, he seemed to have a veil over his eyes."

Taylor snorted loudly as she said, "Andria, when Mom told us Andrew was feeling bad about that bitch Brittney and her family drama, we were afraid she would somehow get him to stay there with her. Mom's very sentimental around the holidays and likes her family around. I told mom we should have that skank in Virginia so we could figure out what her game plan was."

Erin chimed out. "Oh, and no one knew Andria would be there!" She clapped. "It all worked out perfectly."

"I knew the whore would make a move once she saw Andrew had truly moved on. It was obvious that she still had hope. Andrew is a dumb ass, Andria. We all saw she was still in love with him—narcissistic bitch—Andrew wouldn't believe it. Stupid, dumbass, mother—"

"Taylor!" Rebeca frowned before looking back at me. "I have never seen Andrew this happy until you. I also have never seen him this torn up. He called me, desperate for help. He didn't know how to fix things between the two of you. That's when I knew how deeply in love my son was. He called his *mother* for help." She smiled.

We all laughed.

"So you're here for Andrew?" I wanted to clarify.

"We're here for *both* of you. Andria, Andrew has made many mistakes—obviously," she glanced at the ridiculous amount of bouquets spread around Keira's suite that Andrew had sent. "But one thing's for sure. He does love you."

"That's true. He even left me a couple of messages, and I threatened to cut off both of his balls." Erin said too cheerfully.

The look on Rebeca face was priceless as Erin looked at her apologetically.

The next morning, while I took part in an afternoon book event, the girls went shopping. I was surprised when they showed up later that day. I was at the table signing books when Rebeca gave me a quick hug and a hello. There was press from the local newspapers, and apparently one reporter recognized Rebeca as he came barging over. "Mrs. Hughes. Are you a big fan of A.P. Moore?"

"Well, of course I am." Rebeca beamed proudly.

That grabbed the other journalists' attention and they crowded around us. "Mrs. Hughes, is that what brought you to London?" Another reporter asked, shoving his mic in her face.

Rebeca pushed the mic aside as she said, "I came to support Andria."

A lady's voice chimed in from the back. "What is your take on *Deception*?"

That's when I realized Rebeca could have read my book. A book that was a complete fantasy of what I wanted to do to her son. If I could have crawled under the table and left, I would have.

"Well, my daughter read a few blurbs to me when it first came out. I'm embarrassed to say I haven't had the time to start *Deception*, but I plan to," she looked over at me and winked. "The parts my daughter read were beautifully written. I did ask her to skip over the fun parts," she laughed to herself, "but you could feel the love between the two characters." Rebeca's words really touched me.

"Dr. Hughes are you happy that your son, and Brittney Price are back together? As reported in The Tattler."

Everyone turned and looked at Rebeca as she held every single person's attention. "I don't comment on my son's personal life, and I do not read trash. I'm here to support Andria, and I encourage all of you to pick up her book and leave the trash in the garbage where it belongs." She gave a tight smile and walked past the crowd of reporters.

Immediately, I stood up and followed her. I gave her a hug as I whispered. "I'm sorry, Rebeca."

"You have nothing to be sorry for. *That* is what comes with Andrew's career choice."

I pulled her to a quieter corner. "I'm starting to see that, and I'm not sure if I can deal with all of...that. And, I am still angry with Andrew."

She pursed her lips and narrowed her eyes before she said, "Oh, I know dear. You will be upset for a while, but that will pass. I'm sure of it." She gave me the same knowing look that my mom gives to me. "Andrew's life is full of intrusions, and it can be hard to swallow. I can't say that you will ever get used to it, but I know you can handle whatever comes your way. You love my son, and I know you two will work things out. But...for now, you need to focus on yourself. Andrew can wait." I gaped at her. "Oh, dear. Did you think I was going to pressure you into forgiving my son? Andria, Nelson and I have had our fair share of heated arguments and misunderstandings. I have found that it does a person good to think over *his* misdeeds." A sly grin graced her face. "Come along," she said walking away from me as I continued to gape at her. "You have a crowd of anxious readers waiting for you."

When we joined the others, I noticed one reporter curiously looking at the two of us. You could see his mind spinning as he blatantly stared between Rebeca and me.

Erin came skipping in the next morning with coffee and newspaper in hand. "Hey, you made the front page of the entertainment section."

She plopped the paper down on the bed. "Wow, that is a surprise, and you're up early."

She gave me the coffee that she was holding. "I think Rebeca had something to do with that."

I took the paper and read, 'Rebeca Hughes and Taylor Hughes Robinson arrived in London yesterday to support their good friend, and author, A.P Moore at the launch of her new book, *Deception*.' There were several pictures of Rebeca and Taylor, as well as Rebeca and me talking. I had no clue that the press followed Andrew's family, as well. Erin had to explain that to me.

Keira and I had another book signing, and then I planned to meet the girls for dinner in Chinatown. I loved this little hole in the wall place I had found during my last visit. Keira needed a well-deserved night off, and she was excited to pass me on to the others for a while.

The restaurant was better than I had remembered, and it was nice to just laugh and enjoy myself. The pain of thinking about Andrew didn't go away, but it was numbed by the laughter and Japanese sake provided by my friends. My heart also warmed up at the fact that Andrew's mom and sister cared enough to spend time with me, and I was falling in love with his family. Now, I only had to figure out what to do about Andrew.

I hadn't had a decent night's sleep since I had arrived, and I was ready to head back to a very welcoming bed after dinner. But, the ladies had other plans. They were going to a very exclusive club. I told them several times that I didn't want to go, but Rebeca said she rarely gets to go to clubs, and she was going to go with all of us. She insisted, and I finally relented. So after dinner, we went back to the hotel to get dressed. Of course, Erin came in to pick out my dress. It was short and revealing, but I was too tired to argue with her. I put on a short, dark purple dress, with long sleeves that were slit open at the top, and placed a fake smile on my face. The last thing I wanted to do was to go out, but I was doing it for them.

The driver came, delivered us to the front of the club, and we walked in past the velvet ropes without waiting in line. The club was dark inside, and lit by glowing red and yellow lights. Candles flickered on the small cocktail tables, and the loungers placed throughout the small club were printed in black and white patterns. Jazz played in the front room while classical music played in the piano room. The dance floor was downstairs, and you could feel the vibration of the music under your feet.

Taylor looked stunning as always. Even pregnant, she radiated natural beauty in the red empire waist dress that she wore. She had inherited her looks from Rebeca. Even though she was Andrew and Taylor's Mother, Rebeca looked hot in a short, dark blue sequined dress. I could see why Nelson always had problems keeping his hands off of her. Erin towered over me, wearing ridiculously new high heels she had found at *Dover Street Market*. The avant-garde shoes and cap sleeved black dress was a showstopper.

We ordered a few cocktails at the bar. Taylor drank diet soda, while I scanned the room. You could tell by the crowd that it was a distinguished clientele. Taylor explained that it was a 'members only' club, and there were several of them located around the world. It was a place where the rich and famous could be themselves without watchful eyes on them.

We talked and laughed for a while. Yet, my thoughts drifted towards Andrew, and I wondered what he was doing. Erin caught me not paying attention a couple of times, and gave me a sympathetic smile. She knew me. Even though I was saving face in front of Rebeca and Taylor, she knew that I was hurting inside. I missed Andrew, and I needed to figure this crap out.

Several men approached the table during the evening, as they asked one or the other of us to dance. We each declined, but it didn't stop the oohs and aahs from the others every time one of us was approached. When a very nice looking younger man approached Rebeca, she turned red before saying that she only danced with her husband. We teased her for a bit afterward, but continued to drink and enjoy the light conversation. My phone suddenly buzzed, which surprised me at that late hour, and then my heart skipped. I looked immediately at it, wondering if it was Andrew. But, I was disappointed that it was only a reminder about a task to complete for tomorrow.

"Why don't you call him?" Erin asked.

She could always read me. "I can't. I told him I didn't want to speak to him until I got back to the States."

"Have you decided what you're going to do?"

Erin's question sparked the attention of the entire table. I looked at all of them as I said, "All I know is that if Andrew and I are going to work, Brittney can't stay in the picture."

They all nodded in agreement. "Are you going to tell *him* this?" Taylor raised a brow.

I thought about it. "I will. *After*, I get back."

Rebeca smiled to herself and Taylor shook her head, but looked pleased. Erin narrowed her eyes and she smiled.

I loved Andrew, and if he wanted this to work, Brittney had to go.

CHAPTER EIGHTEEN

We had arrived back to our hotel a little after two in the morning. I didn't even bother taking off my make-up; I flopped onto the bed, and didn't wake up until I heard Keira's voice. Even though my body screamed out in exhaustion for more sleep, we had an art event to prepare for that evening. All the proceeds collected were being donated to one of our charities, as well as honoring my most devoted readers. It was being held at a local art gallery, and I would follow after the auction with a reading and book signing.

Even though I felt like crap, and was mentally exhausted, I was excited to attend this event. It was a more intimate engagement, which included a group of my biggest supporters; those who were with me from the beginning, and who followed me early in the game. It was a thank you for supporting me and spreading the word about *Deception*. These were my die-hard fans. I loved meeting and talking to them, and I couldn't wait for this event. It was a welcomed change and a highlight of the trip.

Elena and her team spared no expense for the art event. It was similar to my first launch in LA. There was a red carpet, and a few local celebrities who attended. The press was allowed to take pictures and ask questions outside of the venue only. Even though the event started late in the afternoon, everyone was glammed up. It seemed that I was the only one underdressed in a simple, yet elegant, blue dress Erin had insisted that I wear. I thought, hey, who was I to argue with her? Especially when she kept saying, I know what I'm doing. It makes your blue eyes pop.

Along with Erin, I spent most of the evening talking with the readers and taking pictures. We had a fun time taking some silly candid shots, and I enjoyed listening to their theories for the next two books—some were way off, but a few nailed it on the head. I made a mental note to rethink some of my plot ideas.

Rebeca and Taylor arrived later to show their support before heading home. Rebeca's patient, whom she had performed surgery on wasn't doing as well as expected. Even though she had been able to remove the tumor, the eleven-year-old girl wasn't responding in the way she'd hoped. Rebeca and Taylor were flying out the next morning, and couldn't stay long. Rebeca needed to be alert for surgery the moment that she arrived back in Virginia.

Last night, I mentioned that I had soon planned to move to Virginia or to the Washington DC area. Rebeca's joy and excitement was heartwarming. I even gained a smile from Taylor. She mumbled something about Wade being happy with that.

The auction started to wind down, and it was my turn to end it with a speech. We were off schedule, as the book signing took longer than originally planned. One would think speaking in front of a crowd could become easier, but it doesn't. Although I wrote most of my speech down, I was still nervous. At least standing at a podium helped me to concentrate on the words a little more. I kept to the standard script I normally used, thanking everyone that made it all happen. I did waiver off of the script when I thanked the readers for all of their support. This group of people was special, and I wanted them to know that what I was saying came directly from my heart.

I was winding down, and almost to the end of my speech, when I noticed that familiar pull—like a prickly sensation—floating over my flesh. I had felt it many times before when.... My words stumbled out as I began to lose my focus. I tried to locate my place on my notes, and continued on until the sensation grew stronger, but this time it attacked my heart.

My eyes instantly flew up from the paper and began to scan the room. I homed in on his hair, which was sticking up, before seeing the rest of him. Andrew was a tall man, and he usually towered over people, but he seemed to be slumping. I narrowed in and focused on his eyes. The pain and hurt displayed in them choked me.

Keira walked over and handed me a glass of water. I took a sip, and mumbled out, "Andrew." Her eyes widened, and she searched the crowd quickly until she saw him. She dashed over to Rebeca and Taylor, before they all headed in Andrew's direction.

I apologized to the crowd, and drank another sip of water, before rushing through the remainder of my speech. The moment that I said my last thank you, I quickly walked away, and headed to the first door I could find. I couldn't breathe, as I entered the darkened room. It felt as if I said all that in one breath, and my lungs were burning for air.

"Andria."

The last thing that I wanted to hear at that moment was his voice. It cut to my core, as the emotions of anger, love, madness, hope, and sadness all came flooding over me.

I was drowning. "Andrew," I couldn't turn to look at him. "I told you if you tried—"

"I had to," he whispered behind me.

He was too close. His scent penetrated the air, and the heat radiating from his body seared my skin. "I'm not ready..."

"I love you. I will wait if I have to. But, I can't live without you."

I shook my head. "Andrew..." I could taste the warmth of his breath as it poured over my body.

"I love you. I can't continue on like this. *Nothing* happened between Brittney and me."

"You hurt me." My voice betrayed me showing the weakness I have for him.

"I will never hurt you again."

As I turned to face him, his eyes locked to mine. "I will *not* fight with Brittney over you."

They widened. "You won't have to—"

"How do I know that for sure?"

"I told Brittney that I *never* loved her. I never knew what love was until I met you. I made it very clear that I would always pick you. No matter if it was now or then. I would have *always* picked you, Andria."

Rivers of tears fell as Andrew's hands cupped my face. "I love you, Andria. I love you so much." He placed a soft kiss on my lips. "I love only you."

Andrew showered my face with kisses, as I stood still unable to move. He stopped, and for the first time I saw fear in his eyes.

"You are *everything* to me. I cannot live without you. Please, baby..."

He pressed in closer, searching my eyes for something that he must have found as our lips met again. This time, I relented. I was starved from the lack of contact my body desperately needed from him. My mind protested, as my body gave in, going limp in Andrew's arms as he held me. The weight of everything overcame me. We sank to the floor as his arms cradled me.

I wasn't sure how long we stayed like that, but I knew it had been a while. I heard footsteps pass by the door as hushed whispers filled the air. When I felt Andrew slightly release me, I grabbed onto him. I wasn't ready yet. I needed a little more time before the inevitable happened. We would have to completely talk it through, but right then I needed to feel him.

"Andria, I'm sorry to umm...to interrupt, but we need to let them clean up."

I raised my head off of Andrew's chest looking over at Keira, and saw Erin, Taylor, and Rebeca standing in the doorway. Rebeca had tears in her eyes as she gave us a timid smile. I nodded, Andrew and I stood, and he took my hand as we walked out of the gallery without uttering a word. Keira put us in a car to ourselves, and Andrew held me until we reached the hotel room.

When we entered my suite, I went straight to the sofa and sat down. Andrew took off his sport coat and poured a glass of cognac for him, and a glass of white wine for me. "Do you want me to go first?" he asked as he sat next to me.

I shook my head. "I need to say this. My mind and heart didn't agree on what they saw in that trashy magazine. But, my heart knew that I could trust you, *despite* what things looked like. I do love you, Andrew, but not telling me everything about you and Brittney wasn't right."

"I know. But, I did eventually—"

"You should have told me that she came to see you that night. In fact, you should have explained how you felt about her in the beginning."

He moved closer to me. "Yes, I should have shown better judgment that night. But Brittney, and her manager, Hailey *surprised* me. The only reason I agreed to go to dinner was that Frank was in town. I needed to confront both of them as to why there was a lack of urgency in dealing with the press lately. When they stepped out for a smoke, that's when it seems those pictures were taken."

How convenient, I thought, as I watched Andrew ponder over his words.

There was a subtle headshake as he continued. "Andria, what was I supposed to say in the beginning? My ex-girlfriend and I have a complicated friendship? We dated, things didn't work out, but we stayed friends? She helped me sort my damn mess out, and I feel like I owe her for that?"

"Yeah. That would have been a start."

He chuckled to himself. "Yeah...and you would have run. It wouldn't have helped me at all being Andrew Hughes."

I wanted to tell him that he would have been wrong, and I would have understood, even if he was Andrew Hughes. I took a better look at him, studying his face for the first time. It looked as if he hadn't slept in days; dark, sunken circles surrounded his eyes, as his lids grew heavier. His cheeks were drawn, and he had lost weight. Andrew was a very handsome man. His looks were unreal at times, but the man who was sitting in front of me was broken. I thought, did I mirror him? Was this what people saw when they looked at me?

The two of us weren't too much different at that moment. It was evident that we loved each other, but we both had no clue as to how to fix things. "Andrew, I need you to do something for me."

"I'll do anything," he sounded hopeful.

"Just be honest with me, okay? No matter how hard or how difficult it may be for me to hear it. Just tell me the truth. If you think I'll be upset, or you get angry with me or if I do something that agitates you, whatever." Then I choked out, "If you stop loving me...tell me, okay?"

He looked at me before placing his forehead to mine. "I promise I will tell you *everything*. You are the first woman I have trusted in a very longtime, outside of my family."

We stared into each other's tired eyes before I surrendered, and placed a kiss on his chapped lips. He leaned in more, absorbing every part of me as he hungrily captured my mouth.

Exhausted by everything, I sat back as I searched for air, looking into Andrew's tired eyes. "We're both exhausted. Let's go to bed." He raised his brow. "We both need to *sleep,* Andrew. You look as bad as I feel, and I want to have a clear head when we continue this discussion in the morning."

When we were settled into bed, I laid in Andrew's arms. It felt like I was home again, and we both fell instantly asleep.

It was warm, and I felt a scratchy, prickly substance on my face. That's when I remembered Andrew. He was scraping his unshaved scruff along my face as he slept. I looked, for a moment, at the fallen angel that was sound asleep. Before I slowly moved out of bed, and made my way into the living area shutting the door behind me.

Restful sleep didn't come as easily for me. My dreams turned to nightmares that were filled with images of Brittney and Andrew together.

I called down for breakfast and coffee, while sending Keira a text that I didn't want to be disturbed. We were off today, and I knew she would want to use the free day to see more of London. I also texted Erin, and asked if she wanted to join Keira for the day. She was heading back home tomorrow. Erin was happy to get to know her better, and she told me good luck with Andrew. Lastly, I called Rebeca. "I just wanted to say thank you for everything before you left."

"Andria, no need. As long as you and my son talk things out, that's all I can ask. Oh, and Andria?"

"Yes?"

"If my son hurts you again, you have my permission to slap the stupid out of him. See you soon, dear."

I laughed, "Have a safe trip."

I was surprised that Andrew wasn't going home with them, but I didn't ask. I knew they were concerned with Taylor's pregnancy, and then I thought about Wade. *Of course*, he came with Andrew.

Our food had come, and I was showered, dressed, and pouring my second cup of coffee when Andrew walked out of the room. "Why did you let me sleep in?"

I swear it didn't matter how mad I was at that man, he was sexy as hell when he woke up. He had lost weight, but he still looked like walking sex in his boxers. "I thought you needed the sleep. The time change is a bear to deal with."

He smiled before walking over, and hesitated before placing a kiss on my lips. "I was umm, going to get dressed. Do you mind if I have my things brought over? I just need to get some clothes."

That felt awkward even if we had slept together last night. "No problem."

He walked back into the bedroom. I took my time sipping the coffee, fumbling over what to say to Andrew, when I heard a knock on the door. "Andria." Wade's dimpled grin was a pleasant surprise. "I heard you ladies had a good time?"

"We did, come in." He had a suitcase in his hand. "Andrew's in the bedroom," I nodded in that direction.

I made myself comfortable on the sofa, flipping through the stations on the television. Wade came out after a while. "Well, I have to head to the airport, but it was a pleasure as always, little one."

I smiled. "It's always good seeing you too."

"Can't wait for you to move closer."

Andrew walked in now fully dressed. "I'm excited about that too, Wade."

"Well, I'll be seeing you." He smiled, winked at Andrew, and walked out the door.

As I stood up and started to pour Andrew a cup of coffee at the table, I felt him before I knew he was there. His chest was extremely close to my back. I felt the warmth of his body everywhere, and his hot breath saturated my hair. I looked down, and saw that his hands were curled over as if they were in pain. It was obvious that he was fighting an internal war with himself. To touch or not to touch? "Andrew..."

"Andria..."

"I can't do this right now. I know I invited you into my bed last night, but I was being selfish. I needed you."

"And what about now?"

"We have a lot of crap to sort out."

He pressed in closer. The heat radiating from his body was burning my soul. I leaned forward over the table as his entire body dominated mine. I knew that if he touched me, I would cave. "Andrew...please...give me a moment."

Andrew's searing breath climbed up my neck until he whispered in my ear. "I need you."

I closed my eyes, willing my body to not give in. "It looked as if Brittney needed you as well."

I heard a sigh of frustration blow out from him. "It's over."

"For you, maybe. How did Brittney's lips get on your neck?"

There was a pause before he answered. "She said I had something on me, and began to wipe it off. She leaned in closer to see it—I thought—and before I knew it..."

I laughed to myself. "You are such a dumbass."

He touched my shoulder. I glared down at his hand as he moved it away. He started to run his hands through his mess of hair, as I turned and looked at him. "I made a mistake. I didn't listen and ignored all the signs. But, I made it very clear to Brittney that if she wanted to stay my friend, she had to respect the fact that we are together, and nothing was going to happen between the two of us ever again."

"Right."

"Trust in me." I actually did trust Andrew. Just not Brittney. I wasn't sure how to proceed with Andrew staying friends with her. "I wasn't thinking clearly. Work has been brutal, and I was physically, and mentally exhausted. I barely had time to sleep. When Brittney showed up at my hotel room and insisted that I come join them, I was shocked that she was even there! She said her new director wanted her to join them in scouting out locations. He's that kind of director. Involving the lead actors with pre-production ideas to get a sense and feel of how things will develop." I couldn't help thinking that there was more to it than that. Yet, Andrew still didn't see it. I became even more frustrated with him. "What?"

"When will you get it? That woman doesn't do anything by chance. Look at how she used her Mother's death to get you to be with her."

"Andria! Brittney didn't cause her Mother's death to see me."

Do we know that for sure? I cringed, before shaking that absurd thought out of my head. "Andrew, I'm not saying Brittney caused her Mother's death. I'm saying that she used it to her advantage. It seems she's been using *a lot* of things to control you—manipulative bitch..." I mumbled the last words under my breath.

"No one controls me. *Except* you," he said sternly. "It's been hell being away from you. I know that we've talked to each other daily, but sometimes I need more. The video chats were starting to make me go mad. To see you, and not be able to touch you, Andria...it was as if the monitor was holding you hostage behind the screen. I felt like I was in a prison being kept away from the woman I loved."

I remembered thinking the same thing. My heart ached every time I had to say goodbye to Andrew. Seeing him used to make things easier, but it started to mock me. The moment the screen went black, I felt the pain of his absence down to my soul.

Andrew took a step closer to me. He slowly brought his hands up to my face as he cupped it. "Andria, if you let me, I will spend every day making this up to you. You are the only person I want. *The only person that I love.*"

Looking into his pleading eyes softened my heart. I knew what I was getting into when I fell in love with Andrew. I knew that he would be photographed, and his life scrutinized and picked apart. I wanted us to stay in our bubble, but when that bubble broke, the reality of what it all meant became painfully clear. This was Andrew's life. If I was going to be with him, this was my life now—as long as Brittney wasn't a part of it—and I was sure as hell going to make sure of that.

"Andrew, I forgive you for being a dumbass." I smiled. "I love you, and I do trust you. But...honestly, I can't accept Brittney..."

"I told her I couldn't work with her again."

I looked up at him confused. "What?"

"When we were at dinner, she also wanted to tell me that she was offered a part in the next movie I am slated to begin."

I stepped away from him, and took a deep breath before stating as calmly as possible. "If you work with that...woman again, I won't be around to watch!" I growled out that last bit.

He nodded as he approached with caution. "I thought you would feel that way, so I told Frank to make it clear to them that I would not be working on the project if Brittney was involved."

I sighed in relief. Thinking about them working together again would have been a deal breaker for me. "I hate that she makes me doubt us."

"*Never* doubt us again, Andria." He stepped in closer, pinning me between the table and him. "May I kiss you know?"

I narrowed my eyes before nodding my head as he placed his lips on mine. After Andrew kissed me, he thought sex was soon to follow. You should have seen the look on his face when I stopped him—cold. I needed time before we became intimate again. I reassured him it would eventually happen, but my heart needed a little more time to mend.

He understood, and said that he wouldn't pressure me. Until, I told him that he wasn't sleeping in my bed again until further notice. That's when he started to question if I had really forgiven him. Of course I had forgiven him. He made a poor judgment, but I blamed

Brittney more. Men seldom realize just how crafty and cunning women are until it's too late.

That night, I debated over the idea of Andrew staying friends with *her*. Could I really give him an ultimatum? I knew Brittney would never concede to defeat and leave Andrew alone. I hoped with a little push, Andrew would cut all ties with her, but I may have to push a bit harder. The fact that she still had lips was a miracle. If I were back in the States, I would have cut them off by now.

We had two more days of book signings and personal appearances in London. Then we head off to Paris for a few days, ending the tour in Italy. There was a total of eight days left, and I was determined to make the best of it. It was a once in a lifetime experience, and I heeded the girls advise to take things slow, and soak it all in. Which was easier said than done. No matter how I looked at it. I would once again be away from Andrew, and that thought clouded my mind.

He was supposed to head back the next day, and I would see him again when we made a detour stop in Canada. If we were going to make things work, we needed to spend more time together, so I decided to take a few months off. I could use the time to finish writing my next book, as well as prepare for the move to Virginia.

The next day, I rushed back from the bookstore later that afternoon to see Andrew off. I went to drop off my things, when I noticed the surprise that was waiting for me in my hotel room. There was a new dress laid out on the bed, with a shoebox below. Yet, it was the jewelry box that captured my attention. The dress was breathtaking, and I knew Erin picked it out, but I didn't know why.

I picked up the jewelry box, which displayed a necklace identical to the bracelet Andrew gave me, with a card inside:

> Three rings of pink, yellow, and white gold,
> intertwined forever to symbolize a trinity.
> Three symbolic colors: pink for love,
> yellow for fidelity and white for friendship.
> Our love, forever.

As I ran my fingers over the description, I thought about *forever*. Something about that scared me, yet warmed my heart at the same time. Then the oversized bouquet of flowers, which were sitting on the nightstand, caught my attention as I noticed the attached note:

> *Alexandria Moore,*
> *It would be an honor if you joined*
> *me for dinner tonight.*
> *I'll pick you up at six.*
> *I love you, Andrew*

After rereading his script, I looked over at the clock, and realized it was less than an hour until he would be here. I instantly picked up my cell, sent Andrew a text asking him about his flight. His only response was:

Have dinner with me, Andria.

Strangely, it felt like our first date all over again. I had butterflies in my stomach as I put on the final touch of my garter belt. I bought it for Andrew when I was in New York, and was dying to wear it. I thought tonight was the perfect night for it, as I played with the delicate necklace around my neck. The more I touched it, the more my will power was quickly becoming non-existent.

Andrew kept to his word, and hadn't pushed the sex, but deep inside of me, I wanted him too. I wanted him to take me in every way. It had been a very longtime; even his musky scent turned me on.

I snapped the dark blue thigh highs to the garter, and looked in the mirror at the blue-laced bra and panty set. I then put on the shoes for effect and thought, *damn I looked good.* That was how worked up I was. So worked up, I missed hearing the knocks on the door. It was when I heard my name from a distance that I threw on a robe, and opened the door to the sex god known as Andrew Hughes. He had on a black suit and tie, and his eyes sparkled when they saw me showing more of the green undertones. My heart melted, becoming a puddle of goo, and at his mercy.

I stood, obviously sizing up every inch of him as he leaned against the door; and he let me. When I reached *that* smirk...that was it! My girly bits literally started to growl and weep, while my breasts were fighting their way out of the form fitted bra. I moved the hand that was holding my robe together, and let it fall open reviling exactly what was underneath. The look on Andrew's face was priceless. The smirk was long gone, and his eyes darkened as they bugged out of their sockets.

Andrew started to fidget as his hand gracefully swept across the front of his pants. "Ah, Andria," he forced out as the other hand tugged at his hair. "Ummm, your robe, baby..."

I looked down at it, and back to him. "What about it?" I grinned.

Andrew stepped forward, pushing me backwards, as he closed the door behind him. I watched as he loosened his tie before taking it off.

Hmmm, there was so much I could do with that tie.

As he continued to prowl forward, I stepped backwards, hit the sofa and slid over the armrest. I lay back onto the sofa, legs crossed over the armrest, as my stilettos kicked up into the air. Andrew focused on my shoes for a moment, before his eyes hungrily slid up my body, studying every last inch of it. I stayed still, watching while he unbuttoned his shirt, until our eyes met.

Sitting up, I pulled at his pant waist, bringing him closer in front of me. I unfastened his belt slowly, making sure that I brushed along every inch of him. My mouth watered in anticipation as to what I wanted next. I unbuttoned his fly, then slowly pulled down his zipper as I yanked his pants and boxers down, mesmerized at the sheer size of him. He seemed bigger, and I smiled to myself.

Mine.

Without warning, Andrew pushed me back on the couch, and grabbed my ankles as he placed them on each of his shoulder. He then placed kisses up and down my calf, while his hands roamed up to the edge of my panties, as his fingers swept back and forth over the blue lace. Andrew carefully, and gently, scooted them down before positioning each leg to bend as he took it off.

Placing my ankles back on his shoulders, my stilettos dangled behind him.

I looked in amazement as the most sinister expression graced Andrews face. "My mouth is going to remind you exactly what you mean to me. But my tongue is going to take what is mine." I arched my back at his words as he pushed me down. "Ah, ah, ah. Lay back like a good little girl, while I make you forget your name."

Andrew stood up taller as he lifted my body upward. Each leg in his hands, my lower torso came off the couch, as he brought me directly to his mouth. The lifting motion surprised me, while his mouth shocked the hell out of me.

He devoured me like a starved lion until I cried out. Again, and again Andrew feasted. His hands tightened as I started to writhe, and his strength felt inhuman as I tried to wiggle myself free. The sensation was too much, and I couldn't breathe. Climax after climax came, and each and every one deliciously ached more and more. After awhile, I couldn't sound out words. The man was determined to kill me with his mouth. The last climax hit me like a freight train. I screamed so loud, I knew the entire hotel heard me. Yet, I didn't care. My body went completely limp, and I gasped for air as I chanted Andrew's name over and over again. He gave me one last kiss, before setting my legs down over the armrest, as he walked around the sofa. I looked at him gasping for air as I asked, "Can you give me a minute?"

He shook his head—the ass—and lifted me up as he carried me into the bedroom. He placed me gently on the bed before he crawled in. "I finished your book, Andria."

My heart stopped. Not just at his words, but at the sinister smirk splayed along his face. "The concept of an

American woman meeting an Englishman in a bookstore was a good start. But how their interest for new and darker things brings them together," Andrew grinned wider. "How she's exploring her sexuality after a frigid failed marriage, and he's sharing a new lifestyle with her...well, that gave me a few ideas."

A chill ran through my body ending at the very tip of my toes. Was Andrew thinking what I was hoping? It didn't escape my mind that we had just fulfilled chapter twelve in my book a few minutes ago. "What kind of ideas Andrew?" My voice cracked and I knew it gave me away.

"I think it may be better if I show you."

Erin called to let me know that she had made it back safely—a day later. She didn't say goodbye, stating Andrew and I needed to talk.

"Tell him, Andria."

"I will! I just...I don't know. Every time I think this is a good time, the words won't come out of my mouth."

"You're making too big of a deal about this. Tell Andrew that he was the reason you wrote *Deception*, and get it over with."

"It's not that easy—"

"It is. What are you afraid of?"

"I'm not sure." I thought for a moment. "I will, Erin. I'll tell him soon."

"I hope you do."

"When the time is right."

Keira decided to meet me at the airport to give Andrew and I some time to say goodbye. He postponed his trip back so that we could leave together the next day. She also called to warn us that something was going on in the hotel lobby. There were a lot of reporters, and people standing around; the hotel was hosting some kind of royal event that evening. She suggested Andrew and I slip through the back entrance, and made arrangements with the hotel management to assist in our departure. Even though Andrew and I decided that it was time to take our relationship public, we both wanted to hold on to the time we had for just a little longer.

We rode to the airport together in a taxi driven by a distracted driver, but used the time to just hold each other. Eight days. It would only be eight days until I was back in his arms. Andrew and I were so consumed with each other that we never paid attention to where the driver was taking us. The moment he stopped, Andrew exited the car after kissing me, and hundreds of camera flashes went off. "What the hell?"

I looked out my window to see a slew of photographers awaiting our arrival. How *could they have known?* Then I looked at the taxi driver who hadn't looked up once. Well, isn't that a bitch.

Andrew leaned in looking at the driver. "Thanks asshole! Now, we know why you were too busy looking at your cell versus the road." Andrew looked over to me, and surprisingly didn't look upset. "Well, Andria. Are you ready for this baby?"

I looked in Andrew's eyes, as flashes of our time together entered my mind: The Anchor. The beer stained blouse. Andrew's premier. Our first kiss. Our first date. Andrew in Baltimore. Andrew at my door in Dallas.

Andrew making love to me. Meeting the parents. Seeing his face in the art gallery.

Everything flashed by quickly.

When I focused back on Andrew's eyes, there was no other answer than, "With you, I'm ready for anything."

He smiled, and stretched out his hand as I took it. We exited the car straight into the lion's den.

The End...

...I don't think so.

THE TROUBLE WITH MARRYING
A MOVIE STAR

Book Two in the Red Carpet Series

"Hey Andria?" Keira yelled from the entrance of my suite. I heard the door close.

"Keira, in here."

She walked into the bedroom. "You have a visitor coming up?"

I stopped writing, and looked up confused. "Do you know who it is?"

She shrugged. "He said that he was a friend of Wade's and was asked to stop by."

"Okay? It's weird that Wade hasn't mentioned anything to me."

"It probably just slipped his mind," she said exiting, and suddenly turned back around. "Oh, and that crowd of people who I saw in the lobby of our hotel in London— they weren't for that event like I had originally thought. They were paps and reporters looking for Andrew."

"How..."

"It was on the local news this morning. Apparently, your relationship has gone global. You may want to give your family a call," she said sympathetically.

"Thanks, I'll call—" There was a knock on the door. "Well, after I see what this guy wants."

I went to answer the door and was greeted by a tall slender man, with long brown messy hair who was snarling at me. "Is *that* how you answer the door?" he hissed out.

"Excuse me?"

"You didn't ask, who was at the door. Did you even look through the peep-hole?" he asked, and crossed his tattooed arms.

I crossed mine. "Umm, who are you?"

"Exactly, Andria. I know who you are, but you don't know who I am."

What was this guy's problem? "Look, I have a lot of things to do, so, if you want to interrogate yourself..." He walked past me uninvited. "Hey! I don't care if you *are* so-called friends with Wade, I'm going to call security—"

He turned around with a Cheshire grin splayed on his face. "I *am* security," he said, as he stood staring me down.

"Whatever. Look, I'm going to make that call—"

"Go ahead. Like I said, I am security. Actually, I'm *your* security."

It was a standoff. I didn't know what to say next, and then I said, "I'm going to call Wade."

"You do that." He walked over and made himself comfortable on the sofa.

Wade picked up after the first ring. "Bonjour, Andria. How's Pareee?"

"Some guy is here and says he knows you."

"Do you mean Connor?"

I looked over at the man who was now snooping around the suite. "Is your name Connor?"

"You should have asked me that before opening the door."

Jerk.

"That's Connor," Wade laughed out. "He's your new bodyguard."

"What? I never asked for a bodyguard."

"Andrew insisted."

"He what?" I yelled, as Keira now entered the room. "Andrew never told me this. Why do I need a bodyguard?"

"You said it all little one. Andrew. Your relationship is out."

I started pacing around the hotel room. "I know that Wade, but that doesn't explain why I need a bodyguard."

"Andrew wanted you to be protected 24/7."

"This guy is going to be with me all the time? Where is Andrew?"

Keira walked over to me, sitting down in the closest chair. "He's in the trailer going over his script."

"Thanks." I hung up and dialed Andrew.

His sexy voice came through. "What are you wearing?"

"Nothing that you're going to see if you don't explain why you hired a bodyguard and didn't tell me."

"Connor arrived then?"

Acknowledgements

To an incredible team of ladies who have supported me from the beginning: Connie, A.G., April, Ella, Tinsley, Deborah and Meredith. Along with my patient and talented editor, Donna.

ABOUT THE AUTHOR

I'm the girl who has seen more than she has ever wanted, yet decided to add to that world by writing Hollywood romances. A northern girl, but a southerner at heart, I love anything and everything about love and romance. So much that once upon a time I had a career as a wedding and events coordinator. When I decided to do something I was passionate about, I added my love for travel to the mix. An avid shoeaholic, deep down I'm a sappy romantic who happens to believe that love can truly conquer all.

Znwillett.com

Made in the USA
Columbia, SC
16 August 2017